Swap Night

ON

Union Station

Book Nineteen of EarthCent Ambassador

Swap Night on Union Station

Foner Books

ISBN 978-1-948691-32-1

Copyright 2021 by E. M. Foner

Northampton, Massachusetts

One

"In conclusion, it is the view of Union Station embassy that ambassadors reaching the traditional Earth retirement age of sixty-five years should be allowed to hire an additional special assistant, or, if they currently employ a special assistant who does the work of three people, to double her compensation before she decides to return to her homeworld and resume her royal—do you think I'm being a little too transparent, Libby?" Kelly interrupted herself.

"If you're hoping that EarthCent will believe your suggestion is meant for all embassies and not just your own, it would have been wise not to mention Aabina by name so many times in the examples you gave," the station librarian replied.

"Aabina is the perfect special assistant and she's already turned down a number of better job opportunities to continue working here. I know she's not in it for the money, and I doubt what EarthCent pays even covers her rent on the Vergallian deck, but I don't want her thinking that all of her hard work goes unnoticed."

"I'm sure she already knows how much you appreciate her. I don't think I would be violating anybody's privacy by telling you that I've heard Aabina say that you're her dream boss. In addition, she recently renewed her lease."

"For how long?" EarthCent's ambassador to Union Station asked.

"Three years," Libby replied.

"Thank you, thank you, thank you. Scratch the last fifteen minutes and let's go with the report I recorded this morning."

"You were just getting to the conclusion when Joe dropped in to take you to lunch."

"You're right, and I still haven't made up my mind about the whole thing," Kelly said. "Where did I leave off?"

"You were speculating about whether one of the advanced species might gamble on providing humanity with an unsecured loan for a few trillion creds," the station librarian told her.

"It doesn't sound very realistic when you put it that way." Kelly sighed and took a minute to compose her thoughts. "In conclusion, it is the view of Union Station embassy that the purchase of Earth Two would provide limitless employment opportunities to humanity while allowing us to build equity, but the down payment is beyond the resources of our backers, and I consider it unlikely that any of the aliens will be willing to advance us the money or act as co-signers on a planetary mortgage."

"Coded and sent," Libby reported. "It does seem a shame to let a world that was custom-terraformed for your species slip away entirely."

"Thanks to Donna's daughters and Aisha putting up their cash, we still have an option to counter the Alt's bid. But even if the girls mortgaged InstaSitter and Aisha sold the residual rights to *Let's Make Friends* back to the Grenouthians, it wouldn't be enough for a trillion cred down payment."

"Then perhaps you should think of an alternative, but first it's time you make up your mind about the ambassadorial exchange," the Stryx station librarian said.

"I'm thrilled to be the first EarthCent ambassador chosen for the honor, but I'm concerned about accidentally giving offence to embassy staff and visitors alike," Kelly said. "Do you think I'm just being a worry wart?"

"I suspect you're over-thinking an established tunnel network tradition for outstanding ambassadors who reach the seventy-five percent mark of their estimated tenure," Libby said.

"It feels like more than seventy-five percent."

"You're sixty-five years old and you made ambassador at thirty-five. You have ten years to go before reaching the current EarthCent retirement age for diplomats, so thirty years served out of forty projected is seventy-five percent."

"I can still do that much math in my head, Libby. I just meant that I feel old. And the truth is, I'm worried that the other ambassadors will take advantage of their position when they come here."

"Although visiting ambassadors assume the full authority of the office during the exchange, the tunnel network species have had hundreds of thousands of years to establish safeguards against abuse."

"But I'm the first EarthCent ambassador who's been invited to participate," Kelly pointed out. "We don't have any such safeguards in place."

"Nor do you have war fleets for anybody to cause mischief," Libby said. "I shouldn't be surprised if the Drazen and Horten ambassadors engage in a little tit-for-tat recipe sabotage since your embassy controls the All Species Cookbook, but diplomats accepting an exchange are honor-bound to do their best for the host species."

"All right," Kelly said, "I'm in. I've always believed that the key to diplomacy is forming personal relationships, and I can't do that sitting around my office all day waiting for retirement."

"Donna asked me to pass on that she had to leave early, and Dorothy pinged while you were recording to remind you that it's your turn to cook Friday dinner."

"I knew I was forgetting something," Kelly groaned. She grabbed her purse from the deep drawer of her display desk and headed for the door, where she disabled the security lock with a wave. "Could you tell Aabina that—there you are," she greeted her special assistant, who was waiting just outside the office. "I was about to ask Libby to tell you that I'm cooking tonight. Would you like to join us for supper?"

"I'm afraid I have a prior engagement," Aabina replied a little too quickly. "Do you want to look at the new space before you go?"

"Why is it that when Aisha cooks, you make the time, but when I cook, you're always engaged?"

"I'm sure you're misremembering," the Vergallian girl said. "If I had known you would be inviting me I would have scheduled my interview at the Open University for another time."

"Interview?" Kelly grabbed Aabina's wrist. "As in, a job interview?"

"It's just an adjunct faculty position lecturing once a week about royal training in the Empire of a Hundred Worlds. I'm perfectly happy with my job here, but the dean of Vergallian students asked our ambassador to recommend somebody for the position and she gave them my name."

"I knew Aleeytis was going to cause trouble eventually," the EarthCent ambassador said. "You can't trust lawyers."

"Ambassador Aleeytis fell in love with inter-species law and abdicated the throne to her younger sister in order to practice on Union Station," Aabina reminded her boss. "She ran a law office here for over a century before replacing my mother as our ambassador."

"Whenever I agree with her in a meeting, I always find out afterward that she's tricked me," Kelly complained. "But what did you say about a new space?"

"The office on the other side of our conference room is finally vacant and Associate Ambassador Cohan signed the lease this afternoon. You were on a tunneling conference call and it all moved so quickly that I guess he forgot to check with you."

"We've spoken about it enough times lately that he knew I approved. The Conference of Sovereign Human Communities work Daniel does has been generating so much walk-in traffic that it's beginning to disrupt our operations and it's not fair to Donna. She's just a year younger than me and she has twice as much work managing the embassy as she did thirty years ago." Kelly paused, pointed at her ear, and remained silent for almost a whole minute, but the Vergallian girl was capable of reading the subtle movements of the ambassador's throat caused by subvocalization and had to look away to avoid unintentionally eavesdropping. "Okay, dinner is set. Let's look at that office."

"Did you ask your husband to barbeque something?" Aabina asked.

"I ordered take-out from the new Indian restaurant in the Little Apple that Aisha said we have to try. Are you sure you don't want to come to dinner?"

"Maybe I'll stop in after the interview if it goes quickly. I think they just want to make sure that I'm not a princess."

"But you are a princess," Kelly observed as she followed her special assistant out into the corridor.

"I meant it in the sense of a stuck-up Vergallian royal who talks down to the lower castes," Aabina said. "To be perfectly honest, I wouldn't have even considered accepting a teaching position if it weren't for the experience I've gained in your embassy working with so many different segments of Human society. I don't think I was ever a snob, but my mother's friends and family were all from the upper caste."

"I'm glad to know you're getting something out of working for us. Are we all authorized for access?" Kelly asked when her special assistant stopped to wave open the door to the right of the corridor entrance for the embassy's conference room.

"Yes. Daniel checked with EarthCent and received permission to add the new space to the basic embassy lease." Aabina led the way into a small anteroom with a glass reception window soaped to make it opaque and indicated the wall to the left. "He wants to cut through from this side so we can share the conference room, but the Stryx only allow structural changes between spaces when they're leased by the same entity."

"Good fences make good neighbors," Kelly said, nodding her understanding. Then a sudden chill came over her and she found herself shivering. "Did the last tenants use this place as a refrigerator? I thought it was a retirement counseling service."

"According to Associate Ambassador Cohan, the last occupant sublet the space from Golden Years after the owner retired early with a few months to go on the lease," Aabina said. "Daniel told me it was another counseling business of some sort or another." Then the Vergallian girl frowned and her complexion turned slightly red.

"I think the draft blew out into the corridor because I feel warmer now," the ambassador said. "Are you blushing?"

"I increased my metabolism and dilated my capillaries to compensate for the cold, but now I feel hot so you're probably correct about the corridor air mixing in. I'd ask the station librarian to duplicate the climate settings from the embassy, but the Associate Ambassador is always complaining that it's too warm."

"You're right, we should leave well enough alone," Kelly said. "Poor Daniel is practically sweating at the temperature that Donna and I find comfortable. Are you looking forward to taking over his old office when he moves in here?"

"I'm not sure," Aabina said. "The advantage of having my desk in the reception area with Donna was that I saw all of the visitors, and you and Daniel always stopped to tell me the latest when you were coming or going. There will be fewer distractions in an office, even if I leave the door open, but I suspect it will make me less accessible."

"That's a debate that people have been having for centuries, whether productivity is better with an open office plan, cubicles, or individual offices like we have," Kelly said. "I know that the Galactic Free Press and EarthCent Intelligence both favor the open-office concept for most of their employees."

"Daniel mentioned that he's thinking of an open office plan here, with shared workspace for any visiting members from the Conference of Sovereign Human Communities." She swept her hand past the door that led from the small antechamber to the main office, and then repeated the gesture with the same lack of result. "There seems to be something wrong with the door."

"That looks like an old-fashioned doorknob from Earth," the ambassador told her special assistant. "Try turning it and pushing."

Aabina followed Kelly's instructions and the door opened inward on hinges, but the room was strangely dark. "How odd. First an antique door, and now there appears to be something wrong with the illumination."

"Am I imagining things, or is the whole room painted black?" Kelly asked.

"You're right," Aabina said. "I've never seen anything like it. I think that the light sources have been covered with black filters as well."

"At least it's mainly empty," Kelly said, following her special assistant into the space that was devoid of furniture, though there was a bit of paper litter strewn about. "It feels rather theatrical, if you know what I mean."

"I don't like it," Aabina stated bluntly. "I can't even tell if there are other office doors in here. It seems much smaller than the embassy space, but Daniel said it's the same size."

"I think that could just be the dark color making it feel smaller." The ambassador walked over to where her office door would be located if they were in the EarthCent Embassy and began running her hand over the wall. "The paint feels very odd. It's almost like I'm touching glass rather than metal." Then a panel suddenly slid aside and revealed an office with white walls that were almost blindingly bright. "Whoever decorated this place had serious problems."

"I found the other office," Aabina said from off to Kelly's side. "Ugh, it's painted solid red."

"I hope that Daniel has a budget for renovations because I'm too old for a painting party." Kelly rejoined her special assistant in the main area and said, "Let's get out of here."

A piece of paper that must have been caught in a draft from the ventilation wafted up from the floor, fluttered about for a moment, and then seemed to race forward to paste itself to Kelly's stomach. She peeled it off in annoyance and crumpled it up, but failing to spot anything resembling a recycling receptacle, she just held onto it. Aabina headed off for her interview at the Open University, and the ambassador entered the nearest lift tube. "Mac's Bones," she requested. The doors were just closing when a brown hand with two thumbs slipped in the gap, triggering the doors to open again.

"Bork," Kelly greeted the Drazen ambassador. "I'm sorry I didn't see you coming up when I entered the lift tube."

"I was approaching from behind you and stopped for a moment to discuss our schedule with Aabina," Bork said. "I came as soon as the station librarian notified me that you are going ahead with the exchange. May I accompany you?"

"Certainly, and you're welcome to Indian food in about forty-five minutes if you care to join us."

"Did Aisha make it?"

"It was my turn to cook the family meal this Friday," Kelly told him.

"I should probably wait a few more hours since I had a late breakfast," the Drazen said.

"But I was running late so I ordered take-out from a new place."

"Maybe just a taste then. You know I like to keep up with the Human food scene." Bork glanced down at Kelly's hand and asked, "Are you picking up litter in the corridor again?"

"That was the one group of tourists from Earth, and it was just by chance they visited the embassy right before our last meeting," Kelly said. "This was in the new office space that just became vacant on the other side of our conference room. Daniel is going to move over there and turn it into the main office for the Conference of Sovereign Human Communities."

"Is this CoSHC's reaction to your son basing the Human Empire on Flower?"

"The one doesn't have anything to do with the other. Even though the sovereign human communities are officially members of the Human Empire, CoSHC is their main business organization, and it will remain that way for at least the next century."

"In either case, why bring their trash home with you?" Bork asked.

"Daniel hasn't moved in yet and the office space is badly in need of remodeling. This," Kelly raised the crumpled ball of paper, "sort of floated up and blew into me. I think there's something wrong with the climate controls."

The Drazen frowned. "That doesn't seem likely. May I see it?"

Kelly handed over the paper as the doors opened on the corridor outside of Mac's Bones. "I'm sure it's just an advertisement."

"You didn't read it?" Bork asked as he began carefully flattening out the sheet.

"I don't need to. Humans have a sixth sense for advertisements that's evolved through hundreds of years of people shoving flyers at us when we walk down city streets. I don't know what it is—maybe the combination of fonts and colors—but our brains can recognize a hand-out ad without reading the words."

"Well, my Humanese is far from perfect, but I'll give it a try," the Drazen ambassador said as he walked alongside Kelly to the entrance of Mac's Bones. "Madame Zarathustra, Palms Read, Fortunes Told."

"See?" Kelly said. "It's an ad for one of those psychic frauds. I wonder if she was the one who sublet the space for the time remaining on the lease."

"Specializing in communication with loved ones who have passed over to the other side. Proof of relationship required before attempting contact," Bork continued reading. "Certified psychic by the joint EarthCent-Verlock tourism agency. License P421XY."

"Let me see that," Kelly said, taking the wrinkled flyer back from the Drazen ambassador. "The nerve of that woman. She's invented a connection to EarthCent and the Verlocks to drum up business. I'll bet that's why she took the space next to the embassy. I'm going to have Donna ask her daughters to look into it."

"That's an interesting chain of command you have, and I'll have to remember it when we do the exchange. But why do you assume that Madame Zarathustra is a fraud? I just ran that license number through my implant and it comes back as valid."

"How can it be valid when there's no such thing as a joint EarthCent-Verlock tourism agency?" Kelly asked, and then added, "Libby?"

"Yes, Ambassador," the station librarian replied.

"Does EarthCent have some kind of deal with the Verlocks that I don't know about to certify psychics for the tourist trade?"

"It was set up a few months ago at the insistence of the Verlocks who were concerned about their tourists to Earth being defrauded by charlatans," Libby replied. "The Verlock Academy of Mages provides a standardized test to separate the legitimate fortune tellers from the pretenders."

"But there's no such thing as psychics, and even if there were, you could hardly figure out which ones were real by having them take a multiple-choice test," Kelly objected.

"I wouldn't be so quick to argue with the results of an objective test prepared by a Verlock academy," the Drazen ambassador cautioned her. "They may not be the best cooks, but they do have the most reputable education system on the tunnel network."

"A psychic who advertises that she can communicate with the dead?" Kelly asked skeptically as she braced for Beowulf's greeting. "And what was all that about proof of relationship?"

"It only makes sense," Bork said, fending off the Cayl hound. "You wouldn't want to license psychics who were willing to violate the privacy of the deceased. I know enough about your people to say that celebrities would be cheated out of their eternal rest."

"Now I know you're just pulling my tentacle," Kelly said, unconsciously adopting the Drazen expression. "The dead are dead, and nothing you can say is going to convince me otherwise. I have yet to hear of anybody ever being reincarnated—" she shoved away the dog's massive head again "—other than Beowulf, and his first incarnation was half-alien, so it doesn't count."

"How does being half-alien make it not count?" Bork demanded, and then dropped the argument to greet the EarthCent ambassador's husband. "Hello, Joe. How's business?"

"I mainly watch Paul do the work these days, and the kids only let me brew enough beer to supply Pub Haggis," Joe said. "On the bright side, if I was an EarthCent diplomat, I'd have another five years to go before I could retire. Why are you carrying that crumpled-up flyer, Kel?"

"What do you make of this?" she asked, handing it to her husband.

Joe took a moment to read the ad and then shrugged. "Maybe if I thought my parents had buried a treasure they wanted me to know about, but other than that, why disturb them?"

"I didn't mean it that way. This Madame Zarathustra was subletting the office next to the embassy's conference room for months and I didn't even know she was there."

"That's because you're not interested in psychics. Did you ask Donna about it?"

"I haven't seen her since I found out, but you're right. If anybody knew what was going on next door, she's it."

"Are you joining us for dinner, Bork?" Joe asked. "I have a small batch of breakfast stout flavored with coffee that everybody says is too bitter, but it could be just right for you."

"Thank you, Joe. I'd like to give that a try. I'll just ping my embassy to tell them I'm taking an early lunch and not to expect me back."

Two

"Has it really been six months?" Kevin asked his wife as she placed the baby in the bassinet.

"It felt more like six years," Dorothy said as she tucked the tiny quilt up to her infant son's chin. "Are you going to miss Daddy?" she asked the baby.

"Ritchie is going to miss me," the boy's older sister said. "Why can't I come to work with you?"

"Because you ask so many questions, Margie. I'd never get any work done," Dorothy said. "Ritchie just eats and sleeps."

"I know I promised not to bring it up again," Kevin began, "but Jeeves offered—"

"La, la, la, la, la," Dorothy sang while covering her ears. "Somebody needs to look up the definition of promise."

Kevin sighed and held up his hands just over shoulder-height in a gesture of surrender. "Come on, Margie," he said to his daughter. "Let's get the chandlery open, and then Billy and Rachel's parents asked if you could play with them again today."

"Preschool starts next week," Dorothy reminded them. "You're going to love it, Margie."

"I want to go to REAL school," the four-year-old said over Kevin's shoulder as her father carried her out. "With Stryx."

"Two more years," her mother said, holding up two fingers. Then she slung the work bag with her over-sized sketching tab over one shoulder, her purse over the other shoulder, and took up the bassinet. "Let's go, Richard. Your first day at work."

Ten minutes later, she set the bassinet down on the conference room table in the new offices of SBJ Fashions. Shaina and Brinda, the sisters who contributed the 'S' and 'B' to the name of the business, knew better than to wake up a sleeping infant just to make a fuss, but Baa, the Terragram mage who had been given a minority stake due to the importance of her enchanted "Baa's Bags" brand, whisked off the quilt.

"Just a quick check," she told Dorothy, inspecting Richard's hands. "I can count his toes through the snuggly."

"If a fairy replaced my baby with a changeling, I assure you I'd be the first to know," Dorothy said tiredly. "I don't understand how the so-called advanced species can be so superstitious."

"It's not just Baa?" Shaina asked.

"Affie gave me a Vergallian ugly-infant mask for him at the baby shower, which is the same thing she gave me for Margie. And Flazint's matchmaker did the digit-counting thing when she was checking my family's suitability to act as chaperones."

"It's not a superstition," Baa said, replacing the quilt after satisfying herself on the count of Richard's toes. "There's more to the universe than meets the eye, especially the eye of a primitive like yourself."

"On that note of mutual respect, I declare this post-maternity leave orientation meeting in order," Jeeves said. The Stryx floated past the women to his accustomed spot at the head of the table and gestured to the younger Hadad sister with his pincer. "Brinda?"

"As the head of sentient resources for SBJ Fashions, I officially declare the end of your six-month maternity leave and reauthorize you for access to the office," Brinda told Dorothy.

"You could have just trusted me to stay away," the EarthCent ambassador's daughter said.

"I'd believe that if you hadn't made three attempts to get in when nobody was here," Jeeves retorted. "Did you think I wouldn't notice an unauthorized individual trying to swipe open the door?"

"I was just going to look through the scrap bin for quilting material," Dorothy said.

"At four in the morning on your clock after pinging first to see if anybody was in the office?"

"I was up with the baby and I pinged first just to be polite."

"Listening to you arguing with Jeeves makes it feel like you never went out on maternity leave at all," Shaina said. "I know that the time I took off from work after having my children helped to give me a fresh perspective when I returned, which is the reason we wanted to hold this meeting right away. Before you go back to your design station, have you had any epiphanies you want to share?"

Dorothy immediately pulled her sketch tab out of her work bag and swiped it to life. "Ever since my mom published the All Species Cookbook with tribute recipes from people living on alien worlds I've been working on an idea for tribute clothes. All of our cross-species designs have been intentionally aimed at the largest possible audience, but I've been thinking that it would be better to

16

come up with a concept that could be customized for each species."

"You know that we don't want to hold a lot of inventory," Brinda said. "Even if there was a way to maintain a coherent brand with species-specific clothes, we'd have to stock seven or eight times as much merchandise to reach the same number of customers."

"That's where the Gem nanofabric comes in," Dorothy said. "How many representatives are we up to?"

"Sixty-three," Shaina told her, "but it's still a Beta program, and ninety percent of them are humans operating virtual boutiques on open worlds. It took the Gem a little longer than we thought to work the kinks out of the rediscovered technology, but now they're able to supply as much nanofabric as we can buy."

"Just imagine when we have thousands of sales reps, or tens of thousands. Inventory won't matter because we'll always be shipping the product and everybody will expect delays. It becomes a question of compelling fashions that are worth waiting for. The nanofabric fittings will provide all of the data that Jeeves needs to do the math to map my designs to a Frunge fabric cutting machine, and then—"

"Excuse me?" Jeeves interrupted. "Do you actually expect me to spend my time doing dress math?"

"Just while we're engineering the workflow," Dorothy said. "After that, we can replace you with a computer."

Baa made a noise in the back of her throat, swallowed it, and then burst out laughing. "I think that mapping the data from custom-fit Gem nanofabric to numerically controlled cutting machines would be an excellent use of our Stryx overlord's time. Don't forget to leave extra material for the seams, Master of the Multiverse."

"Putting aside the supply chain and on-demand sewing, I'm not convinced that you have a viable business model," Jeeves said. "I'm more concerned with Brinda's initial question, namely, how you are going to maintain a sense of brand styling while attempting to design for a dozen species all at once. And don't tell me it's enough to embroider the SBJ logo somewhere to go after customers who only buy designer fashions. Our market research has shown time and time again that our fashions are bought for purpose, not for social signaling."

"I'd show you right now if my sketch tab would link to the projection system," Dorothy said, paging through the little-used 'Settings' menus in frustration. "Are you sure you've reapproved my company credentials for all systems?"

"Positive," Brinda said. "Have you ever connected using that tab before? I don't remember seeing it."

"Paul and Aisha gave it to me for a maternity leave gift. It's a Dollnick artist's tab, two sizes up from the student tabs the Open University standardized."

"And you don't have any problem connecting at home?"

"I only use it for drawing so I haven't had any reason to connect to the station networks," Dorothy said. "I guess I haven't tried before."

"Allow me," Jeeves said, extending his pincer.

Dorothy gave him a distrustful look, but she handed the tab to Baa, who passed it on to the young Stryx artificial intelligence. Jeeves set it down on the conference room table and moved his pincer back and forth just a hair above the surface as if he was dowsing for water.

"I had the tab in my hands for less than two seconds and I diagnosed the issue," Baa told him. "You're an embarrassment to your kind."

"The connectivity issue is obvious," Jeeves retorted. "The cybercriminals put a lot of effort into hiding their tracks and I'm trying to tease out who they were."

"Cybercriminals?" Dorothy asked. "You mean somebody has been spying on my design process?"

"That's exactly what I mean," Jeeves said, then gave up in disgust and passed the tab back. "The tab will connect now, and I installed a block that will keep snoopers out, but I can't go any further while limiting myself to techniques known to Human cyber sleuths."

"Why would you stop there?"

"You know that we allow both diplomatic and industrial espionage on the station because interfering would confer an unearned advantage to the less sophisticated party. Even though I have a material interest in SBJ Fashions, my elders don't allow me to use advanced techniques that go beyond what you could conceivably do for yourselves."

"Fortunately, I'm not Stryx," Baa said, holding the tab up to the side of her face. She closed her cat's eyes in concentration, and a faint glow appeared between her skin and the tab's surface.

"Don't erase anything," Dorothy pleaded. "The only backup is my memory."

"I'm not that incompetent," the Terragram mage replied irritably. "There's no biological fingerprint, so the culprit could be artificial intelligence, but not a form I recognize."

"You mean from outside the tunnel network?"

"Or primitive, like a Human-derived AI. Do you get many artificial people coming through Mac's Bones?"

"Just the ones who work for EarthCent Intelligence," Dorothy said. "Thomas has been recruiting more of them the last few years, but I'm sure he does background checks and all of that. Wouldn't the hacking techniques used by an artificial person count as being developed by humanity so that Jeeves could trace them?"

"Not if the artificial person is working as an agent of another species and using their toolkits," Baa said, returning the over-sized tab to Dorothy. "I suggest that you turn your tab over to Thomas and see if EarthCent Intelligence can detect any traces that will lead them to the double agent. If they can work out the time your tab's code was altered, that could be sufficient, since the hacker must have been in close proximity."

"Did you have any of our marketing information and customer lists on the tab or was it just your new designs?" Shaina asked the EarthCent ambassador's daughter.

"Just my new designs?" Dorothy bristled. "I've been working on them for six—well, maybe three months." The baby made a little noise and everybody froze until he resumed his regular breathing. "I got the tab after you locked me out of the company systems, so, no, I didn't have any confidential information on it."

"That's a relief. We pay serious creds for the station librarian to store all of our data so that it's one hundred percent secure, but anything downloaded to tabs is fair game for industrial spies."

"So what do you have to show us?" Brinda asked.

"It's more of a concept than a finished idea," Dorothy said. She linked her tab to the conference room's holographic system which projected a grid of figures wearing skirts and blouses, all drawn in broad strokes, with just the barest bumps for facial features. "Vergallian, Horten,

Drazen, Frunge, Human, Gem. These are the six tunnel network species we've been targeting with cross-over fashions because our humanoid forms have similar measurements, aside from the occasional tentacle." She swiped the tab to bring up a new grid of figures. "We also sell handbags, hats, and shoes to the Verlocks, Dollnicks, Grenouthians, Cherts, and Fillinducks, but their bodies are just proportioned too differently for dresses, and the bunnies rarely wear clothes in any case."

"Even Dollnick fashion houses have difficulty designing for Dollnicks," Shaina said. "The bone structure supporting the lower set of arms presents a real challenge for creating clean lines. That's why so many of them go with the two-piece tops."

"I've never been able to adapt my dresses for Dollnicks, and whenever I scale a design to fit a Verlock female, it ends up looking like a tent," Dorothy said. "The Fillinducks and Cherts almost fit in the first group, but their proportions are off just enough that even with alterations, our fashions just don't look right. Same with the Sharf, if we start including non-tunnel network humanoids."

"Why not, it's only money," Jeeves said, imbuing his artificial voice with a despondent note.

"But this won't cost you a cred," Dorothy said triumphantly, and swiped to a new grid of sketches. The projection included all twelve of the species she had mentioned so far, and the drawings almost looked like they had been done with crayon. But even the shoulder-to-hip sash featured on the Grenouthian somehow conveyed the impression of matching the skirts and blouses worn by the other eleven.

"What exactly am I seeing?" Shaina asked. "Is it just a trick with color coordination that won't hold up if the drawings aren't all grouped together?"

"Ye of little faith," Dorothy said, and swiped the screen for a new projection where the colors and hints of patterns on every figure were different.

Baa half-stood as she peered at the hologram. "As impossible as it sounds, you appear to have stumbled onto a Golden Ratio for cross-species fashion design. I've seen a similar method used by Cayl artists when they depict a multi-species group of individuals in a portrait, but it's a highly advanced concept, and you're millions of years away from understanding the math."

"If the idea is copied from the Cayl we may need to get a license," Jeeves said. "Give all of the details to Tzachan for a legal opinion."

"I didn't copy anything from the Cayl," Dorothy said, "and Tzachan already saw my designs when I chaperoned his date with Flazint last weekend."

"I'm willing to pay some grudging respect to your artistic instincts, Dorothy, but you don't come up with a breakthrough like this fooling around for a few months on maternity leave," Jeeves said.

"I didn't exactly stumble on it, but it's not exactly original either," Dorothy explained. "Plus I had help." She swiped past a few of the images in her presentation to one that had obviously been captured from another display device via the camera. "Myst signed up for a Gem History course at the Open University because she thought it would be easy. This is one of the pictures from her text that discusses the stagnation of the Gem Empire after they reduced their population to clones of a single individual."

"So they're all wearing the same thing," Shaina said. "How do you go from copies of the same individual all dressing identically to creating a look that maintains its essence across a dozen different species?"

"Look again," Dorothy said, and began tapping her fingers impatiently when nobody spoke up. "Don't you see? They aren't all dressed identically. You just think they are."

"Because they all look alike?" Brinda asked.

"No, that wouldn't prove anything. The reason you think they're all wearing the same jumpsuit is that they're all cut to the same ratio and feature the same focal points—here, here, and here," she said, making marks on the tab with a stylus that were immediately duplicated in the hologram. "This particular group of Gem included representatives from all of their colonies, and if you look closely, you'll see that those jumpsuits are sewn from different fabrics, and the clones themselves vary by at least twenty percent in body mass due to available food sources, gravity, and different oxygen levels on their worlds."

"Impressive," Jeeves broke the silence. "Who helped you with this?"

"Myst and Lancelot, of course. He took the history course too so they could do their homework together. Paul explained how math comes into it, and my dad pointed out the bit about the effect of gravity and oxygen since he visited so many worlds before he came to Union Station." She tilted her head a little and squinted up towards the side as if she was trying to recall something. "You know, it might have been Dring who—"

"I knew it," Baa interrupted. "Without the Maker, this would have been the old tale about four blind men describing a dragon based on the part they happened to be touching."

"Well, Dring couldn't have shown me what I had wrong if I hadn't already gotten it mainly right," Dorothy said defensively. "He just gave me a few pointers based on all of the sculpting he's done."

"You've surprised me again, Dorothy, and I didn't think that was possible," Jeeves said. "Thanks to Dring's involvement, the Cayl would never push an intellectual property rights claim, so this isn't going to cost SBJ Fashions an arm and a leg to try. Shaina? Brinda?"

"I can recognize the potential even though I'm confused over what it is I'm not seeing," the elder Hadad sister said. "I suppose I don't need to understand it to work on a marketing and production plan. If we can start recruiting alien entrepreneurs willing to represent our lines and equip them with the nanofabric, we'll end up with more orders than we can handle."

"That's the beauty of running a lean business," Brinda said. "We can always take pressure off the hand-sewn tier simply by raising prices, and the rest of our manufacturing is contracted out, primarily to Chintoo, where the artificial people can rapidly ramp up to almost any production volume."

"As long as it doesn't steal resources from my enchanted LARPing products, I have no objection," Baa said. "But all I've seen so far are a few clever sketches on a tablet that I must remind you have already been stolen by a competitor. I'll reserve my final judgment until I see models from those twelve species wearing a fashionable new outfit that creates the same effect."

"I forgot about the hack," Dorothy said, her face falling. "What if somebody beats us to market? Can we file for a patent now?"

"You didn't ask Tzachan when you showed him your designs?"

"I didn't think of it because I didn't know somebody else had already stolen them."

The baby suddenly woke up, perhaps triggered by the distress in his mother's voice, and began to vent his disappointment at finding himself in a strange room with an uninteresting ceiling.

Baa popped to her feet. "I have some bespoke enchantment orders to fill for a big raid. And don't forget to bring that tab to your intelligence people," she added over her shoulder as she fled.

"Shaina and I should probably start on a business plan right away," Brinda said, edging towards the door, only to bump into her sister who had come around the other side of the table. "Beautiful baby, when he's not screaming."

Dorothy took Richard out of the bassinet and almost had her eardrums burst for her trouble. "Not afraid of a little crying, Jeeves?" she asked her Stryx boss, who remained floating at the end of the table.

"I filter it out," Jeeves replied. "I'm not sure how you Humans manage without going insane, or maybe it explains a few things. Besides, I have a surprise for you."

"You bought me that new Frunge cutting table I asked for?"

"I have to show you. Bring the baby."

"Did you think I was going to leave him here doing his imitation of a siren?" Dorothy asked, and then, holding Richard in both hands, extended her arms and pulled him back to introduce a Doppler effect to his steady cries. "Pretty neat, huh?"

Jeeves floated past and led the way to the mystery door next to the design room that Dorothy had never seen open. It slid aside at his approach and revealed a diaper changing station, a narrow bed, and the latest in crib technology, complete with a Frunge Fascination mobile.

"Welcome to the official SBJ Fashions nursery," Jeeves said. "I would have preferred if you stayed home for a few years, but if you're going to insist on coming into work I need you to take care of yourself and the baby, or I'll never hear the end of it."

"It's lovely, Jeeves," Dorothy said. "But why does my voice sound funny?"

"It's the soundproofing. I want my other employees to remain sane as well. There's a Dollnick audio suppression field built into the crib that you can switch on and off with the clown's head. If you need to use it every day, you're probably doing something wrong as a parent. Take your time settling back in, but try to talk to Tzachan today as the patent issue is time-dependent, and don't forget to drop your tab off at EarthCent Intelligence."

Three

"Good morning, Ambassador Crute," Donna greeted the towering four-armed Dollnick ambassador when he entered the embassy. "Associate Ambassador Cohan is next door in our new space making a to-do list, and Ambassador McAllister should be here any minute. Can I get you something to drink?"

"I'm set for the moment," Crute responded as he strode past the reception desk. "I'll just wait in my office."

"She's not in yet," Donna repeated as the Dollnick approached the door to Kelly's office, which slid open despite the fact it should have been locked. Then his words sank in, and she jumped up and chased after him. "What do you mean, your office?"

"We're exchanging," the alien said, setting his valise on Kelly's desk and removing a device that reminded the embassy manager of a ping-pong paddle. "I'll be working here this week and Ambassador McAllister will be taking my place."

"But we didn't receive any notification!"

Crute began moving the paddle over the display desk, staring intently at a series of status lights on the back. The device also emitted a steady tone until he reached the edge of the desk, and then the frequency rose to a shrill note and Donna winced.

"Sorry about that," Crute said, laying the paddle aside and kneeling to examine the edge of the desk. He took what looked like a jeweler's loupe from his belt pouch, screwed it into his eye socket, and then used a pair of tweezers to remove a tiny speck of something from the underside of the desk's edge. "Grenouthian, I believe," he said, depositing the listening device into a plastic envelope.

Donna squinted at the envelope, unconvinced that the Dollnick had found something. "EarthCent Intelligence swept the embassy last Friday."

"The Drazen detection technology they use might be good enough to find Horten and Gem bugs, but that's about it," Crute said. He picked up the paddle again and started doing a circuit of the office walls. "The Drazens are fine singers and relatively good at mining operations, but intelligence hardware?" He shook his head.

"How did you get the door open just now?" Donna asked. "I'm sure it's locked when nobody is in here."

"The station librarian updated my implant with all of Ambassador McAllister's local access codes when the exchange officially started at 9:00 AM Human Standard Time," Crute explained. "For all intents and purposes, I am she for the next week on your calendar. As soon as I finish scanning my office for bugs we can go over my schedule."

"Kelly," Donna said with relief as the EarthCent ambassador entered the office. "Ambassador Crute is here for your exchange but I didn't receive any notification."

"I just heard about it when I woke up this morning and I was going to tell you when I got here," Kelly said. "I thought I had time because the exchange was set to begin after lunch."

28

"That's when the staff will arrive at the Dollnick embassy, but the exchange runs on your clock," Crute said. He removed a picture of Kelly's parents from the wall with his lower arms and used the hands of the upper arms to extract a listening device embedded in the frame. "It's traditional for these exchanges to go by the home ambassador's schedule."

"You mean I'll have to work a fifty-hour day?" Kelly asked in dismay.

"In accordance with the standard rules, you remain the home ambassador even when you're away," Crute explained. "Didn't you read through the information package?"

"It only showed up on my heads-up display an hour ago. I haven't had time yet."

"Then you can read it when you get to my embassy. Other than security, there won't be anybody there to distract you." The Dollnick replaced the framed picture of Kelly's parents on the wall and resumed scanning for bugs with the paddle. "Was there anything else I can do for you?" he asked over his shoulder.

"I'm not sure," Kelly admitted, shooting a look at Donna, who shrugged. "Do you want to tell me what's on your schedule for the next week?"

"I haven't discussed it with my embassy manager yet."

"Your people don't know I'm coming?"

"Do try to get into the spirit of the thing," Crute said, and the slight note of impatience in his whistle was perfectly replicated in the translation Kelly and Donna heard over their implants. "As the temporary EarthCent Ambassador to Union Station, my embassy manager is standing next to you. Your embassy manager, Gruke, by name, is sleeping at home and won't be waking up for another two hours. But the doors to *your* embassy on the Dollnick deck will grant you access, so if you want a quiet place to read the rules of the exchange, I suggest you head there."

"Is there any reason I should sit in an empty embassy rather than just reading the rules in our, I mean, the EarthCent conference room?"

"Only that it would be an odd breach of protocol for the Dollnick ambassador to monopolize the EarthCent embassy's conference room, not to mention that I'll soon be conducting a confidential meeting there with all of my staff," Crute said.

"All right, I can take a hint." Kelly sighed, wondering what she had gotten herself into. "Good luck, Donna. Ping me if you need anything."

"You prefer to be addressed without reference to your job title?" Crute asked the embassy manager.

"Yes," Donna replied. "And the associate ambassador will insist that you use his first name as well."

"Daniel, Donna, and Aabina," the Dollnick recited as he slid the paddle back into his valise. "Very well, Donna. Shall we go over my schedule for the week?"

"There's really not much to it," the embassy manager said apologetically. "I can tell you without looking that Kelly's only appointment today is with an academic researcher from Earth who is writing his dissertation about EarthCent, and that's not for another five hours."

"How about the rest of the week?" Crute asked.

"Tomorrow and Thursday she has tunnel network committee meetings, but you would have them on your schedule back at the Dollnick embassy, and I suppose now Kelly will attend in your place."

"Exactly," Crute says. "I hope she does a good job explaining why a new regulatory overseer for terraforming projects is a bad idea that would result in fewer worlds being made habitable."

"I believe she was going to vote in favor of that," Donna said hesitantly. "We're still hoping to purchase Earth Two, and the feeling is that we would benefit from some, uh, rules."

"Yes, well, I'll take that into consideration when I cast my vote as EarthCent's representative. Other than meetings, what are my duties?"

"Kelly was intentionally keeping her time as open as possible this week to help Daniel get started with the renovations to the new office space," Donna said. "When we expanded into the old travel agency next door a few years back to create our conference room it turned out to be more time consuming than anybody expected."

"It's all a question of hiring and managing your contractors," Crute said. "Why don't you show me the space, and then if it's convenient for everybody, we'll hold an all-hands-on-board meeting to map where I can be of the most help this week."

Donna led the Dollnick out into the corridor and past the exterior conference room door to the new space. Just as they entered the anteroom, there was a blood-curdling scream.

"Wait here," Crute ordered, and as he dashed through the old-fashioned door, Donna had a glimpse of the hand on his lower right arm pulling something that looked suspiciously like a military-grade weapon from his belt pouch.

"False alarm," Daniel shouted, moving between the Dollnick and Kelly's Vergallian assistant in case the former had an itchy trigger finger. "Aabina and I were discussing how this office reminded us of the haunted houses we

31

visited as children," he continued in his normal voice. "She mentioned performing in the haunted house her family sponsored when she was a teenager. We didn't realize you came in, Ambassador."

"Very convincing, Aabina," Crute said, slipping the weapon back into his belt pouch. He looked around at the walls and muttered, "Whoever came up with this decoration scheme deserves to be murdered." Then he flinched and took a step back. "There's something seriously wrong with this office."

"It does feel a bit off," Aabina concurred. "At first I thought there was a high-frequency vibration coming from somewhere, but the station librarian assured us that no active power sources are operating in the office."

"I have a list of painters to contact for bids," Donna said from the door. "Shall I stop at the first three who are willing to come in?"

"The first three who are willing to come in for a quote today," Daniel said. "But we need to cut through to the conference room and install a door before having the painting done. Who did we use for structural work the last time?"

"Union Builders, but they subcontracted the cutting work to a Dollnick construction crew."

"Smart move," Crute said, nodding in approval. "As your ambassador, I'll ping a contractor I know and have him come take care of it."

Daniel and Donna exchanged a look, and then the associate ambassador said, "As long as they can get it done by the end of the week, I suppose we could skip the bidding process this once."

"End of the week? I expect to see plasma torches cutting through that wall before your coffee break. The Dollnick workday hasn't started yet so I know they'll be free for a little job like this. Just show me where you want the opening."

"It's marked there with white chalk," Daniel said, and then frowned when he realized the wall he was pointing at was pure black. "That's funny. Did somebody come in and rub it off?"

"Humans have no eye for this sort of thing," Crute said. "I'll take care of it." He rummaged in his belt pouch and pulled out a silvery metal donut, then strode to the wall that was shared with the EarthCent conference room. After giving the donut a few shakes, Crute pulled a string out of the end. "Aabina, come hold this end up against the wall for me."

"I'll tell you when it's level," Daniel volunteered.

"As if you'd know," the Dollnick whistled under his breath. He transferred the metal donut to his lower left arm, held the string against the wall with his upper left, and then reached out with his upper right hand to pinch the string in the middle of the span. "Does that look good to everybody?" he asked after snapping the line.

"I guess it better since that looks like a permanent mark," Daniel said.

"The plasma torch will take it off. Now for the sides." He passed the string container from the lower left hand to the upper, pulled out more slack with the lower, and crouched to hold the line against the wall where it met the deck. When Aabina moved over to hold her end in place, he reached up with his upper right hand and snapped. They repeated the process on the other side, and then he stepped back for a look.

"I think you got it exactly in the center of the wall," Donna said.

"I adjusted for the anteroom and the office on this side by eye," Crute said modestly. "Now, as long as we're all together, why don't we go around to the conference room. I'll make a quick ping, and then you can bring me up to date on your plans for the week."

Daniel spent almost a half-hour telling the exchange ambassador about the latest developments in the Conference of Sovereign Human Communities, and then Aabina began doing the same with the current revisions she was processing for the All Species Cookbook. The corridor door to the conference room slid open and a Dollnick in coveralls carrying a large work bag asked, "Do you want me to cut from this side?"

"The other side," the exchange ambassador said. "I already marked it."

"I couldn't get in."

"Meeting adjourned," Crute declared. As he was leaving to let the workers into the new office space, the Dollnick turned back to Aabina and said, "Better close the doors to the embassy reception lobby and stay out of here for an hour. The cutting will go quickly, but there's some pretty nasty soundproofing material inside the walls and it will take the ventilation system a bit of time to clear the smoke."

Daniel headed directly for Donna's desk and waited for Aabina to catch up before speaking. "This isn't going as I expected. I thought that the exchange ambassadors would only show up for the tunnel networking meetings. Crute seems intent on taking over Kelly's job for the week, so you better let EarthCent Intelligence know what's going on."

"I'll ping Clive," Donna said. "You missed Kelly this morning, but apparently the Stryx just sprung it on her at the last minute and she hasn't even had a chance to read

34

the rules yet. I should contact her now and see if she can fill me in."

Crute reentered the embassy through the main door, and on observing the little grouping at Donna's desk, commented, "You can't be planning a coup already. I just got here."

"We were sharing our impressions," Daniel said. "I have a tunneling conference call in a few minutes so I'll be in my office if anybody needs me. Don't forget to contact those painters, Donna."

"That won't be necessary," the Dollnick said. "Brule and Sons will take care of the painting as soon as the door is cut in. I told them to use the same color as the conference room even though it reminds me of the tusks of a sea creature that once tried to eat me. That's a story for another day."

"I appreciate your help, Ambassador, but EarthCent has a budgeting process that—"

"—won't be necessary in this instance," Crute cut him off. "I'm sure a little flexibility in contracting for a trivial renovation project doesn't exceed my authority as the exchange ambassador, and if EarthCent has a problem with it, they can complain next week. Now," he said, turning to Donna. "I want you to contact the director of EarthCent Intelligence and arrange for a briefing, today if possible. Tell Clive to bring along the chief of the Dollnick section."

After Crute disappeared into Kelly's office, Daniel asked Aabina, "Do you know anything about this exchange business? I'm getting a little concerned."

"My mother mentioned once in passing that Vergallian ambassadors are instructed to avoid the honor if at all possible," the alien girl replied. "I think that only applied to being designated the home ambassador. Going out as the visiting ambassador is seen as something of a lark."

"But other than the working hours, what's really the difference?" Donna asked.

"Frequency," Aabina explained. "As a visiting exchange ambassador, Crute will be here for a week, and then everything will go back to normal at the Dollnick embassy. As the home ambassador, Ambassador McAllister will have to spend a week at each of the participating embassies, and we'll have those ambassadors here for a week at a time. I imagine it could be quite disruptive."

"Are they all scheduled in a row without breaks?"

"I believe it's the one-on, one-off principle, so Ambassador McAllister will be back here for a week between every exchange."

"All right, I have to get on that conference call, but give me a shout if our feather-crested friend does anything that seems too out of line," Daniel said, and then retreated to his office.

"I better ping my son-in-law," Donna said, meaning Clive Oxford, the director of EarthCent Intelligence who was married to her older daughter, Blythe. "I hope you aren't planning any time off, Aabina. The next few months are suddenly looking a bit hectic."

"It will be my pleasure to serve as the special assistant to Ambassador McAllister's temporary replacements. It's a unique opportunity to see how the diplomats from the other species work."

Several hours went by with Crute popping out from time to time to make an inspection of the Dollnick contractor's work. By the time the Ph.D. student from Earth arrived, the door to the now-shared conference room was installed, the new office had been painted, and the four-armed workers were just putting the finishing touches on a tiled floor.

"I'll meet him in my office," Crute told Donna when she came through the conference room to announce the visitor. "Would you care to be present, Aabina?"

"Yes, thank you," the Vergallian said, wondering what the Dollnick had up his sleeve. They left Daniel deep in conversation with one of Brule's sons who claimed to have a source that could procure human-sized office furniture below wholesale cost. Crute surprised Aabina by stopping in the kitchen adjoining the conference room and loading a tray with coffee and snacks. "Feeling hungry?" she asked him.

"For my guest," the Dollnick replied. "I've found over the years that the easiest way to control the agenda with academics is to feed them. Could I ask you to go ahead and explain the exchange situation lest he believe that EarthCent is run by scary aliens?"

The Vergallian girl saw the logic in Crute's suggestion and she went ahead to tell the researcher that the Dollnick would be replacing the EarthCent ambassador for the week. Donna had already warned the guest while seating him in Kelly's office and he was waiting with a question.

"Should I go to the Dollnick embassy to interview Ambassador McAllister?" the Ph.D. student asked.

"Absolutely not," Crute said as he entered on Aabina's heels. He set the tray down on Kelly's desk and offered the student a handshake. "Before we begin, I'd like to make sure that the ear cuff translator you're using is getting my meaning correctly." He held out all four fists. "There's a twenty-cred coin in one of my hands, and if you guess it on the first try, it's yours. I'll give you one hint, which is upper left."

37

The student immediately reached up and tapped the hand on his upper left, which the Dollnick demonstrated was empty. "But you said—"

"My upper left, not yours," Crute said, showing the coin and then dropping it back in his belt pouch. "Please help yourself to coffee and snacks. I hope it doesn't make you uncomfortable that I continue standing, but my knees don't fit under the desk unless I lower the chair seat until I'm practically sitting on the floor."

The student looked befuddled for a moment before recovering and introducing himself. "My name is Tor Karlson and I'm a graduate student at the New University of Scandinavia. This exchange that you're working with the EarthCent ambassador is fascinating, but it doesn't fit with my dissertation, and I'm only on Union Station for the week."

"So if the facts don't fit your thesis you ignore them?" Crute inquired dryly.

"Not at all," Tor protested. "My thesis involves how the different personalities of EarthCent's tunnel network ambassadors affect their performance, but as an alien substituting for Ambassador McAllister, I won't be able to use any information you provide me."

"I don't see why not," the Dollnick said. "In addition to my working relationship with the ambassador, I've read innumerable intelligence assessments about her from a variety of sources."

"The advanced species share their intelligence reports on humans?" Tor asked.

"Not intentionally, though I understand that the spirit of cooperation on board Flower has gotten a bit out of hand." Crute twiddled four thumbs while waiting for a reaction but quickly ran out of patience "Try me on some-

38

thing. Aabina has been Ambassador McAllister's special assistant for years. She can referee."

"Well, if you insist." The graduate student hesitated and stole a look at the beautiful Vergallian, who gave him an encouraging nod. "I began my research in EarthCent's archives, and I was immediately struck by the number of diplomatic breakthroughs taking place on Union Station after Ambassador McAllister arrived. It can't be a coincidence that EarthCent Intelligence, the Conference of Sovereign Human Communities, and the Galactic Free Press, the three most important institutions holding diaspora humanity together, were all founded here."

"Was there a question in there that I missed?" the Dollnick inquired.

"How would you explain this confluence, if you were Ambassador McAllister?"

"First, I would have you talk to my embassy manager, as the financing behind both EarthCent Intelligence and the Galactic Free Press came from her daughters. Next, I would point out that those daughters were educated in the experimental school run by the station's librarian—a second-generation Stryx. As to CoSHC, you can ask the man in the office next door."

"But I wanted your, I mean, Ambassador McAllister's explanation."

"She's very good at giving credit where it's due," Crute said. "Ambassador McAllister was the original voice to suggest that EarthCent needed a spy agency, and I have a declassified recording of the secret meeting if that would help you."

"I also heard that she's EarthCent's Minister of Intelligence and that the training camp is in her back yard," Tor said.

"I can see that plugging leaks should be at the top of the agenda if I can get the intelligence committee on a conference call this week," Crute said sadly. "I'm afraid I can't discuss any issues related to Earth's security in-depth unless you present a security clearance."

"But you're an alien!"

"Not in the present context," the Dollnick replied, folding four arms across his chest and staring down at the graduate student. "Aabina, if you'll see our guest out."

Four

"So you don't think that Crute is spying on us after all?" Kelly asked, pushing away the half-sour pickle that came with her deli sandwich.

"I don't think he needs to," Donna said. "Blythe and Clive suggested that I test him on EarthCent knowledge, so I ask him something every time he walks past my desk. I swear Crute knows more about humanity than we do."

"It doesn't annoy him that you keep asking?"

"I always start by saying, 'Normally I'd ask Ambassador McAllister,' and then he's all ears. I think he likes showing off because he's given me a lot of helpful tips. He even took me this morning to meet the new Dollnick manager of the Empire Convention Center and put in a good word for us. How are things going in his embassy?"

"He left me detailed written instructions," Kelly said. "I'll have to make sure to do that myself for the rest of these exchanges. His staff has kept to the regular schedule on their clock, so I've only been in the embassy at the same time as them for around twelve hours so far. This morning, Gruke, the embassy manager, walked me through the presentation I'll be doing at the terraforming subcommittee meeting after lunch. You wouldn't believe how much work goes into making a lifeless rock suitable for oxygen breathers. Sometimes they go as far as reheating an old planet's iron core in order to get the eddy currents going again and establish a magnetic field to protect against radiation. Those jobs can stretch tens of thousands of years."

"I guess it must be their passion because I can't imagine they get much return on investment after all that," Donna said. "Have you snooped around their holographic files at all?"

"I meant to, but it just felt wrong. And when I'm there during embassy hours, there's an endless stream of Dollnicks coming in to see Crute about business matters. I never knew how busy he was."

"What do the visitors say when they see that you're substituting for him?" Donna asked, employing the side of her fork to scrape up the remaining potato salad on her plate.

"That's the funny part," Kelly said. "You'd think they would just come back later, but instead they all treat me as if I was Crute. I only wish that the people who come to us with grant proposals to spend the All Species Cookbook money had half the business sense of these Dollnick entrepreneurs." The ambassador covered the remains of her sandwich with her napkin, shot her friend a guilty look, and moved on to the dessert. "The last one was a prince's representative for a new factory producing sub-sea habitats, and I hinted that he pitch his idea on Earth since it's mainly ocean."

"Did you give him President Beyer's contact information? Getting alien businesses to open on Earth is his passion."

"I think I ended up telling all of Crute's visitors to contact EarthCent headquarters and to use my name," Kelly said. She took a mouthful of Boston cream pie and sighed.

"I hope I didn't violate the exchange protocol by trying to steer their business to Earth."

"I wouldn't worry. It only took Crute a matter of minutes to turn the new office into an employment project for his cronies on the station. At the rate things are going, Daniel will wind up with a Dollnick secretary."

Kelly savored the pie for a long moment while getting out the notebook she carried to supplement her memory and flipping to the last page. "There was something I meant to ask you and—do you know anything about that string game the Dollnicks play?" she interrupted herself.

"You mean Cat's Cradle?" Donna asked. "I've seen it, of course, but with eight hands involved it's just too complex for me to figure out what's going on."

"I'm supposed to judge a competition in a Dollnick school tomorrow," Kelly said. "Crute left me a number of recordings from professional competitions to watch, but the hands are moving so fast that I don't have a clue what I'm seeing. It almost looks to me like they're boxing with string tangled up in their fingers, and then suddenly there's a perfectly formed spaceship or a dragon. They've really turned it into a high art form."

"Maybe you can just go by the audience noise. Turn off your implant, and when you hear a lot of excited whistling, it must mean that the players are really good."

"Or really bad," Kelly pointed out. "Maybe I can get Libby to tell me who deserves to win."

"If it makes you feel any better, Crute is on the hook to be my grandson's celebrity guest on Stone Soup for the Friday afternoon show. Had you forgotten about that?"

"Not at all," Kelly lied, flipping back a few pages in her custom printed notebook with a cover from an alien romance novel. "Jonah is planning to make lobster tails with garlic butter."

"In addition to the fact that Crute has probably never been in a kitchen, Dollnicks are allergic to Earth shellfish," Donna said sympathetically. "I tried to tell him that it would be easy for Jonah to rearrange the schedule or change the recipe since the celebrity guest feature is just getting started, but he told me not to worry."

"According to my notes, I agreed to be the guest celebrity every fourth Friday for the next three months," Kelly said, and her face fell. "If this exchange I'm committed to continues every other week, I'll miss all three shows."

Donna put down her fork, a strange look on her face. "Do you think...?"

"That some of the ambassadors planned it this way so they could appear on Jonah's show? I've learned to be skeptical of coincidences when it comes to diplomats. Libby?"

"Yes, Ambassador," the Stryx station librarian replied.

"Did you determine the schedule for the exchange program?"

"The participating ambassadors had a meeting to set the starting date and the order in which the exchanges would take place. It's described in Appendix C of the package I sent to your implant."

"But you knew I wouldn't read the whole thing," Kelly complained. "Which ambassadors are going to end up taking my place on Jonah's show?"

"Crute, Aleeytis, and Czeros."

Kelly looked back at her notebook to see what Jonah had planned for the other two shows she had agreed to appear on. "Vergallian vegan for Aleeytis and wine tasting for Czeros."

"I think we've been had," Donna said. "I don't care how much influence Crute wields in the local Dollnick community. How else could that contractor have shown up to cut through the wall of our conference room faster than I can get take-out food from the Little Apple?"

The EarthCent ambassador took the last forkful of Boston cream pie and was silent for almost a full minute. "I guess it can't be helped." She pulled the pencil out of its holder under her purse flap and turned to the last page of her notebook where she recorded thoughts that struck her as important. "Beware of alien diplomats bearing honors," she said as she wrote the words.

"And that means those businessmen who came to the Dollnick embassy must have been expecting you all along," Donna said.

Kelly put the pencil away. "Turn-around is fair play. Tell Clive and Blythe what's going on and that I want to see them this weekend to talk EarthCent Intelligence strategy. Chastity too, for the fourth estate. We'll go over the schedule for the ambassadors taking my place and—Libby?"

"Yes, Ambassador."

"Can I find out which ambassadors will be swapping with me ahead of time?"

"It's in the package I sent you," the Stryx librarian replied.

"Could I ask you to send the same package to Donna and Aabina?" Kelly asked.

"Got it," Donna said a few seconds later. "We'll all put our heads together and start thinking about what we can get out of the ambassadors while they're filling your shoes. But don't you have to hurry if you're going to make the terraforming meeting?"

"I should pull a no-show. That would serve Crute right for manipulating me like a chess piece." Kelly returned her notebook to her purse and rose to go, but then she stopped and asked, "Why do you think Crute would want to go on Stone Soup if he's allergic to shellfish?"

"Good question. I'll ping Jonah and he can check with his Grenouthian producer. Maybe they have something cooked up between them."

"Of course," Kelly said. "I'll bet that meeting the ambassadors had to determine the exchange order was a real swap-fest. I can almost see it in my mind's eye."

"Don't let it get you down, at least we know the score now," Donna said. "Good luck with the presentation."

Kelly took the lift tube to the Verlock embassy and made her way through the lobby area with its decorative waterfall that featured red-hot lava in the place of water. She arrived in the conference room just as Srythlan gaveled the session open.

"Welcome to the six-hundred and fourteenth meeting of the exploratory committee formed to consider updates to the tunnel network treaty's guidelines for transferring ownership for terraformed planets," the Verlock stated ponderously. "The topic of today's session is proposed changes to Subsection Fourteen Point Five Point Seven, which specifies bid procedures for unfinished terraforming projects suitable for two or more species. Before I open the subject to discussion, I see that the Dollnick Ambassador has submitted a written request to make a small presentation. If there are no objections?"

"I object," Kelly said. "Crute has maneuvered me into the position of advocating for a policy that's the exact opposite of what EarthCent desires."

"As the Dollnick ambassador you cannot withdraw your own prior written request," Srythlan informed her. "Does the EarthCent Ambassador wish to object?"

"I do not," Crute replied.

Kelly glared at the Dollnick, and then rose and moved to the side of the room where the Verlock holographic projector displayed linked presentations. She took the memory unit from her purse, a slender Dollnick device that reminded her of an antique ball-point pen with a spring-loaded button to retract the point, and clicked.

"Earth Two is a partially completed late-phase terraforming project carried out by a newcomer to the business popularly known as the Container Prince," she said, as a hologram of the planet revolved slowly next to her. "EarthCent purchased rights of first refusal, thanks to the generous backing of private entrepreneurs on this station, but humanity is unable to match the Alt offer."

"Still, it was nice of the Dollnicks to give us the opportunity," Crute said, and the other ambassadors murmured their agreement.

"A complaint was lodged stating that the first right of refusal was granted in bad faith since the Alts already had a team inspecting Earth Two when the EarthCent representatives arrived," Kelly continued.

"I withdraw that complaint," Crute stated formally.

"Request granted," Srythlan said, knocking his gavel on the table with relish.

"What do you mean you're letting him withdraw my complaint?" Kelly demanded indignantly. "I'm up here doing his presentation because everybody told me that I have to represent Dollnick interests. Crute should be representing humanity's interests in my place."

"Exchange protocol violation," Srythlan scolded Kelly. "You're trying to serve two masters at the same time."

"But he did!"

"If I may," Crute said, rising to his feet and moving around the stone slab to join Kelly. "I have examined this issue from both sides, and I've determined that the best course is to drop the matter."

"The best course for who?" Kelly asked in frustration.

"EarthCent's best course," the Dollnick said. "Surely you don't question my integrity."

"Perhaps if you explained your reasoning," the Frunge ambassador suggested. Kelly shot Czeros a look of gratitude and the Frunge returned a wink.

Crute produced his own pen-like holographic memory interface device and clicked the button. The previous hologram was replaced with a densely worded contract. The Dollnick reversed the pen-like device, clicked again, and then used it to highlight some holographic text in red.

"I didn't know it could do that," Kelly muttered, looking at her own pen. "I could have drawn a line around the continent at the heart of the dispute."

"This is the text of the right of first refusal contract signed by EarthCent's representative in the matter," Crute said. "As you can plainly see, there is an exclusive jurisdiction clause setting the venue as the Dollnick homeworld."

"He's right, Ambassador McAllister," Bork told Kelly. "Never sign a contract with aliens that requires you to sue in a court on their homeworld if any issues come up."

"Even if you brought suit, which I assure you would be a waste of creds, the Container Prince could easily delay the hearing through legal maneuverings for a century," Crute continued. "I see no possible upside for EarthCent in going to court."

"But that's the reason we went through tunnel network treaty procedures to complain," Kelly said. "There should be a fair and open process for something as important as buying and selling planets. This affects everybody, not just EarthCent."

"You're speaking against the interests of your exchange embassy again," the Verlock ambassador cautioned her.

"Besides, where are the Alts going to get eight trillion creds?" Kelly demanded. "They don't even have money on their homeworld because they run their economy on the honor system."

"The Empire of a Hundred Worlds will provide financing," the Vergallian ambassador spoke up. "My former partners are handling the legal work for the Alts and the Council of Queens since multi-species real estate deals were one of our specialties."

"Is there a reason you're willing to back the Alts and not EarthCent?" Crute inquired, again drawing murmurs of approval from the other ambassadors for the fine job he was doing representing his exchange embassy's interests.

"I'm sure you all recall that the Alts turned down an invitation to join the tunnel network as full members and instead accepted the protection of the Empire of a Hundred Worlds in return for our providing royal management of their business affairs," Aleeytis explained. "The princesses serving as contract queens are in a perfect position to judge the credit worthiness and disposable income of the Alts."

"If humanity accepted contract queens, would you provide EarthCent with the financial backing to bid on Earth Two?" Crute followed up.

"Wait a minute," Kelly objected. "The reason the Alts chose the protection of the Vergallian empire over the tunnel network is that they find business distasteful. Humanity doesn't have that issue, so queens are off the table."

"Perhaps the Humans could work out a plan to share the planet with the Alts," the Grenouthian ambassador suggested. "After all, both species originated on Earth and are capable of interbreeding."

"Unfortunately, the Alts find Humans as distasteful as they find business," Crute said. "Despite the tens of thousands of years that have passed and all of the genes that they share, Alt children still experience a visceral fear of Humans."

"The Alt representative, Methan, will be coming to Union Station to meet my former law partners," Aleeytis said. "I wouldn't dream of telling the EarthCent ambassador how to conduct diplomacy, but perhaps some confidence-building measures wouldn't be unwelcome."

"Thank you for the suggestion, Ambassador," Crute replied before Kelly could open her mouth. "EarthCent will attempt to reach out to the Alts and see if we can resolve our differences without litigation."

"If that's everything?" Srythlan asked, looking around at the other ambassadors.

Then he pounded his gavel into the stone table again. "Meeting adjourned."

Kelly grabbed the wrist of Crute's lower right hand. "What was that all about?" she demanded. "How could you just announce a new policy initiative for EarthCent when tomorrow night you'll be back in the Dollnick embassy and I'll be stuck cleaning up your mess?"

"I am representing EarthCent to the best of my ability, regardless of the termination of the exchange, which remains in force until 9:00 AM Monday morning Universal

Human Time," Crute replied. "I'll leave you instructions for carrying on with any unfinished business I've started."

"But you said it yourself. I can't even get near an Alt baby or it will start screaming. And the children look like they want to run when they see us coming."

"And you think that ignoring the problem will make it go away? I'm just trying to help."

Kelly had a sudden flash of inspiration. "If you really want to help, I'd like you to visit a Dollnick school with me tomorrow. I'm judging a Cat's Cradle competition, but I'm sure they would be honored to have EarthCent's ambassador serve as a guest judge."

Crute pulled a small notebook out of his belt pouch and flipped through the pages. "Friday morning, let's see. I have a meeting first thing with the vendor providing display desks for CoSHC's new office, and I have a lunch meeting with that annoying graduate student, but, yes, I think I can squeeze you in."

"Annoying graduate student?"

"If you ask me, he's probably a spy for one of the other species," the Dollnick said. "He's altogether too well informed about our operations. I insisted EarthCent Intelligence run a background check and have him in for an interview."

"What did they say?" Kelly asked.

"That I was imagining things," Crute said, shaking his head in disbelief. "Well, don't come crying to me when your secrets are spread far and wide."

"I think it's a little late to worry about that."

Five

"If we're going to seriously discuss adding a franchise on Flower, Marilla should be here," the EarthCent ambassador's husband said to Paul. "You did make her a ten percent owner in Tunnel Trips."

"You're right," Paul said. He turned and called to his fourteen-year-old daughter who was attempting to teach Hindi dance moves to a scowling boy. "Fenna? Could you ask Marilla to meet Grandpa and me at the chandlery? You can fill in for her at the kiosk." The girl nodded and took off running with her thick black hair and sari streaming out behind her.

"Is your dad hiring us to clean out rentals?" Mike asked as he ran alongside the girl. "I need to save money to buy my dad a present for his new office."

"Marilla will tell us," the girl replied without breaking stride. "If you would learn the dance moves, we could enter a contest and win a prize."

"Next you'll say I have to learn to sing in Hindi," Mike panted out as they skidded to a halt in front of the kiosk.

The alien clerk looked up and her skin turned light brown with pleasure. "Are the two of you interested in doing some cleaning? We just had a return from a first-time renter who got so sick in Zero-G that he canceled his trip before entering the tunnel and came right back to Union Station."

Fenna grimaced and pinched her nostrils closed between her thumb and forefinger, but Mike said, "We'll do it. How much?"

"It's pretty bad so I guess I can give you a bonus. How about four creds for the two of you?" Marilla offered.

"Each?" the boy asked hopefully.

"No, that would be quadruple what I normally pay you. I was thinking double."

"You can keep it all yourself," Fenna told Mike and turned back to Marilla. "My dad wants you to meet him and Grandpa at the chandlery. I'll watch the kiosk for you."

"Do you remember how to check in a return?" Marilla asked. "I'm expecting two at any time now."

"No problem," Fenna said confidently. "And if anybody comes in with a weird rental question, I'll just send them to the chandlery."

"Alright." The Horten grabbed her purse and turned to Mike. "Don't try to use the power washer by yourself. The mess hasn't had time to dry yet so you should be able to clean it up and then wipe everything down with disinfectant. Okay?"

"I should have just learned the stupid dance," the boy muttered to himself, but he set off for the old Drazen cargo container where Tunnel Trips kept their cleaning supplies.

Marilla headed in the opposite direction to the chandlery owned by Dorothy's husband. When she got there, Joe and Paul were already perched on the high stools at the counter. Kevin had added the stools when he realized that most of his customers liked to hang around and chat while he put together their orders for ship supplies. The chandler had also added a hot water dispenser at the end of the counter with tasting packets of instant coffee and teabags from the manufacturers of Zero-G self-heating drink boxes.

"I just got in a new shipment of that green tea you like," Kevin told the Horten girl. "The samples are in the basket."

"Thank you," Marilla said, helping herself human-style to a cup of hot water before climbing onto the stool next to Joe. "Is your coffee good?" she asked him politely.

"It's about what I'd expect for free," the EarthCent ambassador's husband said. "I'll get right to the point. We've received an application from Flower to open a Tunnel Trips franchise there. What do you think?"

The Horten girl's skin turned the faintest yellow at the bluntness of Joe's question, but a few years earlier, it would have looked like an alien embodiment of Van Gough's *Sunflowers*. She carefully opened the packet holding the tea bag to buy time before replying, "Do we know anything about the person who applied for the franchise, or is it one of the aliens living on board Flower?"

"Neither," Paul said. "It's Flower herself. She promises to only rent the ships when she's visiting tunnel-connected worlds."

"Flower wants to buy a franchise?" Marilla asked. "I had the impression she was more of a do-it-herself-er."

"Flower is continually traveling between star systems so there's no opportunity for her to develop a local market. She'd have to build out her own network, and that would put her in direct competition with both us and the Dollnick rental agencies."

"I guess it makes sense from her standpoint, and we wouldn't have to worry about her skimping on the scheduled maintenance like some of the franchisees. But I hear from Samuel that she's a bit…"

"Pushy," Joe supplied the word that the Horten was too polite to say out loud. "You'd expect a twenty-thousand-year-old AI that the Dollnicks couldn't put up with to be a handful, but my concern is how our existing franchisees would see it. Many of them operate in star systems where Flower stops, and I could just imagine her undercutting their pricing while she's there."

"There could be an advantage to working with Flower," Marilla said slowly. "You know how some destinations are simply more popular than others. Over the course of a few months the franchises in those star systems accumulate too many ships from one-way trips. We end up having to pay somebody to take them to a franchise that's short on inventory because the Stryx won't let us send rentals through the tunnels without passengers."

"So you're saying that a franchise on Flower could function as a second distribution center for keeping the fleet in balance," Joe said.

"She only stops at the same places twice a year so it wouldn't be a complete solution, but with proper planning, it could save everybody some creds," the Horten girl said, and her skin began to shade towards blue with excitement. "I could work up a mathematical model using game theory and submit it for the final project in the graduate business course I'm taking at the Open University."

"We'll need to make some sort of deal with the Stryx for tunneling bandwidth to keep in touch with Flower," Paul said. "Otherwise we'd get stuck issuing refunds if people rent a ship to visit Flower and she's already moved on to the next system before they arrive."

"Another variable," Marilla said, her eyes shining. "This will be so much fun."

Joe caught the chandler's eye and they shared a smile at the alien girl's enthusiasm for logistical challenges. Then Kevin asked, "What are you going to tell Flower if she wants to use the rental fleet in the courier service she's building? Almost all of the small traders and family ships who stop on Flower end up carrying packages for her, and I've already gotten stuck acting as a transfer station more than a few times."

Paul nodded slowly. "I had the feeling there was something more to it. From what Samuel said the last time Flower stopped here, she's addicted to multi-tasking. Even though most of our fleet consists of reconditioned Dollnick space taxis, there's certainly enough room on board for a couple of packages. But I can't imagine that our renters will agree to act as delivery people."

"The packages I've seen are usually small items, like commercial samples from the businesses Flower has started, or M793qK's branded placebos," Kevin said. "Sometimes there are gifts sent to family by people living on board." He reached under the counter and pulled out a plastic box with a label featuring artwork of a Dollnick colony ship. "I'm holding this one for a trader heading to Bits who's supposed to stop here today."

"Is Flower paying you to act as a transfer station?" Joe asked.

"I get an alcohol-soaked fruitcake for every ten packages I pass along."

"What a fun logistics network she has!" Marilla enthused. "We should definitely work with Flower."

"I'll ping Jeeves and see if he's available to come and explain our communications options," Paul said. He got up to put a polite conversational distance between himself and the chandlery counter, and his place was immediately taken by a skeletal Sharf who appeared to be in a hurry.

"Are you the Human?" the alien demanded of Kevin.

"Which human?" the chandler responded.

"You know, the one with the package."

"You're the trader going to Bits?" Kevin asked. "I didn't realize that Flower was hiring aliens for deliveries."

"Don't play dumb with me. I'm here for the special package," the Sharf said angrily, and the translation of his naturally sibilant speech made the word come out "Sssssspecial."

"Sorry. Just a second." The chandler went into his back storeroom and returned carrying a metallic envelope with what looked a bit like a hand-held gaming device attached to one side. He placed the envelope on the counter, flipped open the bottom of the device, and told the alien, "You know the drill."

The Sharf looked extremely irritated, but he jabbed a finger into the opening, and then pulled it out and stuck it in his mouth. The device took almost a full minute to analyze the genetics of the blood sample before letting out a happy chirp, at which point Kevin handed over the envelope. The alien departed without another word, still sucking his finger.

"Don't tell me," Joe said, putting his palm to his forehead like a bad psychic. "Flower also has you acting as a post office for spies."

Thomas, the artificial person who ran the training camp for EarthCent Intelligence, arrived at a trot before Kevin could reply. "Wasn't that Yaender?" he asked. "He's on our banned list. We caught him trying to recruit double agents among our trainees."

"I never got his name, but he's definitely Sharf Intel," Kevin said. "He was just here to pick up a package from Flower. If you think that's his name, I'll make a note of it on the file." He picked up his standard tab, brought up the interface for the surveillance camera that covered the chandlery's counter area, and saved the clip of the Sharf along with the possible identity.

"You're working for EarthCent Intelligence now?" Marilla asked Kevin. "I'll have to be careful of what I say around you."

"I'm just a middle-man tasked with supporting that crazy deal that EarthCent made to host alien spies on Flower. Their intelligence services save a ton while keeping an eye on the sovereign human communities, and they pay the difference to EarthCent to help offset Flower's operating costs. I guess sometimes the spies have something other than information they want to send back to their headquarters, and from Union Station, their local ambassador can forward it anywhere in a diplomatic pouch."

"So you're saying that some of our Tunnel Trips renters returning from Flower could be unknowingly carrying espionage materials?"

"Maybe you could add a lockbox to the ships," Kevin suggested. "It wouldn't need to be a safe or anything, just enough to keep the curious out."

Joe shook his head and turned to Thomas. "Any progress on tracking down whoever hacked my daughter's tab?"

"If Dorothy doesn't get it back soon, she's going to buy a new one, and those things are expensive," her husband added.

"I have good news and bad news," the artificial person said. "The good news is that our information technology team backed up her data before they began their forensic analysis."

"I'll tell her to start shopping," Kevin said. "Are you sure it's not repairable?"

"You could try bringing it to Rupe, the Dollnick in the Shuk who does screen repairs," Thomas said. "It's just kind of embarrassing for EarthCent Intelligence if one of us brings it to him."

"Rupe's good people, repaired a screen for me when I first came to Union Station," Joe said. "I'd offer to take it in myself, but the last time I saw him, I think he was pretty upset by how much I'd aged."

"How about tracking down the hacker?" Marilla asked. "Do we need to worry about Tunnel Trips data security?"

"That's all contracted out to the station librarian," Joe told her. "I suppose you might want to make sure the security on your personal tab is up-to-date if you use it in here. I'm not sure where Hortens rank in terms of encryption technology."

"Don't tell anybody you heard it from me, but we're about on the same level as the Drazens," the Horten girl admitted.

"So did you learn anything from destructively examining Dorothy's tab?" Kevin asked the artificial person, who had been EarthCent Intelligence's first hire.

"All we could determine was that the hack occurred the morning we held an open recruitment event for artificial people," Thomas said. "There are hundreds of possible suspects, and that's assuming some clever alien didn't sneak in and pass himself off as AI."

"Could a biological agent really do that without your knowledge?" Joe asked.

"If an artificial person can pass as human, an alien can certainly pass as an artificial person with the right gear. It's not like we walk around x-raying each other all of the time. If the intelligence service of an advanced species wanted to build a device that created the sort of electro-magnetic field leakage we show while we're moving, yes, I think it could be easily done."

"It sounds like I got here just in time," Jeeves declared, floating up to the counter from the other side. "A suit that would allow a biological to pass as an artificial person is an interesting idea, though I'm not sure I see a business model for it in the fashion industry."

"We were discussing the possibilities as to who might have hacked Dorothy's tab," Thomas said. "Don't you have a vested interest since the stolen intellectual property belongs in part to SBJ Fashions?"

"Yes, but I had to promise my elders that I wouldn't upset the competitive balance of the tunnel network if I went into business with Humans."

"I thought that you gave Baa a minority stake in SBJ Fashions in return for her work," Paul said, retaking his seat at the counter, which was becoming quite crowded. "Doesn't that allow you to use knowledge and technology up to the level of a Terragram mage?"

"It doesn't work that way," the young Stryx said. "And Baa took a close look at Dorothy's tab before EarthCent Intelligence damaged it, but I thought you had another reason for inviting me here."

"Flower wants to purchase a Tunnel Trips franchise and we realized it will require real-time communications," Joe said. "Her idea of holding to a tight schedule has become increasingly flexible since that problem with the Wanderers."

"If I had a forehead, I'd be slapping it with my pincer right now," Jeeves said. "Just what we all need in our lives—more Flower."

"Marilla pointed out that with the proper logistical planning, the fact that Flower visits so many of the sovereign human communities with Tunnel Trips franchises could help us reposition inventory," Paul said. "And now that Flower has an operating shipyard on board, we could send her the overhaul jobs we don't have time for here."

"I'm sure Flower will be thrilled to get the business. The question is, will she end up running Tunnel Trips?"

"Not while I'm a minority owner," Marilla said defiantly. Then she glanced up as the overhead bay doors began to slide open and two small ships penetrated the atmosphere retention field at practically the same instant. "I better go back and watch Fenna check these in. She's never had to deal with multiple customers at the same time before."

"So how is everybody adjusting to my daughter returning to work?" Joe asked the young Stryx. "Does she have you teetering on the edge of bankruptcy yet?"

"Dorothy's latest idea hasn't cost me anything so far, and I'm hoping it stays in the research phase for a good long time," Jeeves replied. "The truth is, she's our best salesperson and trainer for the nanofabric franchise idea she came up with last year, and we've just started scheduling seminars to expand the business."

"But is it really possible to tap into some sort of universal aesthetic?" Kevin asked. "She kept running off to ask Paul about the math when she was working on it because I couldn't help her. I'm not even sure I understand the point."

"You know I can't answer your question. Dorothy stumbled on a concept that humanity won't be equipped to fully understand for some time. To confirm or deny anything beyond that would be unfair to the competition, especially when my own business interests are involved."

"I couldn't solve all the critical variables myself," Paul said. "Just enough for an approximation that she could show to Dring. He's been a little more forthcoming on technology questions since attending the test of humanity's first interstellar jump drive with you."

"It was altogether the most pleasant vacation experience I've had," Jeeves said. "And if I was looking for a remote business opportunity, I'd consider opening my own Tunnel Trips franchise in Earth orbit. The rental worked out quite well, whereas if we had taken Dring's gravity surfer we still wouldn't be back."

"Elegant technology, though," Joe said. "Dring told me that the Makers used to stage gravity surfing competitions around the event horizons of black holes. I can't even imagine what sorts of speeds they achieved."

"You never told us what you thought of Earth Two," Kevin said to Jeeves. "Dring mentioned that the two of you hitched a ride out with Flower before returning to Union Station from her next tunnel network stop."

"As long as you're in competition with the Alts for the planet I really shouldn't say anything," Jeeves replied, and then he lowered his artificial voice in a conspiratorial fashion as if that would make a difference. "But as a friend, I might point out that opportunities like Earth Two don't come along every day."

"You know that we don't have that kind of money," Joe said. "Aisha got together with Blythe and Chastity to buy the first right of refusal from the Dollnicks, but the Alt bid is on the order of a thousand creds for every human being alive today. Maybe a planet that's already seeded with Earth's flora and fauna is worth it, but the average person just doesn't have that kind of cash lying around, and they couldn't all move there even if they did. The terraforming is only finished on the one small continent."

"I think the real issue is the success of the open worlds," Kevin said. "If our only choice was to live on Earth or on Earth Two, a couple of billion people would have stepped up, and even if they didn't have the cash, they could have managed a down payment and taken out a mortgage. But I'm always talking to traders who visit open worlds, and they all say that the humans living on them wouldn't leave for a world of their own."

"If you think there's something new about Humans not knowing what's good for them, you're less intelligent than I take you for," Jeeves said. "The thing that defines great leaders is that they take their followers places that they wouldn't have gone on their own."

Six

"It might help if you blew on them," the Thark ambassador suggested, holding his hand out in Aabina's direction. Kelly's special assistant, who stood almost a head taller than the new exchange ambassador, took a deep breath and complied. Then the shorter alien crouched on his heels, muttered, "Daddy needs a new colony ship," and threw the dice against the wall. They bounced off and rolled to a halt, each displaying a white surface uppermost. "Light again," he grunted in disbelief.

"I guess I don't understand the Thark version of shooting craps," Daniel said. "Each die has three white faces and three black faces, so when you're throwing two of them, there are only four possible outcomes, and two of those are the same. How does the betting work?"

"These aren't gambling dice, they're for measuring probability," the alien explained as he scooped up the little cubes. "It's similar to flipping a coin, but more accurate because the weighting is perfect and there are two of them."

"What do you mean, measuring probability? The math is exactly the same as if you were flipping two coins. There's a twenty-five percent chance that the outcome will be both white, the same for both black, and a fifty percent chance you'll get one of each."

The ambassador threw the dice again, and as they rolled to a halt, one of the two seemed to hesitate on edge for a moment before tipping back towards the wall and coming up white. "Light," he said again. "That's five times in a row."

"Tenth of a percent chance," Daniel said. "It's not likely, but not impossible."

"Nothing is impossible, and it's not a tenth of a percent, it's a thousand and twenty-four to one," the Thark corrected the associate ambassador. He picked up the dice and threw again. "Four thousand and ninety-six to one."

"Are you sure the dice aren't loaded?" Aabina asked. "Maybe somebody swapped them on you as a joke."

"Tharks don't joke about gambling, and these are my tamper-proof set from our Bureau of Standards. I use them for my side gig calibrating the table games in the casino." He threw a seventh time. "Light again!"

"So we're at one chance in over sixteen thousand," Daniel said, again rounding down the figure. "How long are we going to be here before you admit that there's something wrong with the dice?"

"There's nothing wrong with the dice, that's the whole point," the Thark ambassador said. He straightened up and led the way from the new office space into the shared conference room and threw the dice against the closed door that led to the corridor. They bounced to a halt, one coming up white, the other black. "See? I came in early to check the office since it's my first day, and I've been going back and forth for the last ten minutes testing. There's definitely something wrong with the probability in that room."

"How can probability work on one side of the wall and not the other?" Aabina asked. "We didn't even close the door."

The Thark ambassador shrugged. "If this was a casino, I'd void your certification. Since it's an embassy, I'm tempted to invite some punters over to shoot craps for real."

"Are you saying the new CoSHC office isn't safe?" Daniel asked. "Could there be some sort of electromagnetic radiation in there affecting the dice?"

"These are probability dice," the Thark repeated slowly, as if he was explaining something to a particularly obtuse child. "The only thing that affects them is random chance, and there's something wrong with the odds in that room."

The associate ambassador shrugged. "I guess that means I won't be hosting a poker game anytime soon, but other than that, I don't see the problem."

"Don't see the problem?" The alien ambassador replaced his dice in a small golden box which he deposited in his belt pouch. Then he chose the highest chair at the conference table for himself. "Sit," he told Daniel and Aabina. "If the issue isn't obvious to you, this could take a while."

Daniel nodded to Aabina, and they both took their customary places. "I know that gambling is in some ways central to Thark culture, but CoSHC is strictly a business organization," the associate ambassador said.

"There's something about talking business with Humans that makes me feel like a parent explaining the facts of life, but I'm surprised you don't see the difficulty, Aabina," the Thark said to the Vergallian.

Aabina's eyes went wide. "Ambassador McAllister showed me the notes she took when she went to you for advice about investing the windfall from the All Species Cookbook. Are you suggesting that anything involving probabilities won't work right in that office?"

"Let me put it this way. I wouldn't use that office for work if you paid me."

"The main reason I rented it is to provide a place for CoSHC members visiting Union Station to conduct business," Daniel told the Thark. "When the furniture arrives, I'll move my display desk over from the embassy and hire an office manager, but if there's some probabilistic defect in there—" he pointed back over his shoulder with a thumb, "—I'll have to put the whole thing on hold until we get it straightened out. If this is some kind of diplomatic prank, you should tell us now."

"You can rest assured that during my one-week term as the exchange ambassador here, EarthCent's interests are my interests," the Thark said.

"Could you sell us liability insurance that would cover if something went wrong?"

The little alien boggled at Daniel as if the associate ambassador had suddenly grown a pair of horns. "Are you insane? You want me to make book on events in a space where the laws of probability are suspended? It would render our actuarial expertise and millions of years of underwriting experience worthless. I'd rather just hand over all of my money right now, because at least that way, my losses would be limited to what I have on me. Selling you a liability policy on that place would be like writing a blank check."

"The station librarian already told us that there's nothing wrong with the office from a technical perspective," Aabina said. "I have to admit that I've never encountered anything like it before. Have you heard of any similar situations where the laws of probability didn't apply?"

"You mean other than rigged casino games?" The Thark ambassador slumped in his chair and seemed to hug himself. "Are you both familiar with my people's history?"

"You're talking about the civil war that destroyed your empire," Daniel said.

"There was nothing civil about it," the ambassador told them. "We were once the primary military power for thousands of inhabited star systems, and our empire would have rivaled that of the Cayl if it hadn't torn itself apart. One of my nieces is a historian, which isn't a common career path among Tharks because it's just too depressing. She studies with the Verlocks who analyze history based on proven mathematical principles. Even after taking into account the peculiarities of the culture we came from, she couldn't find a basis in the math for every significant family group in our empire turning on one another in a hollow cycle of honor and revenge."

"It doesn't sound that outlandish to me," Daniel said. "We have a saying on Earth that before embarking on a journey of revenge you should dig two graves."

"Confucius," Aabina confirmed. "I read him when I was studying up on Humans."

"Keep in mind that we're talking about Tharks here," the exchange ambassador said. "My niece's dissertation adviser is one of the top Verlock historians, and he checked all of her equations. Although it's impossible to be definitive about the facts surrounding events that took place so long ago, the working hypothesis is that our empire was destroyed by a powerful curse."

Daniel coughed to cover up the beginnings of a guffaw. "You're telling me an advanced species that built some of the most powerful warships the galaxy has known was brought down by magic?"

"When you have eliminated the impossible, whatever remains, however improbable, must be the truth," Aabina said. "Sherlock Holmes to Doctor Watson in multiple books."

"I like that one," the Thark ambassador said, perking up a bit. "Ambassador McAllister loaned me a few of her favorite novels a while back but I'm afraid I didn't finish any of them. Too many intercepted letters and mistaken identities for my taste. Perhaps I'll have to peruse her shelves again."

"Putting aside literary criticism for the moment, how does all of this impact the new office?" Daniel asked. "Are you suggesting that if we open it to visiting CoSHC members they'll end up at war with each other?"

"It's a distinct possibility, but forewarned is forearmed."

"Somehow, I don't think that arming ourselves would be appropriate in this case."

"*Igitur qui desiderat pacem, praeparet bellum*," Aabina recited. "Therefore let he who desires peace prepare for war."

"Is that one of ours too?" Daniel asked.

"Publius Flavius Vegetius Renatus from his tract De Re Militari," the Vergallian girl said, and then blushed. "Sorry. I was telling my class about the quotations game that royal trainers employ and I guess I'm still locked in."

"Fascinating," said the Thark ambassador, who had clearly recovered from his brief bout of depression over his people's ancient history. "If you had asked me yesterday whether I'd ever quote a Human, I would have bet against it, but maybe there's something I can recycle in a speech.

69

Can you recommend a single book with quotable lines for me to try, preferably short?"

"Ecclesiastes is short, though it loses something in the translation," Aabina told him.

"I picked up Humanese when Ambassador McAllister loaned me those novels of hers."

"The original is one of their older languages, Hebrew."

"How many letters does it have?" the Thark ambassador inquired.

"Just twenty-two," Aabina said, seeing the direction the exchange ambassador was going. "I worked up a concordance when I was studying that I can send to your implant. It should only take you a few hours to puzzle out the book."

"But what do we do about the problem with our office?" Daniel persisted.

"Have you announced an opening date?" the Thark asked.

"Not yet. Our renovation for this conference room a few years ago didn't go as planned so I didn't set any deadlines. The only reason the new office is otherwise ready for occupancy is because Ambassador Crute took over the project when he was here the week before last."

"I thought I recognized the Dollnick by the shadow of his crest. Very well. My suggestion is that you avoid using the new office space until probability returns to normal." He took the golden box out of his belt pouch and handed it over to Daniel. "Don't lose the dice. They cost more than you earn in a year."

"How will you calibrate casino games without them?" Aabina asked.

"I can sit down and play for a few hours," the Thark ambassador told her. "It's time consuming, but profitable."

Daniel took the dice out of the box and examined them closely. "So I can monitor the problem with these and hope it goes away, but what if I want to do something more proactive?"

"That's outside my area of expertise, and my official starting time as exchange ambassador began five minutes ago. Could somebody invite the embassy manager to join us and we'll discuss our plans for the week?"

Aabina opened the door to the embassy lobby and summoned Donna, who brought with her a standard tab.

"Kelly left a to-do list for us," Donna said. She linked the tab to the conference room's projection system, and a hologram of bullet points materialized.

"I don't have any network appearances scheduled?" the Thark asked in disappointment. "I thought Ambassador McAllister had a guest slot on Stone Soup every other Friday."

"She's only on once a month," the embassy manager said apologetically. "I could ask my grandson if there are any openings this week."

"If he's willing to cook up some soap, I'd be honored to serve as the official taster." The exchange ambassador ran his eyes down the list of bullet points again. "She forgot the most important thing."

"What's that?" Daniel asked.

"I'll be performing an audit of the All Species Cookbook. The embassy has signed contracts with a dozen species for translations and various subsidiary rights. While you're doing an admirable job keeping the cookbook itself up to date with new recipes, corrections, and most importantly, current advertising, my intelligence reports show that your accounting and invoicing are in disarray."

"That's my fault," Aabina said. "Ambassador McAllister put me in charge of dealing with the day-to-day cookbook operation as it pertains to the other tunnel network species. The Galactic Free Press handles printing and distribution for Humans, and their accounts are always up to date."

"She's trying to cover for me," Donna told the Thark. "Aabina is responsible for customer relations with our alien cookbook partners, and she does the negotiating for new licensing agreements, but I'm the one who's supposed to keep track of the money. I didn't realize there was a problem."

"That's not terribly surprising, given the complexity of the contracts," the Thark said. He pulled a small tab out of his pouch, linked it to the display system, and brought up a document with the heading, 'All Species Cookbook Horten Grant of Rights. EarthCent Confidential.'

"As our exchange ambassador, would you be willing to explain where you obtained that document?" Daniel asked.

"I did a little homework last night to prepare for my service here and found that all of the grants and licenses for the cookbook have been published on one of the public networks. Remind me to audit your information security if I have time."

"I remember these contracts," Donna said. "The way they were negotiated, the other species all paid us substantial advances. With the reserve against returns, we weren't expecting any further payments for at least a year or two."

"It's been two years, and the All Species Cookbook has outperformed its predecessors, especially in the Horten and Drazen editions," the Thark said. "You can't expect the publishers to queue up to pay their bills. It's up to EarthCent to request the current accounts from all of the translation rights holders and then to invoice them for the amounts due."

"I guess I thought that being advanced species and all they'd just pay us," Donna admitted.

"You don't get to be an advanced species by doing everybody else's work for them. I'll contact the publishers in question and demand a data dump. They'll comply with that because we can revoke their rights otherwise—at least somebody got that part of the contracts right."

"But won't you have returned to your own embassy by the time they generate the reports?" Daniel asked.

"They have one business day to comply," the Thark ambassador said. "Unfortunately, the contracts specify the business day of the licensees, so some of the data won't get here until the end of the week. But that will give me time to take care of a few other things I have in mind."

"She was very keen on getting you to look over her investment portfolio for the cookbook money," Donna said.

"Of course, but that won't take long. I think my spare time here would be best used working on that final bullet item, investigating an alternative financing arrangement for Earth Two."

"Do you really think it's possible? The Dollnick owner is asking eight trillion creds."

"According to our intelligence assessment, the ground work is less than twenty percent complete," the Thark said. "One small continent is substantially finished, though it's not clear that a natural balance has been achieved. I understand that the owner is willing to grant sweat equity for the remainder of the planet."

"You mean if we're willing to provide labor for the terraforming work we can earn the other continents?" Daniel asked.

"Equity, not ownership. It wouldn't make any sense for the owner to provide resources for Human workers to do the job and then simply hand over the improved continent. No. I suspect that at best, your labor could be substituted for a down payment. And there would still need to be a large cash payment for the finished continent, which is why you should share the planet with the Alts."

"But they can't stand being in the same room with us," Donna reminded him.

"I can only point you in the right direction," the Thark said, looking back at the list again. "Coming from a species that came close to committing suicide, I may not be the best individual to advise you on interpersonal relations."

"But they've insulated themselves from the tunnel network by agreeing to be a Vergallian client state and hiring contract queens to handle all of their interplanetary business affairs," Daniel said. "My son, Mike, probably spent more time in close proximity with an Alt child than any other human when Methan's daughter was a guest on *Let's Make Friends* four or five years ago. He said she told him that he smelled funny."

"All girls that age think boys smell funny," Donna said. "It just means that we and the Alts share more in common than a few genes."

"She spoke directly to him?" the Thark ambassador asked. "That's better than I thought. I'll have to adjust the odds on the big board when I return to my embassy."

Seven

"Whatcha betting?" the Thark behind the window asked brusquely.

"I'm not here to gamble," Kelly said. "I'm—"

"Don't want to know," the clerk cut her off. "Next."

"But I'm here to—"

"Next, please!"

A leathery-skinned hand with claws settled on the EarthCent ambassador's shoulder and gently moved her to the side. The Huktra who owned the hand bellied up to the window and began placing rapid-fire bets. Kelly sighed and stepped back so she could survey the cavernous hall of the off-world betting parlor in hopes of spotting a floor manager. She settled on a leathery young alien who was sweeping up discarded plastic betting slips.

"Excuse me," she said. "I'm exchanging with the Thark ambassador this week, and as far as I know, he uses this facility as an embassy. Could you tell me if he has a private office behind the counter?"

The sweeper, who was even younger than she had realized, replied, "I don't understand whatever language you're speaking. Do you have an implant?"

"Yes," Kelly said, and gave him an encouraging smile.

"Does that mean yes?"

"Yes," she repeated.

"Does that mean no?" the young Thark tested her.

"No," Kelly said, shaking her head in the negative.

The youngster leaned his broom against the closest table, reached in his belt pouch, and showed the EarthCent ambassador a coin. "I'll bet you five creds I can guess what you want in ten tries, but you have to answer my yes-or-no questions."

"Yes, I suppose we can do that," Kelly said, in part to humor the youngster, and in part because she wanted to avoid asking Libby to translate. She knew most aliens didn't like being addressed by the Stryx out of nowhere.

"First question. Are you here to gamble?"

"No," Kelly said, shaking her head side to side in an exaggerated manner.

"Second question. Are you lost?"

"No."

"Third question. Are you here to meet somebody?"

"Maybe," Kelly said. "I don't actually know whether the Thark ambassador has any staff."

"Have you already forgotten that I said I can't understand you?" the young Thark asked. "I'll rephrase the question. Do you have an appointment to meet somebody here?"

"No," the EarthCent ambassador said, shaking her head.

"Are you looking for work?"

"In a sense, but—" Kelly cut herself off in frustration when she remembered he couldn't understand her. "No."

"Confused about whether or not she's looking for work," the young Thark said to himself. Then he looked around, lowered his voice, and asked, "Are you a prostitute?"

"No!" Kelly retorted angrily. "You have five questions left."

"Don't get mad. You don't have enough wrinkles to be a prostitute, but maybe your species is into smooth skin."

"Oh, uh, in that case, thank you."

"Did you lose something here?"

"No," Kelly said.

"Are you here for the gambling workshop?"

"No. What's a gambling—never mind."

The Thark began ticking off Kelly's answers on his fingers. "Not lost, not here to meet anybody, not gambling, not a prostitute, didn't lose anything. It must have something to do with work. Are you a salesperson?"

"No."

"Sizing us up for a competitor?"

"No."

"Last question. Are you here to exchange with our ambassador?"

"Yes," Kelly said in amazement. "How did—you knew the whole time," she accused him, her eyes narrowing.

"I'm sorry, I didn't understand what you're saying. If you want to go double or nothing, I bet I can guess your meaning in ten tries."

"No," Kelly told him, digging around in her purse. "I'm sorry. I only have my programmable cred."

"That's fine, we have a register," the young Thark said, and then clamped a hand across his mouth.

"I knew you had an implant," Kelly declared triumphantly, and then displayed the five-cred piece that she had been hiding in her closed fist. "And I'll bet that you did know that I was coming."

"I wasn't going to keep your money," the young Thark said sullenly. "Our ambassador asked me to watch for you, and he said you have a good sense of humor for a Human."

"And does your ambassador have an office?"

The sweeper took up his broom and the long-handled dust pan. "This way." He led her to a table right in front of the enormous tote board that displayed the odds and results for sporting events all around the tunnel network. "He usually sits here to keep an eye on things."

"Thank you," Kelly said. "You wouldn't know if he left me any instructions, would you?"

"Of course I'd know. He's my great-granduncle, isn't he?"

"So he gave you a list?"

"I'm the list," the Thark ambassador's great-grandnephew said, pointing at the side of his head. "Do you want the whole thing, or just what's on schedule for this morning?"

"Let's start with this morning."

"Put a hundred creds on Fierce Warrior, on the beak, in the third race at the Imperial—"

"Hold on," Kelly interrupted. "You can't mean to say that the Thark ambassador left a list of bets he wants me to place."

"There are also a few meetings, but most of the list is wagers. He only made me memorize a couple hundred, so it's a light week."

"I'm sorry, but I can't spend the week gambling in your great-granduncle's stead."

"Humans," the youngster cursed, slapping his thigh. "He bet me you'd say that. I was sure that you'd ask about your end first."

"My end?"

"You know, your percentage of the winnings for placing the bets."

"You mean your great-granduncle was willing to pay me a commission to gamble with his money?" Kelly asked. "That doesn't sound like a very good investment for him."

"Who said anything about his money? He gave me a list of tips. You bet your own money and you get to keep ninety percent of what you make."

"But what if I lose?"

"That's why we call it gambling," the young Thark said in exasperation. "If you don't want these tips I'll try to sell them. Great granduncle is the best handicapper on Union Station."

"I think I'll stick with the meetings," Kelly said. "Anything this morning?"

"The gambling workshop I mentioned. The members should start trickling in around now."

"But I can't teach gamblers how to pick winners. I really don't know the first thing about it."

"Who said anything about picking winners? The workshop is for punters who have a problem," the young Thark said, making something that looked suspiciously like air quotes with his fingers when he said 'problem'. "Here comes the first one now."

Kelly looked in the direction the young alien pointed and didn't see anybody coming. When she turned back, the Thark ambassador's grandnephew was nowhere in sight. At this point, she wasn't sure whether he had been serious about anything, so she returned to the long row of betting windows and tried another clerk.

"I'm Ambassador McAllister of EarthCent on exchange for your ambassador," she began. "Would you know—"

"What's your bet?" the clerk interrupted.

"I'm just looking for information—"

"Place a bet and I'll tell you what I know. We have quotas."

Kelly realized she was still holding a five-cred coin in her hand so she slid it under the window. "Fierce Warrior on the beak. He's running at the Imperial—"

"Flying, and she's a gryphon," the clerk cut her off again. He tapped the keys of a mysterious device, dropped the coin in a slot, and produced a plastic slip covered in what might as well have been hieroglyphics. "So what did you want to know?"

"I'm here as the exchange ambassador and—"

"Didn't his great-grandnephew talk to you?" The Thark carefully stood up on the rungs of his high stool for a better view of the room, and then climbed up onto the seat so he'd be able to see over the various life forms gathered in front of the windows. "It looks like he's waiting for you at the ambassador's usual table in front of the tote board."

"Oh, maybe he had to go to the bathroom," Kelly said. "I just wasn't sure that—"

"Next," the clerk called, settling back onto his stool.

By the time she worked her way through the crowd of bettors to the Thark ambassador's version of an office, two other aliens had joined the youngster. One was a Drazen with gold bracelets on his tentacle, and the other a well-dressed Frunge businesswoman. On second look, Kelly recognized the dress the Frunge was wearing as something Dorothy had designed for SBJ Fashions a few years earlier.

"That's her," the great-grandnephew told the aliens. "You all have fun sharing. Personally, I'd rather sweep."

"What's that?" the Drazen asked, pointing at the betting slip in Kelly's hand.

"Oh, I'm not a gambler if that's what you're thinking," Kelly said as she sat. "It's just that nobody at the windows would give me any information unless I placed a bet, and the Thark ambassador left me a tip about Fierce Warrior—"

"To win?"

"On the beak, whatever that means."

The Drazen and the Frunge exchanged a look, and then they both made a dash for the line of betting windows.

"Nice going," the young Thark said. "For five creds, I'll forget it ever happened."

"For ten creds, I won't tell your great-granduncle you tried to bribe me," Kelly retorted. "How many other members are there in this workshop?"

"There's another Drazen who usually comes, a Chert, though she keeps the invisibility projector on so it's hard to know if she's here, and a couple of Grenouthians."

"Grenouthians? I had no idea they gambled."

"I'll bet you didn't."

"There's no call for sarcasm," Kelly said. "I'm telling you the truth."

"Humans," the young Thark said, standing his broom against a nearby table and taking a seat across from the EarthCent ambassador. "I meant exactly what I said. I'll bet that you didn't know Grenouthians gamble. Will you take the bet?"

"Of course not. It's a sure thing for you."

"And that's my own little gambling problem. All of the other kids call me Locky because I'll only bet when I know I'll win."

"Did you mean Lucky?" Kelly asked. "Translation implants sometimes have problems with names that mean something."

"Locky, as in when the outcome is a lock—it's locked in."

"That's very wise of you, Locky. You'll never need to be a member of a group like this."

"Why do you think I sat down?" the young Thark asked. "I am a group member. My great-granduncle made me join."

"I can't even begin to explain to you how confused I'm getting," Kelly said. "Take pity on an old woman and explain to me the purpose of this gambling workshop. From what you said earlier, I thought it was for problem gamblers."

"It is," Locky said, and the EarthCent ambassador's implant picked up his tone of growing frustration. "All of us have a problem with taking risks. My great-granduncle is trying to help us get over it."

"But the way those two ran for the betting windows…"

"Because it was a tip from the best handicapper on Union Station, practically a lock. How much did you bet?" he asked, looking at the slip that the EarthCent ambassador was still holding.

"Five creds," Kelly said.

"I'll buy it from you for six."

"Are you serious? I'll make a twenty percent gain without having to wait for the race results."

"Then it's a deal?" Locky asked hopefully.

"I can't encourage somebody your age to gamble, and besides, you could just walk over there and buy a ticket."

"The betting just closed," the young Thark said, pointing up at the board. "We also have a rule about employees gambling."

"So you're asking me to place your bet because you aren't allowed to gamble," Kelly concluded, trying to sound stern, even though the young rogue was starting to grow on her.

"Who said anything about not being allowed to gamble? They encourage it, but the minimum bet for employees is twenty creds because they want us to set an example."

"Something tells me that you're worth more than twenty creds."

"I am, but I can't bring myself to bet that much in one go," Locky admitted. "That's the other reason I'm in the workshop."

The slightly out-of-breath Drazen with the gold bracelets returned, brandishing a fistful of plastic tickets. "Thanks for the tip," he said.

The Frunge woman arrived right behind him. "I feel like today's meeting is helping me already," she added, fanning herself with her own betting slips.

"Let me see those," Locky demanded, squinting across the table. "They're all for minimum bets to show, aren't they?"

The Frunge woman's hair vines paled. "You didn't have to out us as lightweights in front of the Human," she said with a pout.

"I've exchanged with the Thark ambassador," Kelly reassured her. "Anything you could tell him you can tell me."

"What did you put everybody on?" a massive Grenouthian boomed as he took a seat.

"Excuse me?" Kelly asked, assuming that the giant bunny was accusing her of prescribing drugs without a license. "I don't know what the Thark ambassador did, but while I'm running the group, we'll be sticking with talk therapy."

"She's a bit of a square," the young Thark told the Grenouthian. "Everybody's on Fierce Warrior at Imperial

Dragonways, but the gryphons are already on their starting perches, so you're too late."

"Why doesn't it switch over," a high-pitched voice demanded out of empty space near the EarthCent ambassador's left elbow.

"Imperial Dragonways charges for their video feed by the picosecond," the grandnephew explained. "The tote board will switch over when the race starts."

"What's with the Human?" a new Drazen asked, settling on one of the remaining chairs. "I've heard they have this weird problem that when they start gambling they can't stop."

"Not exactly our problem, eh, Harf?" the other Drazen asked rhetorically. "The Thark ambassador left her a hot tip, but I could only make myself put down ten creds."

"To show," Locky added.

All of the aliens appeared slightly deflated by this news, and they looked to Kelly.

"Well," she said. "While it's difficult for me to understand how cautious betting can be construed as a failing, I suppose we could try some exercises."

"Are you saying I have a weight problem too?" the Frunge woman demanded.

"Not at all. I have some experience with workshops and I've always found that the best way to get over our fears is to act them out. I'm afraid that the term 'exercise' in English covers too much ground to be translated properly, but I thought we could take turns role-playing the actions that we find difficult."

"The Thark ambassador never did that. He just gave us tips and then pointed out how much more we would have won if we bet with confidence instead of trying to limit our losses."

"And that helped you?" Kelly asked.

The aliens all exchanged glances. "Not really," Locky said. "But this is only our third meeting, so maybe it takes time."

"I'd like to start by asking each of you to tell me what you see as your biggest obstacle to, er, becoming the gambler that you want to be," Kelly said. She took her notebook and pencil out of her purse, flipped to a blank page, and looked up with a bright smile. "Who wants to go first?"

"And they're off," the Drazen with the gold tentacle bracelets said, staring up at the tote board.

All of the aliens began watching the race, so the EarthCent ambassador put down her pencil and turned in her seat to see what the excitement was all about. A flock of gryphons wearing brightly colored crash helmets were racing around a complex track that included moving hoops and flaming barriers. The lead gryphon fearlessly accelerated towards a hoop that couldn't possibly fit her, but at the last moment, she folded her wings tightly against her body and shot through.

"Don't be Fierce Warrior. Don't be Fierce Warrior," the Frunge woman chanted.

"That's the tip the Thark ambassador left us," Kelly said.

"But I bet her to show. Do you know how much more I could have made if I bet her to win?"

The EarthCent ambassador watched for a moment as Fierce Warrior stretched her lead. "But you'll still win something, right?"

"Winning less than you could have if you had the courage of your convictions is even worse than losing," the

Grenouthian explained. "That's why we're in the workshop."

"She'll win going away," the Drazen groaned, staring at his handful of plastic slips like he wanted to throw them on the floor. "How much did you bet?"

"Me?" Kelly asked. "Five creds, on the beak." The workshop members all brightened up considerably, and the Grenouthian even did a drum roll on his belly. "Why? What's so funny?"

"You're only going to make three creds," the Frunge woman said gleefully. "It's ten times my payout, but it still won't buy you a decent dinner."

"If you had bet a hundred like my great-granduncle instructed, you would have made sixty," the young Thark said as Fierce Warrior streaked past the finish line. A groan went up around the off-world betting parlor and thousands of plastic slips were tossed into the air like confetti. "Hey, somebody has to sweep those up, you know," Locky shouted, but nobody paid him the slightest attention.

"Who do we have in the next race?" the second Drazen asked.

"Please," Kelly said, holding up both hands. "Let's take a break from gambling and talk about your problems placing bets."

"Our problems?" the young Thark said. "You're the one who only put down five creds."

"Then I'll go first." The EarthCent ambassador took a deep breath and let it out slowly before she began. "I've never been that interested in gambling because I believe it's wrong to get something for nothing. I'll play poker with my husband and our friends to be social, but my idea of a good outcome is breaking even."

"She's in worse shape than us," the invisible Chert at the EarthCent ambassador's elbow said. "At least we want to win."

"Are you sure about that?" Kelly asked. "I've heard that problem gamblers don't care whether they win or lose. They're just in it for the thrill."

"Humans are weird," Locky said. "Of course we want to win. Someday I want to become an underwriter for the family's insurance book, but they won't even consider me until I make my first million gambling."

"I would have made over a million by now if I could just increase my bets," the giant bunny said. "Sometimes I feel like I have nothing to show for the last two hundred years."

"Aren't you a producer for the Grenouthian news?" one of the Drazens asked.

"Yes, but everybody in my clan works for the network. I'm talking about doing something completely on my own."

"If it's not prying, how much have you earned on your gambling so far?" Kelly asked.

"Sixty-two thousand and fourteen creds," the Grenouthian said. "I never bet more than ten creds at a time."

"Are you crazy?" Locky demanded. "If you had let it ride, or even followed a half-and-half progression, you'd be rich by now."

"A half-and-half progression?" Kelly asked.

"It's the coward's approach to betting. You pocket half your winnings on every bet and let the other half ride."

"I don't want to hear you use disparaging language like that again," the EarthCent ambassador said. "We're here to support one another. I won't tolerate any shaming."

"I wasn't talking about him, I was talking about me," the young Thark said. "I always take half of my winnings off the table.

"We're all losers," the Frunge woman groaned.

"But why do you feel that way?" Kelly asked, and then took up her pencil again and wrote 'SHAME' in block print. "Let's try to narrow this down. Do all of you feel shame about not being able to take bigger chances?"

"Yes," the members of the group chorused.

"And after you win a small bet, what do you feel?"

"Guilt," the Drazen with the gold bracelets said.

"Sorrow," the invisible Chert chimed in.

"More shame," the Frunge contributed.

"Very good," Kelly said, listing the replies in her notebook. "Can you identify any triggers that lead to your behavior?"

"Could you give us an example of what you mean?" the Thark ambassador's great-grandnephew asked.

"Triggers. Like, have you ever been placing a bet for more than you normally would only to have somebody you're with question your intentions? Or it could be sights and sounds, like a problem betting here that wouldn't necessarily be the same at the casino."

"I'm not old enough to gamble in the casino," Locky told her.

"How about internal triggers?" the Grenouthian asked, and even through the translation, Kelly recognized the producer's excitement. "Every time I go to the betting window, I hear a little voice in my head saying, 'Ten creds is a lot of coin.'"

"That sounds more like your conscience than a trigger," Kelly said. "Deep inside you know that gambling is wrong."

"Hey, what kind of support group are you running?" the second Drazen demanded. "You just said we shouldn't be judgmental."

"Sorry, it slipped out," Kelly apologized. "But don't we all have the same voice in our heads warning us when we're about to do something unwise?"

"You have my father's voice in your head?" the Grenouthian asked in astonishment. "How is that possible?"

"I meant in general, not the same voice you're hearing," Kelly corrected herself. "But if your father warned you against gambling, it's no wonder you're having a problem."

"He didn't warn me against gambling, he was just cheap. It didn't matter whether I was talking about eating out or buying school supplies, he always repeated that line about ten creds. He still does when I feel guilty enough to go visit."

Eight

"Where were you all week?" Dorothy asked Affie. "I swear I saw more of you when I was on maternity leave than I have since returning to work."

"It's the Alts," the Vergallian said. "They don't have a government in the traditional sense, so it's taking a lot of hand-holding to get them through the process of buying a partially terraformed planet. I'm hoping that when Methan gets here we'll be able to clear up the remaining issues in a few weeks."

"Why don't you just make all of the decisions for them and get it over with? I thought that's what they hired you for."

"They didn't hire me. Aabina's mother hired me for them while she was still our ambassador here, and she didn't leave me any choice in the matter if you recall."

"Well, she tricked Dietro into becoming our sales manager at the same time, so I guess it was a fair trade." Dorothy put down her scissors, took up the swathe of sash she'd just cut out, and stretched it diagonally across her torso. "What do you think?"

"Very Grenouthian," Affie said. "Is Flazint off somewhere working on clasps?"

"She went on a lunch date with Tzachan. They're pretending it's a business consultation to get around chaperoning so it doesn't count against their quota."

"And Baa?"

Dorothy snorted in amusement. "One of the professional LARPing teams we sponsor lost their mage and begged Baa to fill in at the last minute."

"Oooh. They're going to regret that." Affie flinched delicately at the memory of the LARPs she had gone on with the Terragram mage as the magical damage dealer in the party. "What about Myst and Lancelot?"

"They're either in class or doing homework, neither of them will be in today. Why all the questions?"

"Our current ambassador, Aleeytis, advised me to brush up on Humans, and you know how I hate reading," the Vergallian girl said. "I thought if you had some work to keep your hands busy I'd take advantage and ask you some questions."

"I just put the baby to sleep so—were you waiting outside until he stopped crying?" Dorothy asked suspiciously.

"Me? You know I love your baby. I'll even hold him while we talk if you want."

"No, that would just keep him up. Why does the Vergallian ambassador want you to brush up on Humans?"

"She wouldn't say, but I'm sure it has something to do with the Alts and the whole Earth Two deal," Affie said. "It's a shame your two species don't get along when you have so many genes in common."

"We get along with the Alts fine, they just don't get along with us," Dorothy said. "Besides, you must know more about Humans than any Vergallian on the station, unless you include my mom's special assistant," she amended herself.

"I would have gone to Aabina, but Ambassador Aleeytis cautioned me that it could be seen as collusion."

"Alright," Dorothy said, taking up her scissors again and starting to cut out a new pattern. "What do you want to ask me?"

"Back before the Stryx removed the Alts from Earth, how did your species get along?"

Dorothy put the scissors right back down again and turned to stare at Affie. "Are you joking? How would I know anything about events that happened tens of thousands of years ago? That's Earth's prehistory. We don't have any written records, just the odd bit of bone or cave art. I only know that much because we read about it in Libby's school."

"But it's only been forty or fifty thousand years!" Affie said in dismay. "I know that Humans were a bit slow to discover iron-working and all that, but don't you at least have stories and songs going back that far?"

"No, and back then there weren't very many of us or of them, so I doubt we ran into each other that often. I remember Libby telling us that there were periods in our history where we hit genetic bottlenecks, with only a few thousand breeding pairs on the whole planet. That may be how the Neanderthal genes got mixed in, and vice versa."

"If the station librarian told you that, doesn't it mean the information is from Earth scientists?"

"I suppose, but I don't think she would have passed it along if it was wrong," Dorothy said. "You're really asking the wrong person."

"Could you explain how 'Neanderthal' became a pejorative term?" the Vergallian asked. "When I turn on my implant, it gets translated as a loutish male who treats women badly. You can see how that would bother the Alts."

"I'm not an entomologist, Affie."

"Etymologist. An entomologist studies insects."

"Which just proves my point that you're asking the wrong person," the EarthCent ambassador's daughter said. "Besides, nobody refers to the Alts as Neanderthals anymore, and some people think of them as super-humans."

"Really?"

"The Alts figured out their own interstellar drive without help, they live longer than we do, and they're incredibly nice."

"Do you mind if I tell them you said that?" Affie asked.

"I guess not," Dorothy said, taking up her scissors again. "Sorry I couldn't be of more help."

The Vergallian girl checked that the door to the design room was closed and pulled over the stool from her neglected workbench so she could sit down. "I thought maybe you could help me with another thing. You know, the way you helped Flazint."

"You're dumping Stick and you want me to visit a matchmaker for you?"

"Where do you get these—it's the opposite, as usual. Now that Dietro and I have had real jobs for a couple of years, my family may be willing to open preliminary negotiations."

"You've been working for SBJ Fashions ever since we started," Dorothy pointed out. "That didn't count as a real job?"

"Not to my family," Affie said with a sigh. "When one of my older sisters stopped at Union Station a few years back, she referred to my working here as 'slumming with Humans.' That's why I didn't introduce you."

"I always thought that Fleet Vergallians were more open-minded than the ones from the Empire of a Hundred Worlds."

"As far as my mother is concerned, I'm throwing away decades of royal training. But when Aabina's mother got me the job working as a contract queen for the Alts, I went right to the top of the list."

"What list?"

"The princesses-available-for-marriage-negotiations list."

"Is that a real thing or just a figure of speech?" Dorothy asked, carefully snipping through the last bit of fabric before starting to remove the pins holding the pattern to the cloth.

"It's a real list," Affie said. "One of my cousins sent it to me because she thought I'd be pleased."

"But now that you're on it, you don't find being objectified as a princess and married off to make family connections that appealing anymore."

"It never was. Not for me, not for any members of royal Vergallian families. It's just the deal we're born into. But after my older sisters had daughters, I moved too far down the line of succession to matter. That's the only reason my family allowed me to come to Union Station and attend the Open University in the first place."

Dorothy finished stripping the pattern from the fabric and set everything aside to turn her full attention to her friend. "So let me make sure I have all of this straight. When Aabina's mother was the Vergallian ambassador, she tricked you and Stick—I mean Dietro," she corrected herself, "—into taking on new jobs to prevent your family from interfering in your relationship. But now that you've made a name for yourself representing the Alts as a contract queen, your family is shopping you around for political gain."

"It's not that simple," Affie said. "My mother has what she sees as my best interests at heart, namely giving me a chance to put a daughter on the throne."

"How can that happen if you don't become a queen yourself?"

"If I marry the son of a queen without sisters or daughters, my daughter would be the next in line, though we would probably have to fight off a cousin or three," the Vergallian girl explained. "But it's not only that. They're trying to save me from Dietro."

"Why?" Dorothy asked. "I used to think he was kind of a stoner, but since he started working for us and quit burning Kraaken sticks, he's turned into some kind of alpha-alien. I've even seen Baa back down from arguing with him when he gets his blood up."

"So here's the thing. Dietro doesn't talk about his past and nobody knows where he's from."

"How is that a big deal? You can tell he's upper-caste just by looking at him, and I know from LARPing that he can duel with the best of them. What are the other two things Samuel said every Vergallian gentlemen needs to know?"

"The three D's," Affie said. "Dueling, dancing, and diction. He was always good at the first two, and his diction came back when he cleaned up."

"I'm still not seeing it," the EarthCent ambassador's daughter said. "If your mother is willing to overlook his lack of royal family connections, what difference does it make if he wants to keep his privacy?"

"Because we've been civilized for millions of years and it's not that easy to be anonymous. Aabina's mother tried running him down through Vergallian Intelligence, but they couldn't come up with anything. Later, my mother did the same thing through Fleet."

"Doesn't that just mean he's not a spy?"

"If anything, it means he might actually be a spy, but I don't think he would hide that from me," Affie said. "I think I have it figured out, but I need you to confirm it."

"How am I going to do that?" Dorothy asked.

"I'll tell you, and then next time we all get together, you bring it up casual-like and I'll know from his reaction."

"Bring what up? You're driving me nuts."

The Vergallian girl lowered her voice. "I think he was a monk."

"You mean one of those Live Action Role Playing guys who wears a robe and does all the fancy staff tricks?"

"A real monk," Affie said. "Or at least a novitiate."

"With the tonsure and all that?"

"Not a Human monk from LARPing, a real Vergallian monk."

"I don't remember ever seeing anything about monks in Vergallian dramas, and Sam never mentioned anything," Dorothy said, and then she gave her friend a knowing smile. "I get why your mother is against your marrying Dietro now. He's celibate."

"Sometimes I don't know why I even talk to you," Affie said. "Vergallian monks aren't celibate, it's a warrior caste. Back in the early days of our empire, the monasteries provided a balance to the rule of queens, and most royal families sent their second son to train as a novitiate. There were times in our history when the monks had as much power as the council of queens."

"So what happened?"

"It's complicated, but the monks overreached and fell out of favor, and then they compounded the error by hiring out as mercenaries. After a few hundred thousand years went by, they basically degenerated into a cult for highly-paid assassins. The monasteries had to go underground."

"Like literally underground? In mines and caves?"

"This happened long after we had interstellar travel, Dorothy. The monks were hounded off of civilized planets and they established monasteries in space. Some of them even became pirates, for lack of a better term."

"And drug dealers? You think the monks sent Dietro to Union Station to undermine the tunnel network selling Kraaken Red?"

Affie groaned and dropped her head in her hands. "Next time Flower stops here I'm going to tell her to give you a job writing anime scripts. No, I don't think my boyfriend came here on a secret mission to get everybody high. But I do think he was born in a monastery, and that's why his genetic test came back with markers from half of the royal families in the empire."

"Why did he get a genetic test if he's trying to hide his past?" Dorothy asked, and then took note of the Vergallian girl's blush. "You stole a hair sample from your boyfriend?"

"I rolled him on his back, held his nose, and took a cheek swab," Affie admitted. "He sleeps like a stone after we have sex."

"Don't let Flazint hear you say that or the chlorophyll will explode out of her hair vines." The EarthCent ambassador's daughter frowned. "Wait a minute. What was that bit about half of the royal families in the empire?"

"So there weren't always hundreds of worlds and thousands of queens," Affie said. "In the early days of the empire, there were only a few dozen royal families and the rest of us are descended from them. The monasteries had their own royalty, though they didn't call it that, and their bloodlines would have concentrated during the hundreds of thousands of years they've been in exile. Dietro's genetics include the royal houses that were extant when the monks went underground."

"Okay, so mystery solved," Dorothy said. "Next time Kevin and I chaperone a date for Flazint and Tzachan, you bring Dietro along, and I'll work Vergallian monks into the conversation."

"It's not that—" Affie cut herself off as the door to the design room slid open. "Hey, Flaz. How was your lunch date?"

"It wasn't a date," the Frunge girl replied indignantly. "Tzachan and I were discussing the legal implications of Dorothy's new design philosophy. I even took notes," she added, brandishing her tab.

"The sad thing is that you probably did," Affie said. "I've got to run, but let me know if you hit a stumbling block with the cross-species Golden Ratio that needs my aesthetic sense."

"What's the status of those sword belts you were going to design with Dietro?" Dorothy asked. "Baa was asking whether or not we're ever going to produce them because she had an idea for a magical set."

"I'm working on it, really," Affie said. "I've just been so busy with the Alts."

"I can't start on the buckle hardware or the loops until I know what the basic belt is going to look like," Flazint reminded Affie. "You haven't even said whether it's going to be a shoulder type or double-hung from the waist."

"Both," the Vergallian replied impulsively. "Ask Dietro when you see him. Sword belts have been around forever, you know. I'm mainly interested in the colors."

Dorothy and Flazint shook their heads as Affie slipped past Baa, who was just entering the design room.

"She was always a bit of a dilettante, but at least she used to show up for a few hours each day," the Terragram mage said after the door slid shut behind the departing Vergallian. "If she keeps working for the Alts full time we're going to have to replace her."

"I know, but she's been here since the beginning, and we probably wouldn't have gotten into the fashion business without her," Dorothy said. "I'm trying to get Myst interested in abstract design, but it's proving hard to pry her away from traditional jewelry. How did the LARPing session go?"

Baa shook her pouch, creating the unmistakable sound of heavy gold coins clinking together. "I won," she said with a wicked grin.

"How about the rest of the raiding party?"

"They wiped, but I cleaned out the dungeon so they can go on to the next level when they regenerate. What are you working on?"

"Sashes," Dorothy said, picking up the latest piece of fabric she'd cut and holding it diagonally across her chest. "I think they're the perfect test case because the Grenouthians don't wear anything else. If we want to get them involved, it's sashes or nothing."

"It doesn't look like a sash," Flazint said doubtfully.

"That's the whole point. When you see the sashes displayed in a boutique or a catalog, they'll look like an avant-garde fashion for whichever species the clothing dummy represents. But when members of those different species wearing their versions of the sash are in the same room together, it will be obvious that the sashes are all part of the same lineup."

"This is sounding more and more like the Stryx Dance," the Frunge muttered under her breath.

Baa looked over from her work area where she was weighing the gold coins. "It sounds exactly like the Stryx Dance," she said. "Has it occurred to you that your new cross-species Golden Ratio will only work on the same species?"

"The tunnel network species affected by the Stryx Dance?" Dorothy asked. "If you're right, maybe we can use it in our marketing."

Flazint's hair vines stood on end. "Don't even say it, Dorothy. And look what you did to my hair!"

"I've never seen it do that before. What's so bad about bringing up the fact that somebody interfered with the evolution of our species, likely the Stryx?"

"We don't talk about such things," the Frunge girl said, trying to twine her hair vines back around the trellis. "It's a good thing I already had my lunch date."

"You said you were working," Dorothy teased her. "Besides, this could play into the patent application."

"A new Golden Ratio that creates mass hysteria and rhythmic motion," Baa said dryly. "You know that patents can be accessed by the public, don't you?"

"I didn't mean we'd write it that way, but maybe Tzachan can work the genetic engineering version of panspermia into the claims somehow."

"Not listening," Flazint declared, moving off to her own workstation.

"There, you've scared her away," Baa said, waving her gold stash out of existence. "And while I'm not at liberty to go into details about your evolution, I can tell you that—"

"Baa," Jeeves interrupted from the door. "Didn't we talk about your tapping into station power for multidimensional purposes unrelated to your enchanting work? I'm the one who ends up paying the bill."

"And I don't understand how you can weigh virtual gold," Dorothy said. "I thought it only existed in the LARPing studios."

"My bags of holding are inherently multidimensional," Baa said, holding up the five-feather purse she had just emptied. "I use a little pocket universe around the scale to make sure that the powers-that-be aren't cheating on the exchange rate."

"But where did the gold go?"

"I collapsed the pocket universe without returning the gold to the bag of holding so it manifested back in LARPing space, where it gets credited to my account," the mage said. "When you've been around as long as I have, you learn a few tricks."

"Have you been going over the data from our franchises using the Gem nanofabric for custom fittings?" Jeeves asked the EarthCent ambassador's daughter. "The whole business model was your idea, after all."

"You know I haven't had the time or you wouldn't have asked," Dorothy replied. "Between preparing for seminars to attract new franchisees and working on the new line, I'm flat out."

"If you do find some time, it wouldn't hurt to take a look at what passes for fashion with the Alts. If nothing else, asking Affie to find you examples would keep her involved."

Nine

"Affie," Kelly greeted Dorothy's friend. "What are you doing here?"

"I practically live in our embassy these days," the Vergallian girl explained. "Negotiating a planetary real-estate deal on behalf of the Alts is incredibly time consuming, and then I still have my usual contract queening work to do as well."

"I suppose I never thought about where you had your office."

"Aabina's mother insisted I work out of the Vergallian embassy so she could keep an eye on me, and when Aleeytis took over, she made the arrangement permanent," Affie said. "Technically, I have the final say over Alt business interests on the station so I could have rented a separate space. But when you consider all of the overhead that goes into maintaining an office, it wouldn't make sense from the fiduciary perspective."

"I wasn't aware that the Alts had so much going on here," Kelly said. "I thought they were rather anti-business."

"Oh, no. They're just anti-greed. The Alts are an incredibly productive species, and they never formed the habit of filling their time with passive entertainment content. I've been to Alt a half-dozen times now and I've visited most of their major cities. When you walk around the residential areas at night it's like listening to a thousand orchestras."

"So they're exporting musicians?"

"No, but you wouldn't believe the prices their stringed instruments and woodwinds fetch," Affie said. "They aren't that keen on traveling or being separated from one another. Looking back, it's surprising that they developed an interstellar jump drive given how happy they are at home."

"Then maybe they aren't that interested in Earth Two after all," Kelly said hopefully. "I was told that the Council of Queens is willing to give them a loan or co-sign a Dollnick mortgage, but what's the point if the Alts would rather stay at home?"

"I think it has to do with the fact that the Stryx gifted them with their current planet after rescuing them from Earth. They see themselves as custodians rather than owners, even though the world was terraformed with flora and fauna from home. Unlike most species, they never went through a period of exploiting natural resources for the sake of profit, and—" The Vergallian girl cut herself off. "I'm being rude boasting about my Alts when I should be showing you to your office."

"I'd happily listen to you go on about them all day," Kelly said. "The more I can learn about the Alts, the better the chance I'll have of winning their trust."

"But that's not your job this week," Affie reminded her as she led the way through the embassy. "You're here in exchange for Ambassador Aleeytis to represent Vergallian interests. Let her worry about advancing understanding between Alts and Humans while she's occupying your place."

"I left her a list of priorities. Did she do the same for me?"

"Yes. I have rather detailed instructions for you since most Vergallian diplomacy is accomplished after supper, usually during the dancing. But your exchange goes by the Human clock and the times aren't going to line up correctly for a formal dinner this week."

"That's fine by me," Kelly said, following the girl into the ambassador's office. "When Samuel worked here for Aabina's mother, he came home exhausted from ballroom dancing at all hours of the day and night. I'm afraid I've reached the age where after a waltz I just want to sit and catch my breath."

"Take a seat now and I'll run you through the meetings Aleeytis has scheduled for the week," Affie said, indicating the ambassador's desk. "I think it's safe to say that she's been saving up the Humans for you, and then there's the tunnel network meeting about media access that you would have attended as the EarthCent ambassador in any case."

"Yes, I'm looking forward to speaking in support of greater access. I don't understand why ambassadors should be allowed to dodge the local press when the coaches of professional sports teams are required by their leagues to give interviews after games even when they lose."

"Aleeytis is against expanding access and she trusts you to represent the Vergallian position," Affie told her. "Royals are taught that diplomacy has the best chance of success when it's kept from the public eye. If our populations knew ahead of time what they would be required to concede to reach a compromise, the only treaties that

104

would ever get signed would come out of unconditional surrenders."

"That's a pessimistic way of looking at it," Kelly protested. "Humans believe that a free press is an essential part of government."

"I've been studying up on your history and I'm not sure I see the point you're trying to make."

"I thought you hated reading."

"I'm still recovering from all of the tomes I had to memorize for my royal training, especially the genealogies," Affie said, suppressing a shudder. "Fortunately, you can get an excellent overview of Human history by watching Grenouthian documentaries. Poor Dietro hasn't stayed over in a week because I always have one playing on my home entertainment system."

"I'm not sure—" Kelly began, and then started up from the chair, waving her hands in front of her face. "What was that?"

"Just a hologram," the Vergallian girl told her. "Since for all intents and purposes you're replacing Aleeytis for the week, she thought it would be best if you appeared to be her."

"But does it really work?" Kelly sat back again, craning her neck to look down at her own body. "Is this holographic skin matching her lip movements to mine while I speak?"

"Stand-in technology is more sophisticated than that. It combines the best real-time Horten holographic mapping with a Dollnick audio suppression field and Drazen voice synthesis, the kind they use for choral training," Affie explained. "There's a bit of a lag because the holographic controller has to receive the translation of what you've said before it maps the lip movements to the voice synthesis, so try to remember not to move around too much while you're speaking."

"I'm not sure that I'm comfortable with passing as Aleeytis," Kelly said. "It seems like an imposition, both on the visitors and on her."

"Just try it for the morning and if it doesn't work out I'll show you how to disable it," Affie offered.

"Does this mean that when I've come to see the Vergallian ambassador in the past, I may have been speaking to her secretary, or a security guard?"

"That would be a violation of diplomatic ethics. The only reason it's acceptable now is that from a legal stand-point, you really are the Vergallian ambassador. We usually use the stand-in technology as a training tool for staffers."

"Why would that be necessary?" Kelly asked.

"You know that Vergallian ambassadors are all royals, and that means there's a great deal of etiquette that must be observed," Affie explained. "Embassy staffers are hired through civil service tests and some of them have no experience around royalty before they start work. With the stand-in technology, they can get used to working around a royal without causing a diplomatic incident."

"Very well. And I don't have a problem representing the Vergallian embassy's views on expanded media access, provided Aleeytis follows my instructions to speak in favor of the proposal for EarthCent. Something like this came up just last month when I exchanged with Crute and he used some excuse to do the exact opposite of what I requested."

"What excuse?"

"He claimed to have examined the issue from both sides and to be doing his best for humanity," Kelly said.

"In other words, he didn't agree with me so he did what he wanted."

"I don't think—" Affie stopped and pointed at her ear. "That was security. Your first appointment is here to see you."

"To see Aleeytis, you mean."

"Just remember what I said about moving around too much and that you're representing the Empire of a Hundred Worlds, not EarthCent."

"You're welcome to stay," Kelly offered as Affie moved towards the door.

"I wish I could, but I really have a lot to prepare for Methan's arrival. At home the Alts manage their affairs on the honor system, but when they're dealing with aliens, they want everything in writing."

"Pretty smart," Kelly said grudgingly. She took advantage of being alone for a moment to hold a hand up in front of her face and admire the tasteful rings and a bracelet worn on the holographic wrist that disguised her own. Then she made an effort to sit up as straight as if she'd had royal training herself. A young man who looked vaguely familiar entered the office. "How may I help you?" she asked, doing her best to channel the dignity with which Aleeytis spoke.

"The real question is how I can help you," the young man said.

"I'm afraid I don't understand."

"Didn't your cultural attaché tell you I was coming? Jason Fox? I have an appointment."

"Yes, of course, Jason, but I leave such details to underlings," Kelly said, restraining herself at the last minute from dismissively waving a hand that might have broken out of the hologram.

107

"Well, I told her that I was game, but I wanted a guarantee of citizenship from the ambassador," Jason said. "I've finished the training course at Mac's Bones and I've been approved for field work, but we all know that EarthCent Intelligence is just the Drazen's poodle."

"Excuse me?"

"Sorry, it's an expression meaning that we follow them around for scraps and lick their hands."

"That's not true," Kelly said. "EarthCent Intelligence is an independent agency that cooperates closely with the Drazens, but they also work with other alien intelligence agencies, including our own."

"Right," Jason said, giving her an exaggerated wink. "I know you have to say that because the Empire of a Hundred Worlds officially stopped trying to undermine humanity, but an ounce of prevention is worth a pound of cure."

"And you're offering to serve as our eyes inside of EarthCent Intelligence?"

"That's what the contract said," Jason told her. "My EarthCent Intelligence trainer warned us about the value of promises made by alien spymasters recruiting double agents. I want my guarantee of Vergallian citizenship straight from the mouth of a queen."

Kelly was tempted to slap the turncoat, but instead she said, "I'm afraid I can't do that, Jason. I abdicated my throne over a century ago to practice law."

"You'd rather be a lawyer than a queen? I thought we were the crazy ones," he said. "Thanks for nothing, Ambassador. I'm going to go sell my services to the Hortens."

"Be careful," Kelly called after him. "I hear that their ambassador will be exchanging with EarthCent's. You wouldn't want to show up on the wrong day." As soon as he left, she took out her notebook and pencil and wrote, 'Jason Fox recruited by Vergallians, will try Hortens next. Tell Thomas.' Then the door slid open again and a gaunt young woman entered.

"Yes?" Kelly said.

"Here join Empire Hundred Planets," the girl said in a stilted fashion.

"You want to join the Empire of a Hundred Worlds?"

"Yes. Want Vergallian become."

The unnatural way the visitor's lips were moving tipped Kelly off that the girl was trying to speak Vergallian, though she had probably started learning too late in life to ever gain even rudimentary fluency in the language.

"Please, have a seat," Kelly said, gesturing at the chair in front of the desk. "Tell me why you want to become Vergallian, and let's stick with Humanese if you don't mind."

"I knew I was butchering the grammar, but I learned from watching dramas with subtitles, and they all speak so fast," the girl said. "I love everything about Vergallian dramas. I've been saving for two years to go on a studio tour, and then I thought, what if I could just live there?"

"At a drama studio?"

"In the Empire of a Hundred Worlds. Any one of them would do. I just think that you're all so beautiful."

"What's your name?" Kelly asked.

"Bandya," she said, and then blushed. "Actually, I was born Barbara Tandy, but it's stupid to have two names so I combined them."

"Did you have all of your molars removed, Bandya?"

"To bring out my cheekbones, but I haven't had any surgery beyond that. I'm not trying to pass as high caste or

109

anything, but I'd rather not stand out as Human if you accept me."

"Is there a reason you didn't just sign up for a labor contract to work in Vergallian space?" Kelly asked. "Or if you're self-employed, there are now three open worlds in our empire accepting Humans without any special visas. If you go to the EarthCent embassy and ask for Aabina, I'm sure she can help you."

Bandya sagged a little and said, "I talked with Aabina. She told me I was destroying my health by fasting and that I started learning Vergallian too late to master the intonations. Then she said that there's nothing wrong with being Human and suggested a support group for drama addicts, but I know they would just try to talk me out of it."

Kelly found herself at a complete loss for what to say next, and then something the Frunge ambassador had once told her about dealing with problem cases rose to the front of her mind. "Did you bring your documentation?"

"Do you mean there's a form I have to fill out?" Bandya asked.

"There may be, but that would come later," Kelly improvised. "I'll need to see your education and work history, birth certification, all of the standard documentation. We can't be too careful, you know."

"I have most of that in my cabin, and I think I can get the rest via my teacherbot."

"Excellent. Why don't you return this time next week and we'll resume our discussion."

"Thank you so much," Bandya said, wiping away a tear. "You're the first Vergallian to take me seriously. I always knew that the upper caste would be different."

"Yes, well, I've had special training in empathy," Kelly said, hoping that Aleeytis would let the girl down gently.

She took up her pencil again and made a note to talk with Aabina about the phenomenon of drama fans wanting to become Vergallian.

The rest of the morning passed in much the same manner, and in several cases, Kelly made up excuses for why the people should return the next week when they would be talking to Aleeytis. Then Affie returned and escorted her to the informal dining room where they feasted on Vergallian vegan made by the embassy's chef. When she headed back to the ambassador's office, Kelly found herself just behind an alien with a familiar tentacle.

"Bork," she addressed the Drazen ambassador. "What are you doing here?"

"I came to discuss the new media guidelines," he said, standing aside so she could wave open the office door. "If I can't change your mind, I hope to at least persuade you not to oppose the majority on this."

"But I believe that greater media access to the ambassadors would prove beneficial for everybody," Kelly said, moving around the large desk and taking her seat. "I would have thought that you'd support—what?" she asked, noticing that Bork was staring at her.

"That's a stunning stand-in," he said. "I haven't seen better on set."

"You're talking about your hobby doing historical reenactments?"

"Not the live reenactments. I'm thinking about the minor parts I occasionally pick up in immersive productions during my vacations. Famous actors all have stand-ins so they don't have to remain on set for all of the technical calibration or when the focus is on other actors."

"Maybe they don't want their stand-ins to be too good," Kelly said. "If they were, those famous actors could find themselves out of work."

"That was all resolved long ago," the Drazen ambassador told her. "Actors own the rights to their appearance, and from the technical standpoint, you end up with interference patterns if you try to record a hologram of a hologram. I feel sorry for the old Human actors and entertainers who didn't have appearance rights in their contracts. I remember seeing a Grenouthian documentary that showed your deceased celebrities being resurrected for commercial purposes."

"I think that was more common before the Stryx opened Earth," Kelly said. "Eventually people decided that it was just gross and it backfired on the advertisers."

"Glad to hear it," Bork said, and then his face took on the determined look of a Drazen prepared for a long argument. "I want you to support the new media guidelines and I'm not leaving this office until we come to an agreement."

"But I do support them," Kelly protested. "I was there when you and the Grenouthian ambassador wrote the first draft."

Bork looked around the office, spotted an ornately framed mirror on the wall, and carried it around the front of the desk where he propped it on the guest's chair so that Kelly could see herself encapsulated in the stand-in hologram.

"I'm here to persuade the Kelly McAllister who is exchanging for the Vergallian ambassador," he said. "Do you really believe that supporting the new guidelines is in this embassy's best interests?"

Kelly hesitated. "Aabina's mother believed she never could have put together her grand bargain that got the Vergallians off of Earth's back if the details had been made public before the Council of Queens and the Fleet Vergallians bought in."

"But how often does a diplomatic coup like that come along?" Bork argued. "How many misunderstandings caused by poor communications must we accept in return for the occasional showy reconciliation?"

"It was more than a showy reconciliation—" Kelly began, but the Drazen cut her off with an impatient gesture.

"Please allow me to finish," he said, and produced a pair of rods which he drew apart to display a holographic scroll. "This is today's Galactic Free Press, the news source of record for Humans in the Diaspora. Do you know what it says about your exchange with the EarthCent ambassador?"

"My exchange with—oh, right. I don't remember seeing anything at breakfast."

"That's because there is nothing. I did a little checking and I discovered that the Galactic Free Press sent their top Union Station reporter here last week to ask about the upcoming exchange. You refused to talk to him."

"But I'm always happy to talk with—do we have to do it like this, Bork? I'm just not very good at keeping straight who I'm supposed to be."

"Do you want the new guidelines to be adopted?" the Drazen ambassador asked.

"Yes, I mean, if you're asking me as the EarthCent ambassador."

"I thought it was obvious from context," Bork said as he collapsed the holographic scroll with a sigh. "If I can't convince you as the Vergallian ambassador, you'll be honor-bound to vote against the new guidelines."

Kelly spent a moment staring at the reflection of Ambassador Aleeytis in the mirror and tried her best to imagine what arguments the former attorney would have made. "Why should I care about what isn't reported in the Galactic Free Press? They don't even publish a Vergallian edition."

Bork leaned forward triumphantly. "And what if they did?"

Kelly kept her eyes on the reflection of the hologram she was encased in. "Anybody can set a tab to translate a language, but that's not the same as journalism that fits the cultural context of the audience. Why would anybody outside our intelligence service care about the news that Humans want to read?"

"Why indeed?" Bork asked, and pulled the two sticks apart again. A new holographic scroll materialized, this one in Vergallian. "When the publisher of the Galactic Free Press came to me with the idea of launching a Drazen edition, I said to her, 'Frankly, all the pictures of humanoids without tentacles is a bit of a turn-off, and I only read the food section. If you have the resources to try a new alien edition, I recommend publishing for our Vergallian friends.' Of course, it wouldn't make sense for them to persist in the effort if they can't even get your opinion on important issues of the day."

"I see," Kelly said. "Well, if you put it that way, I'm officially convinced that supporting the new media guidelines for diplomatic access is in the best interest of the Union Station Vergallian embassy, and I'll be pleased to offer my support."

"I thought you'd see the light," Bork said. "I'll just return the mirror to its place."

"Better leave it and I'll practice thinking like a Vergallian. I'm not looking forward to telling Aleeytis about her change of heart in the meeting."

Ten

When Ambassador Aleeytis returned to the EarthCent embassy after the meeting to vote on the new media guidelines, her perfect features gave away nothing of her feelings about being outmaneuvered by Bork.

"Associate Ambassador Cohan was just looking for you," Donna told the Vergallian. "He said you wanted to see him before your appearance on Stone Soup this afternoon because he wouldn't be here when you got back."

"Yes, an exit interview is the normal procedure in these exchanges," Aleeytis said. "Is he in his new office?"

"I think he's checking the probability again," Donna said.

"Humans," the Vergallian muttered under her breath. She maintained a professional smile, and rather than returning to Kelly's office, she cut through the conference room to the new space.

Daniel was squatting on his haunches and throwing the Thark ambassador's binary dice against the wall while Aabina stood observing. From the looks on their faces, it wasn't going well.

"Still defying the odds?" Aleeytis inquired.

"Six straight rolls," Daniel reported. "I checked with a Verlock statistician and he warned me to stop at four thousand-to-one. Going higher than that too many times in

116

the same spot can cause permanent damage to the space-time continuum."

"And you're sure that the Thark ambassador isn't having you on? He's famous for his quirky sense of humor."

"We've tried the dice in a dozen other rooms and they always work fine," Aabina said.

Aleeytis frowned. "The two of you are serious about this, aren't you? I thought it was some strange Human version of hazing the exchange ambassador."

"Try it yourself," Daniel said, extending the dice.

The Vergallian ambassador hesitated for a moment. "Perhaps it would be better if we discussed this in the conference room with the door closed." Once they were all settled around the conference table, she asked, "Have you considered manipulator fields?"

Daniel nodded slowly. "It's possible, I suppose. But in addition to field projectors, it would require real-time imaging. We've already experimented with shielding the dice with our bodies from every possible direction. Is it something the Vergallians would be capable of pulling off?"

Aabina and Aleeytis exchanged a look, and then the ambassador said, "Probably not. As you say, it would require perfect imaging of the dice in motion and highly focused manipulator field lobes, probably employing an expensive and bulky phased array of some sort. Given the imaging, perhaps the Dollnicks could do it, and almost certainly the Grenouthians and Verlocks, but I can't imagine why."

"Crute's contractor had access to the office, and his construction crew could have installed surveillance equipment that's beyond our detection capabilities. The Stryx won't help us with things like that."

"But if one of the other species went to the trouble of setting up such a surveillance and control system, why announce it by affecting the outcome of dice rolls?" Aleeytis asked. "No, there must be something else at play here. I would advise waiting until Ambassador Srythlan comes for the exchange and consulting with him."

"It's just that I hate paying rent for the space and leaving it empty," Daniel said. "It's been over a month already. Maybe we should have sought help from scientists rather than waiting it out."

"If the Verlock ambassador can't point us to a solution, I can try asking at the Open University, but then word would get out," Aabina told him. "I'm afraid to think what would happen if the Grenouthian network gets a hold of this story."

"How ironic," Aleeytis said. "I just attended a meeting where we voted for a trial program to give the local media better access to ambassadors rather than limiting our availability to special requests and press conferences. Against my better judgment, I voted for the new guidelines, but I must admit I was disappointed when Ambassador McAllister cast the deciding vote in opposition to my instructions."

"Kelly did that?" Daniel asked. "I'm sure she must have had a good reason."

"It was—surprising. But Aabina makes a legitimate point about the Grenouthians. I spent a good part of my week here trying to convince their network to submit treatments for planned documentaries about Humans to EarthCent for feedback before proceeding."

"Any luck?"

The Vergallian ambassador gave an elegant shrug. "Time will tell. Did you read through the information I provided about the Alt's planned purchase of Earth Two?"

"It was fascinating," Aabina said. "I never studied the tunnel network treaty laws surrounding terraforming projects and I had no idea they were so complicated."

"I only got through around ten percent of the material before I went home last night," Daniel said. "It was so much more detailed than what EarthCent Intelligence has been able to provide that I'm still trying to wrap my mind around the parts I did read. I have to admit that I'm surprised Vergallian Intelligence responded to your request while you were serving as our exchange ambassador."

"They wouldn't have if I had made the request, which I didn't," Aleeytis said. "I still do the occasional consulting for my former law partners and they asked my opinion about the variances the Alts are seeking."

"So that's why you made us sign the temporary employee agreements with you," Aabina exclaimed. "It was the only way you could show us the information without violating attorney-client privilege."

"And it's why I asked the station librarian to restrict access to the documents to the display desks in the embassy," Aleeytis said. "I'm not enthusiastic about involving the Stryx, but it was the only way to ensure that the originals don't leak out, which would cause my former partners reputational damage."

"Can you explain the whole bit about nonconforming uses of the planet?" Daniel asked. "I don't understand why the Alts have to consult with anybody about what they do there after the purchase is finalized."

"Planets aren't used spaceships that can be easily repossessed and sold along. If the Alts borrow the full purchase price from the Council of Queens, they could buy the planet outright from the Container Prince, and then the only usage limitations would arise from the tunnel network treaty. But if they opt for borrowing the down payment and taking out a planetary mortgage with the Dollnicks, there are restrictions on what they can do with the property until the mortgage is paid off."

"But why? If I bought a house with a mortgage back on Earth, I could do whatever I wanted with it, including tearing it down."

"I suspect that you are misinformed," Aleeytis said politely. "If the dwelling is the primary security for the mortgage, which in my experience is what differentiates a mortgage from other types of loans, the lender would certainly limit the purchaser's rights to diminish the value of the asset."

"So you're saying that even though the planet is only partially terraformed, the Alts will have to check with the Container Prince about any alterations they make?" Daniel asked.

"Did you think my former law partners were dragging their heels on the deal to run up the billable hours? The contract is extraordinarily complex in cases like this when there isn't even a completed terraforming plan on file for everybody to follow."

"I was up late reading through tunnel network case law about variances," Aabina said. "Do I understand correctly that the reason for the terraforming planning board granting variances is so they don't have to change the existing law for special cases?"

"Exactly," the Vergallian ambassador said. "It would be strange if every planet didn't present its own unique problems in terms of complying with tunnel network ordinances. If each solution was codified, it would inevitably create contradictions within the law, not to mention an extremely unwieldy terraforming code. The only practical solution is to grant a one-time variance from the written law on a case-by-case basis."

"Are there similar regulations in place for existing worlds, or is it strictly for newly terraformed planets?" Daniel asked.

"Ah, now you've hit upon the key point." Aleeytis stood up and began to pace as she spoke, no doubt a habit from a century of courtroom appearances. "Planets are long-term assets, and in some empires, the tax codes stick terraformed worlds with multi-thousand-year depreciation schedules. So when you bring in a modifier like 'newly', it's important that we get our terms straight. Newly terraformed worlds are defined as those where the work was done by a current tunnel network member, presumably one who has respected the rules and regulations about permissible actions and usages."

"It's not just about how you terraform a planet? There are also laws about how it's used?"

"Of course. Did you think that ag worlds, resort worlds, and industrial planets were interchangeable?"

"I always assumed it was up to the owner," Daniel said.

"In most cases, the terraforming planning board will grant a request to change the use of a planet, but there is a legal process that includes public hearings that most developers would prefer to avoid," Aleeytis said. "The whole business of planetary development is one of the reasons species sign on to the tunnel network treaty. Take the Venus terraforming project that the Dollnicks are performing under contract to EarthCent. How would you like it if when Venus is finished, some developer creates similar worlds in nearby star systems to choke off your business?"

"I don't think there are any available planets in the right orbits in nearby star systems," Daniel said. "I'm pretty sure we checked."

"You're missing the point. Didn't you ever wonder how the tunnel network treaty functions to keep the peace?"

"If any of the species break the rules, the Stryx will cut off access to the tunnels and the Stryxnet."

"Obviously, but when did the threat of a penalty ever stop a war?" Aleeytis asked. "The tunnel network treaty is designed to prevent members from creating *Casus Belli*—occasions for war—and it does so by promoting the trade and business activities that keep us together."

"But how does regulating the use of terraformed planets promote business?" Daniel asked.

"By preventing the vindictive or destructive use of resources. An obvious example would be the tunnel network ban on planet cracking. If one species went around splitting open rocky worlds to get at the metal core, the whole mining industry would fall into ruins, and those star systems would fill up with hazardous asteroids. Or if the Dollnicks were allowed to terraform ag worlds to the limit of their capacity, the value of the much smaller number of ag worlds terraformed by the Drazens, Hortens, and Frunge would crash. The financial effects would ripple through their economies and fingers would point at the Dollnicks."

"I was aware of some of this, but I find subsection 102-207 particularly confusing," Aabina said. "For planets that were terraformed by non-tunnel network species and then purchased by one of us, it states that the terraforming planning board can allow a change from a nonconforming use to a lesser nonconforming use without a public hearing."

"Hold on," Daniel said. "I thought that planets terraformed by non-tunnel network species weren't covered."

"They aren't, as long as the usage remains the same," the Vergallian ambassador explained. "But if you purchased a world that the Sharf had terraformed for heavy industrial use and you wanted to change it to mixed-use with residential and industrial, you would lose the grandmothering."

"The what?"

"Grandfathering," Aabina interpreted for him. "Vergallians traditionally follow matrilineal language in the law."

"Say the Conference of Sovereign Human Communities bought a previously terraformed industrial planet from the Sharf and we wanted to change the usage," Daniel hypothesized. "We'd have to go before the terraforming planning board and request a variance?"

"It depends," Aleeytis said, coming to a momentary halt in her pacing. "Aabina just brought up subsection 102-207 which addresses this very situation. The tunnel network treaty establishes a hierarchy of uses for planets according to the impact on the galactic economy and quality of life. The original Sharf use would be considered nonconforming because they never went through the tunnel network treaty process to terraform the planet for heavy industry, but if you changed the use to one that conforms more closely with the intent of the planning board, they can grant the variance on a simple voice vote."

"Could you give me an example that doesn't involve planets?" Daniel asked. "I'm just having a bit of trouble wrapping my head around the size of the thing."

"Let me try," Aabina said. "Take our new office. The Stryx allow unlimited commercial use on this deck, which means that by right, we can use it for office space, open a retail store, a restaurant, or even turn it into a warehouse. Now I'm just making this next part up, but say that the station building code required a bathroom for every four chairs in an office or two bathrooms per residential dwelling."

"We'd be in trouble either way because there's only one bathroom," Daniel said. "In addition to the two small offices, we'll have a receptionist and work spaces for up to a dozen visiting CoSHC members, so I'm figuring at least fifteen or sixteen chairs."

"Which would mean four bathrooms, but the last lease holder used the space for an office, so that use is grandfathered and we could get by with just one bathroom."

"Because the previous leaseholder got a variance to only have one bathroom?"

"Maybe, or maybe they started using it as an office before my imaginary building code was established," Aabina said. "Now say you wanted to change the zoning to mixed-use and live in one of the offices. How many bathrooms would you need?"

"According to Ambassador Aleeytis, we would lose the grandfathering," Daniel said, glancing at the Vergallian ambassador, who gave him an encouraging nod. "So two bathrooms for the apartment, and there would still be fourteen chairs, so another three and a half bathrooms."

"Building codes always round up," Aleeytis told him.

"Six bathrooms, which is crazy. We wouldn't be able to use the space at all."

"Unless residential use was considered to be less non-conforming with the bathroom requirement than office use," Aabina told him. "And I think you could make that argument because the bathroom requirement for residential is less demanding than the requirement for office, at least with the open floor plan you'll be using in the main area."

"So you're saying that the Stryx, rather than seeing me continue to use the whole space for grandfathered nonconforming office use, would allow me to switch to a mixed-use because it comes closer to conforming with the bathroom requirement," Daniel said slowly, reasoning it out as he went.

"Correct, and it's the same with planets."

"That's where I lose you," he admitted.

"Consider an artificially created canyon," Aleeytis said. "A canyon large enough to split a continent in half."

"Why would anybody create a geographical feature that large?" Daniel asked.

"I'm not a terraformer, but I've heard of it happening by accident. Sometimes it's necessary to heat a planet's crust, and then if it doesn't cool evenly, the result can be large cracks that are similar to those worn by millions of years of water flow. Such an accidental creation would be nonconforming with the terraforming plan on file, but I've never heard of the terraforming board forcing a contractor to reheat a planet to the molten state to start over."

"Okay, but you're talking about a repair job in that case," Daniel said. "Can you give a recent example of a variance granted because the owners of a world wanted to do something that outright defied the permitted usages?"

"There are terraforming jobs in progress today that began before Humans discovered the wheel," Aleeytis said. "You may think that the activity is more widespread than it actually is because so many Human contract workers have been hired for landscaping jobs on planets nearing completion. In fact, one such variance I've seen in recent years was for your homeworld, but I don't—"

"Wait a minute. I thought you said we could all do whatever we want on our homeworlds?"

"The tunnel network terraforming subcommittee is responsible for the codes regulating work performed by alien contractors on the worlds of primitive species," Aleeytis said. "I suppose it was a little before your time, but when the Dollnicks constructed Earth's space elevators, they had to apply for a variance to locate the stalks away from the equator. Doing so introduces a number of technical challenges and increases both the capital required and the long-term operating costs. The transcript from the public hearing was quite amusing."

"Did that take place on Union Station?"

"Homeworld issues that would fall under the umbrella of zoning or building codes are always handled by the planning board on the nearest Stryx station. For terraforming issues, there is no set jurisdiction, so they tend to be heard on a station regarded as a friendly venue. Union Station has been holding more than its fair share of these hearings in recent years. Why don't you volunteer for a seat on the planning board, Associate Ambassador Cohan?"

"Why didn't I think of that?" Aabina said. She turned to Daniel. "Ambassador McAllister never joined the planning board because she didn't feel qualified to voice an opinion on the technical issues."

"And you think I'm qualified to comment on planetary engineering?" Daniel asked with a laugh.

"I think you'd be surprised how much you've picked up dealing with all of the issues that CoSHC members run into on open worlds."

"They provide an excellent briefing package before each scheduled meeting," Aleeytis said. "The worst thing that can happen is that after a few meetings, you'll decide that it isn't for you and find another diplomat to take your place."

"All right, I'll try it," Daniel said impulsively. "Do I go to the terraforming subcommittee chair to sign up since the planning board works under their supervision?"

"I can take care of it right now," the Vergallian ambassador said. "Librarian?"

"Yes, Ambassador Aleeytis," Libby replied.

"Associate Ambassador Cohan has volunteered for a seat on the planning board. Please update the public record."

"He'll be taking your place?"

"It's a sacrifice, but while I'm here on exchange for the EarthCent ambassador, it's the least I can do to advance the education of a colleague."

"Change registered," the Stryx librarian said.

"Wait a second," Daniel said. "What was that bit about finding another diplomat to take my place?"

"Ambassadorial level," Aleeytis told him with a cat-that-ate-the-canary smile. "Thanks to EarthCent's quaint policy of rewarding employees with new job titles rather than salary increases, Associate Ambassador just makes the cut. Now if the two of you will excuse me, I'm booked as the special guest on *Stone Soup*. Donna's grandson is planning to make Vergallian Vegan, and all of this diplomacy has put me in the mood for some knife work."

Eleven

"For anybody who joined us late today, I originally planned to prepare Vergallian Vegan with the assistance of the EarthCent Ambassador, but she exchanged with Ambassador Aleeytis for the week," Jonah said, looking directly into the front immersive camera. "If you're wondering why the counter is covered with flowers, those are actually carved fruits, and you'll want to replay the first forty-five minutes of our show today to see how our special guest created them."

"They're so beautiful," an attractive teenager enthused from where she was sitting in the front row of the audience with her family.

"But before we continue, I'd like to say a few words about the knives we're using today." Jonah eased directly into reading the voiceover script that appeared on his heads-up display as the Grenouthian engineer in the booth started the holographic projection that appeared over the counter for the live audience. "For over five centuries, the Tanaka family of Japan has been producing knives specially designed for Mukimono, the art of fruit carving. These hand-forged knives are lovingly prepared with special curved tips to aid in carving out delicate flower petals, but you can also use them to cut vegetables for your dinner."

"They're surprisingly well balanced," the Vergallian ambassador contributed.

"These knives carry the All Species Cookbook seal of approval, and are just one of the many reasons to take a shopping trip to Earth," Jonah continued, as the hologram shifted from showing a master craftsman polishing a knife to a bird's eye view of Japanese gardens surrounding the workshop. "Tell your travel agent that you heard about Earth on *Stone Soup* and receive a five percent discount on the space elevator and lodgings."

The hologram going out on the network feeds was replaced with ordering information in the proper language for the audience, and Jonah took advantage of the break to check on the progress Aleeytis was making carving the watermelon, which was almost finished. Then the Japanese garden hologram that the studio audience was still seeing vanished and the host shifted back into chef mode.

"Your watermelon carving could be mistaken for a painting," Jonah praised Aleeytis. "Could you explain a little about your technique?"

"The key in all fruit carving is controlling the color boundaries, and your watermelon gives us several interesting strata to choose from," the Vergallian ambassador said without missing a beat. "The outer skin offers a spectrum of greens, from deep forest to the lightest hazel. The rind provided a thick, brilliant white, and then of course there's the luscious pink of the fruit itself."

"But how do you control the shades of pink to create such a powerful three-dimensional effect?" Jonah asked.

"The boundary between the rind and the pulp is more gradual than you might think, and I'm also taking advantage of the fact that the deeper I carve into the melon, the more the exposed flesh is in shadow. The darkest reds you're seeing are literally due to the shade of the petals I've carved."

"If you placed that melon in a flower bed, I'd think I was seeing the biggest rose blossom that ever bloomed."

"We have larger roses in the Empire of a Hundred Worlds," Aleeytis told him as she made a final incision and removed the bit of rind with the tip of her knife. "There. I'm a bit rusty, but as my fruit-carving tutor always said, it's better to stop one cut too early than one cut too late."

Jonah carefully picked up the watermelon and moved it to the space at the center of the smaller carved fruits he had helped to prepare under the Vergallian's tutelage. The family sitting in the front row burst into applause, and a moment later, the rest of the studio audience, which had been instructed to remain quiet until the 'applause' signs were lit, joined in.

"Who are those people?" the Grenouthian assistant director demanded in Jonah's ear. "If they're relatives of yours, I don't want them back in this studio again."

"Never seen them before," Jonah subvoced in reply, and then tried talking over the noise. "Thank you. Thank you. We don't have much time left, but Ambassador Aleeytis would like to share some general tips about eating Vergallian Vegan." As he spoke, the Grenouthian sound engineer in the booth kept raising the volume until he drowned out the audience, and then seamlessly tracked the noise level back down so that the host never sounded like he was shouting. "Ambassador?"

"It's common knowledge that ordering Vergallian Vegan cuisine is the safest choice for tunnel network travelers, but what isn't widely known is that the food you'll be served isn't fit for the convicts in a queen's lowest dungeon," Aleeytis said. "When preparing food with vegan ingredients, the goal is to cook with intention and to bring out the delicate natural flavors. Most so-called

Vergallian Vegan restaurants boil up some vegetables and drown them in hot sauce."

"But how can we know what we're getting?" the teenage girl in the front row asked, her sincerity shining through her wide eyes.

"The Council of Queens has a certification program for Vergallian Vegan, and the symbol—" Aleeytis retrieved a carrot and placed it on her cutting board "—is the Chef's Chain, which represents a commitment to quality." She cut off both ends of the carrot, quickly sliced down one side to create a flat, and then rolled the vegetable and repeated the slice twice, leaving her with a rectangular block of carrot rounded on one side. "I move in one blade's width and cut forty-five percent through, flip it over, and repeat," she continued while deftly putting her words into action. "Then I move in the width of two blades and cut all the way through."

"So you're left with a pretty thin slice of carrot that's been cut forty-five percent of the way through along the length of both sides," Jonah observed. "I think I see where this is going."

"Now I'm going to make slits perpendicular to the length, about once every pinkie width works for me, but you can use a ruler at home," the Vergallian said as her knife flew across the carrot. "Could you hand me that polypropylene spatula?"

"This?" Jonah asked as he extended the plastic frosting spreader.

"Yes. I'm just going to insert it in the slit so I don't cut through both layers since I'm so out of practice. A trained Vergallian chef would have no need for such a prop."

Jonah watched as she dexterously used the tip of her razor-sharp knife to cut through the carrot between every

132

other one of the shorter perpendicular slits, starting at the end. Next, she carefully gouged out the carrot between the new slits, creating a series of small rectangular windows.

"Now we simply flip it over and do the mirror image operation on the other side, skipping one slit in so that the windows don't line up," Aleeytis said. "Then we turn the carrot around and repeat both operations with the long slit on the other side."

"It looks like you're gouging out the carrot on an angle," Jonah said.

"Yes, forty-five degrees works best." She set aside the knife and picked up the carrot. "As you can see, we now have two ladder shapes that are interlocked through the spaces between every rung. "Now, I'm going to cheat and use the polypropylene spatula again," the Vergallian ambassador continued, "and cut a triangle shape out of the thick end of each ladder rung with two slices. I'll just neaten up the ends, and now we cut through to connect the points of the triangles we just made, being careful not to cut into the interlocked ladder rung."

"Are you getting all of this?" Jonah subvoced to the assistant director.

"Phenomenal knife work," the Grenouthian replied in his head. "I always thought diplomats were all talk."

"There," Aleeytis declared, shaking the links out of the carrot that now formed a continuous chain. Again the teenager in the front row began clapping, drawing the rest of the audience along with her.

"And that's the symbol Vergallian Vegan restaurants certified by the Council of Queens will display?" Jonah asked when the applause died out of its own accord.

"In a hologram, along with a Stryxnet code you can scan to check that it's genuine," Aleeytis confirmed.

133

"That's all the time we have for today, and I want to thank you again for exchanging with the EarthCent ambassador," Jonah said, and then it struck him that his words were open to misinterpretation. "I mean—"

"And we're out," the voice in his head interrupted. "All that applause put us almost forty-two seconds behind schedule so we'll have to run the credits at triple speed to fit in our last commercial spot. Do me a favor and ask that family in the front row not to come again."

"I had a lovely time," the Vergallian ambassador said to Jonah. "If you keep working on your knife skills, perhaps we can have a contest one day."

"Thank you," Jonah said. "As a special guest, you get to keep the apron." Then he removed his own apron, took the back stairs off the set, and went around to the audience seating, hoping that the family would already be gone. Unfortunately, they were still in place, and the teenage girl greeted him enthusiastically, even as her younger siblings seemed to draw away.

The father stood up and hesitantly offered Jonah a handshake. "I'm Methan, this is my wife Rinla, and our children Meena, Antha, and Methanon," he said. "I hope you can forgive Meena's outbursts. She's been taking assertiveness training from a Vergallian princess who was assigned to Alt as a contract queen."

"You're Alts?" Jonah asked. "I thought you were a bit too good looking to be Human, but not quite Vergallian, either. Are you on Union Station for long?"

"It's not decided yet," Methan said, "but you don't have to worry about our being in the audience every day. We're just here early because Methanon is going to be on *Let's Make Friends*. Aisha sent us free tickets to see your show."

"I was on *Let's Make Friends* when we visited Union Station five years ago," Meena said. "It was so much fun, and the aliens were so nice."

"I'll have to thank Aisha for finding me such an enthusiastic audience," Jonah said. "The bunnies, er, Grenouthians, turn around the set faster than you'll believe. You only have ten minutes to wait, and most of that is just to give the studio audience time to get seated. Shall I bring Methanon backstage?"

The youngest Alt, who appeared to be about six years old, tried to hide behind his older brother, and his mother shook her head. "He's still a bit shy of Humans," she said. "The message from Aisha was that the Grenouthians will inform us when the time comes."

"Then I hope you enjoy your time here, and thanks again for watching," Jonah said. He returned backstage, stopping along the way to explain the situation with the Alts to the assistant director, and then met Aisha outside the dressing rooms.

"It sounded like you had a great audience today," the host of *Let's Make Friends* said to him.

"The Alt family in the front row sort of ignored the applause sign," Jonah warned her. "Mainly the teenage girl who was apparently on your show years ago and has been taking aggressiveness training."

"Meena. I remember her, and if I was to recommend aggressiveness training to a former guest, she would have been the one," Aisha said. "I hope the little boy is a bit more rambunctious or I'll have the director in my ear all show telling me to ignore him."

"Are you adding him to the cast rotation, or is it a one-time guest appearance?"

"I suppose we'll see how it goes. The EarthCent embassy asked me to extend the invitation as they're trying to improve relations with the Alts. The funny thing is that with all the exchanges Kelly is doing I'm not really sure who made the request."

"Good luck with the show," Jonah said. "I'm taking Sephia to dinner so I have to run."

Aisha continued to the green room and found that the children were already out of makeup and excited to be back on the show for their second cast rotation. "Where's Hork?" she asked.

"Bathroom," Emanuel said, pointing over his shoulder with his thumb.

"Did you go?" Aisha asked in a lower voice.

"Of course," the seven-year-old replied. "This isn't my first rodeo."

"You've ridden bulls?" the Sharf girl asked, tapping her ear cuff translation device as if she suspected it was defective.

"It's something my dad says," Emanuel told her. "My mom says he's full of it."

"Full of what?"

Aisha clapped her hands to get the cast's attention as Hork returned to the green room. "Welcome back, everybody. Please listen for a moment. We have a special guest today, a little boy whose parents are on Union Station for diplomatic reasons. For those of you who aren't familiar with the Alt species, they originated on my homeworld and we look very similar, but the Stryx moved them to their own planet a long time ago."

"How long?" the broad-shouldered Verlock girl asked.

"I think it was over fifty thousand years," Aisha said.

"That's not long," a number of the alien children said at the same time.

"In any case, this little boy may not be comfortable close to Emanuel, so try to remember—"

"Time to get going," a young Grenouthian assistant called from the doorway. "Live in five."

"Just make sure that one of you is always between Emanuel and the guest," Aisha said.

As the cast members, all of whom tested as approximately seven years old in terms of their relative emotional development began moving out, Hork declared, "Humans have the space cooties," and used his tentacle to keep Emanuel at a distance.

"Do not," the human boy said, pushing back. The Drazen was taking martial arts training and evaded, causing Emanuel to stumble into the bulky Verlock girl, who didn't even break stride at the impact. Then another Grenouthian assistant who was assigned to watch for horseplay backstage plucked Emanuel off his feet and didn't put him down until they reached the set.

The children were all veterans of the show and quickly fell back into the routine. Aisha started as she always did after a cast rotation, asking the children what they learned during their time away. Before anybody knew it, the long commercial break at the halfway point arrived, and it was time to bring the Alt boy on stage.

"Don't worry," Meena encouraged her younger brother, whose fingers their father was gently prying from their mother's arm. "Aisha is really nice, she doesn't even smell Human, and you can just keep away from that Emanuel."

"Go on, Methanon," Rinla told her son. "We'll be right here if you need anything."

With these twin assurances, Methanon finally released his grip, and his father hastened to bring him to the front of the stage and pass him up to the impatient assistant director. The Grenouthian planted the boy on his mark, checked that the Alt's ear cuff translator was still in place, and then dove out of view.

"Welcome back," Aisha said as the cameras went live. "Today we have a guest cast member, and if everybody treats him really well, maybe he'll come back again. Who wants to play the introduction game?"

"Me, me," the four alien girls on set chorused, waving their hands to get the host's attention.

"Why don't you all take a turn, and each of you can introduce a boy?" Aisha suggested.

"I'll go first," the little Frunge girl said confidently and took a step towards Methanon. "I'm Dzerri."

"I'm Methanon," the Alt replied. "What's the game?"

"The one making the introductions has to come up with a word in our native language using a syllable from each of the three names," Dzerri explained. She pointed to the Drazen boy and said, "He's Hork, so together we're Onrikhork."

"United," Aisha said as her implant provided the translation of the Frunge word. "That was very good, Dzerri."

"I'm Nvellab," the Sharf girl came forward to introduce herself.

"Methanon," the Alt boy repeated.

"And he's Lothad," Nvellab said, indicating the Horten boy, who nodded. "Together we're Labanad."

"Companions," Aisha repeated the translation. "That's excellent. You girls are so clever."

"I'm Frnylid," the Verlock girl told the Alt.

"Methanon," he said again.

"And he's Kupe," she continued, pointing at the tall Dollnick boy. "Together we're Mekupelid."

"A triple integral of a function on a hyperrectangular domain," Aisha faithfully repeated the translation from her implant. "That's very—advanced."

"How did you know I just learned triple integrals?" Methanon asked Frynlid. "They're so much fun."

"And I'm Bleena," a shy Vergallian girl introduced herself.

"Methanon," the Alt boy said, adding a polite bow.

"Oh, you mustn't bow. I'm not from a royal family," Bleena said, coloring prettily. "He's Emanuel," she added, pointing at Chastity's son. "Together we're, uh, Eonea."

"A cloth made from a mixture of wool and linen," Aisha voiced the translation, wondering why it rang a bell. "Now that we're all introduced, do you want to tell us why your family is visiting Union Station, Methanon?"

"My dad came for legal counsel," the Alt boy said.

"Are you getting sued?" the Frunge girl asked. "My uncle is a lawyer."

"Maybe they're criminals," Hork said excitedly. "Or pirates."

"I'm sure that's not it," Aisha inserted herself before the speculations could grow out of control.

"It's got something to do with terraforming," Methanon said.

"Do any of you know about terraforming?" Aisha asked.

"Me, me," the Dollnick boy cried excitedly, waving all four hands in the air. "My whole family works in terraforming."

"Have you ever heard of Earth Two?" Methanon asked.

"Yes, but it's supposed to be a secret," Kupe said.

"It's in the Galactic Free Press all the time," Emanuel told them.

"You read Alt?" Methanon asked in astonishment.

"Humanese," Emanuel said proudly. "Mom says she's working now to publish a version in Vergallian."

"I believe there's already a short version of the Galactic Free Press available in Alt," Aisha said, and she looked out at the audience where Methanon's father nodded.

"What did it say about Earth Two?" the Alt boy asked Chastity's son, though he looked at Emanuel's hair rather than making eye contact.

"That there are lots and lots of cool animals and stuff," Emanuel said. "It's really big and there aren't any people, but it's not finished either."

"I guess if all of that is in the Galactic Free Press it's not a secret anymore," Kupe said. "I know that it was the first terraforming job done by the Container Prince, though he's not really a prince, at least not yet. And my cousin said they only finished the smallest continent, but the wildlife is all out of balance. He said the rest of the planet needs a lot of work, so it's sort of a fixer-upper."

"Oh, I thought it was all prepared," Methanon said. "I like gardening, but a whole planet would be a really big job."

"Maybe you could work together with Emanuel," the Vergallian girl suggested. "My mother says that lots of Humans work on Dollnick terraforming projects and you're practically the same species."

"But he's Human," the Alt protested. "They're not—I mean—you know..." Methanon trailed off when he realized he couldn't tell how the Alts felt about their former neighbors, but everybody was waiting, so eventually he said in a small voice, "Humans scare me."

"My mother says that music can fix anything," Hork declared. "We should sing Methanon our song."

Aisha looked for the assistant director out of the corner of her eye to see if he'd object and received the go-ahead nod. The Grenouthian sound engineer in the booth started the theme music, and the children sang to Methanon,

Don't be a stranger because I look funny,
You look weird to me, but let's make friends.
I'll give you a tissue if your nose is runny,
I'm as scared as you, so let's make friends.

The light on the front immersive camera blinked out, and the assistant director hopped up on stage. "Sorry I couldn't count you out to the commercial break but it came direct from the booth," he said. "The director says you should still sing the song at the end of the show, and try to get the new kid to join in. And the director respectfully requests that you play Storytellers before the audience falls asleep."

Twelve

"How are the negotiations with Flower coming?" Joe asked his adopted son.

"Slowly," Paul replied. "I've delegated the detail work to Marilla because she's so excited about the data crunching opportunities. I'm not ready to hand the whole thing over to the lawyers yet, but I have the feeling that Flower has us outclassed."

"She's a twenty-thousand-year-old AI with a lot of recent experience in contract negotiation," Joe said. "And remember that she's in the entertainment business in a big way with her anime studios. That means she's accustomed to playing hardball with some of the toughest Grenouthian lawyers in the galaxy."

"I should probably ask Aisha to look over the latest draft. She's learned a lot about contracts in two decades of hosting her show, but between the new cast rotation and Stevie starting at Libby's school, she's already got enough on her plate."

"It's hard to believe Steve is already five. He's such a quiet boy."

Paul laughed. "You think that because the hull of the ice harvester is practically soundproof and your high-frequency hearing is failing."

As if on cue, Joe pointed at his ear. "Yes?"

"I asked Libby to ping you for me," his wife's voice said. "I need two bodies in a hurry."

"Excuse me?"

"You know I'm exchanging with the Fillinduck ambassador this week and they do everything in trios. He left me a whole list of public events to attend and I can't go alone."

"I'm honored that you thought of me first, Kelly, but you know I don't have too much patience for—"

"The first one is a school science fair," Kelly cut him off. "Plus, you're retired, and if you don't come, I'll be walking around with a blow-up doll under each arm."

"All right," Joe said, and gave Paul a speculative glance. "Who are you getting for the third?"

"EarthCent Intelligence is still a little vague about how Fillinduck trios work, but I think our third needs to be a young female not related by blood. Is Fenna around?"

"Just a minute." Joe dropped his finger and said, "Kelly needs me to go to a Fillinduck science fair so she doesn't scandalize the aliens and we need a third."

"I already told Kevin I'd go out with him in the bum boat," Paul said apologetically. "He's got a big order of Zero-G meals for an ore processing ship that isn't docking."

"Actually, Kelly asked about Fenna."

"I saw her heading for Dring's earlier," Paul said. "Just tell Kelly to ping Aisha so she knows."

Joe jogged over to the passage through the mound of scrap metal that separated Dring's sublet from the rest of Mac's Bones. Beowulf trotted alongside for a while, but the Cayl hound soon figured out that the seventy-year-old man wasn't going to catch a second wind, and dropped out for fear of pushing him.

Dring and Fenna were just resetting the chess pieces when Joe arrived, and the Maker rose to greet his landlord. "Welcome, Joe. Care to take my place for a game? She's getting pretty good."

"She beats me every time now," Joe said. "I'm sorry to break up your fun, but I'm here to ask Fenna if she's open to attending a Fillinduck science fair. Kelly needs us for two bodies."

"Sure, I'll go," Fenna said without hesitation. "Do you want to come too, Dring?"

"Will four be a problem?" Joe asked the Maker, who was knowledgeable about all of the alien cultures encountered on the tunnel network, and many beyond.

"I'd enjoy accompanying you, and no, it won't be a problem," Dring said. "I'm sure the only reason Kelly needs three is that she's exchanging with the Fillinduck ambassador this week. If she was attending as herself, the local Fillinducks wouldn't think twice about her appearing alone. The aliens living on Stryx stations are a cosmopolitan lot by necessity."

"Great, but we need to get going now," Joe said, and pointed at his ear. "Libby? Can you let Kelly know we're on the way and tell me where we're going?"

"Just ask for the Fillinduck deck and then follow the foot traffic," the station librarian replied. "Everybody goes to the science fair."

Kelly was waiting for them when they exited the lift tube capsule, and her face split into a wide smile when she saw that the Maker was along. "I just found out that I'm supposed to be an honorary judge, but when they see you, they'll forget about me in a heartbeat," she told Dring. "You wouldn't mind, would you?"

"Judging at science fairs is one of my favorite things," the Maker said graciously. "It looks like everybody is going that direction."

"What kind of projects do you like most, Uncle Dring?" Fenna asked. "We're having a science fair at Libby's school next year and I want you to come."

"You know how much I enjoy gardening, so experiments on how changes in the environment affect plant growth are always interesting. I recall one project at a Drazen school's science fair where they showed that with the same lighting, fertilizer, and water, seedlings in the choir room grew twenty percent faster than seedlings with no exposure to choral music."

"Oh, I should start singing to our plants."

"Well," the Maker continued, "I didn't say anything about it at the time, but I expect that the higher carbon dioxide and moisture in the choir room from singing may have been the main contributing factors."

"Do you know what age group this will be, Kel?" Joe asked.

"The Fillinduck equivalent of high school, so they're probably pretty advanced," the EarthCent ambassador replied. "I'm expecting a lot of Rinty bubbles."

"And how are you enjoying your exchange with Ambassador Ptew?" Dring asked.

"It's frustrating. The other ambassadors are better prepared for these exchanges than I am because they can consult with the histories of their diplomatic services. I suspect they've been planning this for a while and saving up a certain type of duties for me."

"You don't like science fairs?" Fenna asked Kelly.

"Ambassador Ptew couldn't control the timing of the science fair and a few other things, but I've been dealing with an unending stream of salesmen and solicitors for this or that Fillinduck charity all week. When you consider that my working hours don't line up with their embassy's working hours, all of these appointments must have been prearranged. And my last day there I'm expecting a performance review team from their homeworld."

"The old 'stick the exchange ambassador with the decennial job performance review' trick," Dring said with a chuckle. "They've been doing that one for millions of years."

"But won't the inspectors just come back another time when they realize that Ambassador Ptew tricked them?"

"The Fillinducks are fond of clever maneuvers, and to raise the stakes they don't allow do-overs in situations like this. When the audit team realizes they've been had they'll move on to the next Stryx station. Ptew will be off the hook for another ten Fillinduck years."

"Looks like quite a line," Joe observed as they came to a halt at the back of a crowd shuffling towards the auditorium. The moment he spoke, a passage cleared before them, and a trio in academic robes approached.

"Maker Dring, Ambassador McAllister," the Fillinduck principal greeted them nervously. "You honor us with your unexpected presence, Maker, and if I might be so brave as to impose on your good nature, I know our youngsters would be thrilled if you would judge the fair. I'm sure Ambassador McAllister and the others in her trio would stand aside."

"Of course," Kelly said, unable to suppress her delight.

"The honor is all mine," Dring said.

The Fillinduck trio escorted the visitors through the crowd and into the large auditorium, the very air of which was snapping and crackling with electrical discharges. The first booth featured a giant metal ball on a glass cylinder, inside of which could be seen a belt made from fur. The lower wheel on the belt was attached by a long chain to a bicycle made for three, where a trio of Fillinduck students sat at the ready.

"A Van de Graaff generator," Dring explained the alien text to Fenna. "Put your hand on the ball and don't remove it until I tell you."

The fourteen-year-old reached out and put her hand on the metal sphere, and the Fillinduck students began to pedal furiously. A moment later, the luxurious black hair that normally hung to the small of Fenna's back began to rise, and soon her head was surrounded by a giant halo. The Fillinducks, whose own heads were covered with a type of downy feathers that performed poorly in static electricity demonstrations, burst into spontaneous applause.

At a signal from their teacher, the trio of students stopped pedaling. The tallest one picked up a long dowel made of wood and touched it to Fenna's hand. Her hair slowly fell back into place, and Kelly smoothed down a few recalcitrant strands for the girl.

"Very well done," Dring complimented the students, and then complied with their request to pose with them for selfies.

"Can we build a Van de Graaff generator, Grandpa?" Fenna asked Joe. "I want to show Mike my hair going up."

"We can, but let's see the rest of the fair first," Joe said. "There may be something else you'd rather work on."

"This one looks like the project I did in my high school science fair," Kelly said when they reached the next booth. "I showed that by adding salt to water you can raise the boiling temperature."

"I don't see a heat source boiling their salt water, Kel," Joe said.

"It's a miniature nuclear fission reactor," Dring told them after reading the poster. "The students are demonstrating a containment field method for radioactive decay."

"Is it dangerous?" Kelly asked.

"Not at all," the Maker assured her, stirring the boiling water with a blunt finger. "Well, it's too hot for you to touch, but the containment is excellent. All of my traveling has made me very sensitive to radiation."

The next booth featured a maze where some tiny mammals that resembled rodents were racing through the glassed-over passages at high speed.

"What are they doing, Uncle Dring?" Fenna asked.

"Do you see the little pouches the test subjects are carrying?" the Maker asked. "The students have trained Geezles to efficiently deliver small packages. It's a proof of concept, not a business plan."

"I feel sorry for the next trio," Kelly muttered to Joe, motioning with her head at the three students standing behind a folding table with the burned-out remains of a model skyscraper. "They must have worked so hard putting it together only for it to catch fire."

"They seem to be getting a lot of attention," Joe said as they trailed along behind Dring and Fenna. "Maybe they have video of the fire on those tabs."

A space in front of the booth opened up at the Maker's approach, and one of the Fillinducks immediately handed over a tab. Instead of video, it proved to be a digital lab book of detailed observations made by the students, both in real-time during the fire, and from hundreds of hours of video captured from miniature cameras that were spread through the model skyscraper before the destructive testing began.

"Fascinating," Dring said after swiping through several screens full of data. "The students are part of an advanced credit course where they take architecture classes at the Open University and get credit towards their high school graduation."

"Are they studying how to design fireproof buildings?" Kelly asked.

"The tunnel network species all solved those problems before developing interstellar travel. This skyscraper is modeled on a particular style found on Earth. The title of their project is 'Retrofitting primitive skyscrapers with state-of-the-art fire suppression equipment.'"

"But it didn't work," Joe pointed out.

"They subjected the model to repeated destructive testing until they found the level at which operator failure could overcome advanced engineering," Dring explained. "In the final trial, they examined what would happen if the Humans decided to test the readiness of their fire department by shutting off all of the Fillinduck suppression systems and starting a bonfire in the lobby. It's a very realistic simulation for this age group, and the lab books are extraordinarily neat."

Joe lagged behind for a moment to examine the burnt-out wreckage. He estimated that the model must have employed tens of thousands of rivets in the melted steel skeleton, in addition to being fully plumbed and wired in miniature. "This must have taken years to build," he couldn't help exclaiming.

"We used a three-dimensional printer," one of the students who obviously had a translation implant informed him. "The hard part was finding architectural plans from

Earth that were clean enough to program the printer. The first few buildings we tried had too many engineering change orders, and the printers aren't designed to undo layers that have already been deposited."

"I wanted to do a suspension bridge," one of the other students chipped in. "Earth has lots of interesting ones, even though they need constant repainting."

Joe caught up with his party where in turning to get to the next aisle they had run into another group of special guests.

"You remember my husband, Joe," Kelly said to Methan. "Joe, this is Methan's wife Rinla, their daughter Meena, and their sons Antha and Methanon."

"Nice to see you all again," Joe said, keeping his hands in plain sight so as not to give the Alts any reason to get nervous. "I seem to remember a story in the Galactic Free Press about Antha signing a treaty with the Drazen ambassador while he was here."

"For Ambassador Bork to play himself if we produce an immersive drama about our first contact with the tunnel network," the boy said.

"And Methanon has joined the cast of *Let's Make Friends*," Kelly added.

"My mom mentioned how nice it is working with you," Fenna said to the Alt boy, who like his siblings, was wearing an ear cuff translation device. "And I remember when you were on the show, Meena. My best friend Mike was part of the cast."

"How did you find out about the Fillinduck science fair?" Joe asked Methan.

"Ambassador Ptew invited us last week," the Alt diplomat said. "We weren't aware that he would be exchanging with your wife."

"Not that there's anything wrong with that," Rinla interjected.

"The other ambassadors have been manipulating me since this exchange program started, and I suspect they're trying to bring about a reconciliation between our species," Kelly said, and then hastily corrected herself, "Not that we bear you any animus that requires reconciling."

"So you're saying the problem is all on our side?" Meena spoke up sharply.

"Of course not," the EarthCent ambassador said. "I'm sure there's blame enough to—"

"Please," Methan interrupted, holding up his palm for her to stop, and then addressed his eldest. "I have to say that your aggressiveness training went better than any of us could have imagined, but asserting yourself is one thing, and going full-on Human is another." Too late, the meaning of the old Alt expression he'd used registered, and he turned back to Kelly apologetically. "There's truth in what you said. Our grievances against Humans are old ones, and our scholars tell us that your people had completely forgotten our existence until your paleoanthropologists rediscovered us a mere few hundred years ago."

"For me to discuss this in detail now would be to steal time from my duties to the Fillinducks as their exchange ambassador," Kelly said. "From what I know of the, uh, Humans, I'm sure that EarthCent would be happy to participate in a conference or historical commission to investigate your complaints."

"I shall take your words under consideration," Methan said, and the two parties parted on amicable terms.

"Well, that was more progress than I've made with the Alts in the last half-dozen years," Kelly said. "I wonder if they really are getting used to us."

"I suspect that Methan and his family have had a lot more exposure to humanity than most Alts," Joe told her. "Two of the children have been on *Let's Make Friends*."

"Ah, those look interesting," Dring said, and accepted an odd-looking pair of spectacles with thick Fresnel lenses. There was no chance they would fit over his head, but he held them a short distance in front of his face and gave a chuckle. "Very useful indeed. You try them, Fenna."

The young teen put on the glasses and almost lost her balance, sagging against the Maker. "I'm seeing triple," she exclaimed. "What are they?"

"According to the poster, they're a therapeutic device for young Fillinducks suffering from a rare condition that makes it difficult for them to participate in trios," Dring explained. "The glasses let them practice alone in front of a mirror."

Joe and Kelly tried the glasses in turn, both of them having more or less the same reaction as Fenna. "I guess you have to be Fillinduck," Joe said.

After that came several booths where students had grown different types of bacteria on which to test novel antibiotics, and then there were an equal number of terrarium displays showing the impact of various external elements on soil erosion. The next aisle was given over to tri-state computing, and it didn't help Kelly when Dring explained it was the successor to the fuzzy logic systems that had once been popular fodder for graduate school dissertations on Earth. By the time they had stopped at every booth in the show, she was leaning against Joe for support. After Dring announced the awards, they were free to leave.

"I haven't enjoyed a science fair so much in ages," the Maker declared when they were back in the corridor. "The Fillinducks have made impressive progress as a species."

"Their projects were all super-advanced," Fenna said enviously. "I couldn't do any of them, except maybe the first one with the hair."

"They were excellent students, but I was talking about our encounter with the Alts that was obviously engineered by Ambassador Ptew," Dring said. "The Fillinducks never went through an aggressive period of expansion, but they've always been a bit stand-offish. I wouldn't have expected them to play peacemaker between two less advanced species from whom they have nothing obvious to gain."

"Maybe Ambassador Ptew is just taking his role filling in for me seriously," Kelly said. "As I've never gotten him to explain why he ignored me to the extent of boycotting meetings I attended for twenty-five years, I doubt that asking him why he's involving himself now will get me anywhere."

Thirteen

"Welcome back," Joe greeted the EarthCent intelligence agent. "If half of what I read in the Galactic Free Press is true, you and Ellen must have had a busy time of it on Earth."

"And then some," John said, returning the older man's hearty handshake. He looked around Mac's Bones and shook his head at the changes. "I see the rental business is picking up. Keeping you busy?"

"I'm retired, and most of the fleet is reconditioned Dollnick taxis so they aren't much fun to work on," Joe said with a sly grin. "But Paul keeps bringing in abandoned fixer-uppers from the lot his wife bought from Stryx Gryph at an auction, and those can be a challenge."

"I heard from Larry, Phil's son, that you might have an old Grenouthian four-decker on the market."

"It's still here, but I'd guess it's a bit big for you and Ellen, and Paul is hoping to get the market price. Plus you'd have to talk to my son-in-law, Kevin, because he has first dibs."

"Is he serious about buying it?"

Joe laughed. "He is, but my daughter isn't, and given that they have a new baby, I don't see them going anywhere anytime soon. The ship's just over on the other side of the campground, so why don't I give you the tour, and then you can decide if it's worth talking to Kevin."

"Sounds good," John said, falling in next to Joe. "Do you know how much Paul is asking?"

"He had Thomas check with the EarthCent Intelligence analyst who tracks the second-hand market, and the closest compare was sold in Earth orbit for three-point-five."

"Million?"

Joe nodded.

"Stryx creds?" John's voice rose from its usual baritone to a tenor.

"Oh, that's why you looked so surprised. The transaction was reported in eBucks, so that's something like seven hundred thousand creds at the current exchange rate."

"It's not cheap," John said, but he looked thoughtful. "When I check in with EarthCent Intelligence later, I'll have to stop and ask Blythe if they're still offering financing help for field agents."

"Maybe Ellen could get something from the Galactic Free Press, seeing that her last ship was destroyed in the line of duty. But you didn't answer my question about why you want to upgrade."

"Ellen and I have a family now, a boy and a girl. Maybe I should say a boy and a teenager, and Semmi is a growing gryphon."

Joe stopped walking and took a long look at the EarthCent Intelligence agent to see if he was being serious. "If that's the case, you'll have to bring them all over for dinner tonight. Where are they hiding?"

"Ellen took the kids to Libbyland right after we set down. I'm surprised you didn't see them leaving."

"I thought I heard Beowulf complaining about something, so it must have been your gryphon. I was on grandson duty and I didn't even notice your ship had arrived until Kevin came back and relieved me. You and Ellen may be onto something."

"You mean skipping the diaper years?" John laughed, but it turned into a whistle when he saw the Grenouthian four-decker. "Now that's a ship. There's no problem with us owning them?"

"The Grenouthians will never supply the engineering drawings if that's what you mean. But Paul got Jeeves to go through it with him, and it should be set for the next century or so, as long as you keep up with the scheduled maintenance."

It took the EarthCent ambassador's husband almost an hour to show John through the ship because the latter asked a number of intelligent questions that required detailed explanations. Then they heard Beowulf barking loudly, and Joe said, "That's his alien bark. I'm not sure which species, but that's probably because my hearing isn't what it used to be."

"The dog can identify aliens by species?"

"He can probably identify them by name, but that doesn't mean I understand when he tries to tell me," Joe said. "I can't explain how that popper works in any case, beyond the fact that it's an emergency one-time jump drive."

John was reluctant to leave the engineering deck of the ship that was already starting to feel like his, but he followed Joe to the hatch, which was folded down as a ramp. Outside, the giant Cayl hound was keeping a close eye on an alien whose arms were covered with tiny red and blue feathers.

"Ambassador Ptew," Joe greeted the Fillinduck. "If you're looking for Kelly, she left for your embassy a few hours ago. It's her last day exchanging with you, I believe."

156

"Actually, I came to see your guest, but I also wanted to thank you for bringing Maker Dring to the science fair," the Fillinduck ambassador said. "I'm sure the students will all mention it prominently in their application essays for whatever they do for the rest of their lives."

"You're here to see me?" John asked. "I don't believe we've ever met."

"I understand that you and your common-law wife are the only Humans to have visited Earth Two in person. I'm filling in for the EarthCent ambassador on Union Station this week and I thought I'd take this opportunity to debrief you in person."

"Could you give us a minute?" the EarthCent intelligence agent requested, and took Joe a few steps aside. "What is he talking about?"

Joe shrugged. "The alien ambassadors are taking turns swapping with Kelly. Supposedly it's because she's hit the seventy-five percent mark of her career, but from what she tells me, they're all taking advantage to unload the nuisance work that builds up in an embassy over time."

"So it's a legitimate request?"

"You can ping Clive if you want, but as far as I know, we're cooperating fully and everything is on the honor system. Kelly is sure that the other ambassadors are up to something, but she's equally sure they mean well, so there's not much we can do other than play along."

"At least there isn't a Huktra ambassador on the station," John said, and returned to where the Fillinduck was waiting. "I'm all yours."

"Giving up your personal autonomy won't be necessary," Ptew told him. "Is your wife here?"

"She took the kids and the gryphon to Libbyland."

"You have children?" The Fillinduck frowned and his eyes fixed somewhere off to the side as he consulted his heads-up display. "I see a Tyrellian gryphon named Semmi and a Human who works for the Galactic Free Press named Ellen, but no children. Were they recently acquired?"

"Relatively," John said, which drew a puzzled look from the ambassador. "It's a pun on—"

"I got the pun, even in translation it's obvious, but I've read up on Human reproduction and I don't understand how newly hatched, I mean, birthed children could benefit from a visit to Libbyland."

"They're adopted, informally. Just last month, though I know I reported it to EarthCent Intelligence for the benefits."

"Survivors insurance?" Joe asked.

John nodded. "It didn't reduce Ellen's payout, so why not?" Then his eyes narrowed and he said to the Fillinduck ambassador. "You're not getting your information from EarthCent Intelligence, are you?"

"It seems that in this case I should have," Ptew muttered. "Will your wife and the other beneficiaries be returning soon?"

"I think they're gone for the day," John said. "Is it that important you talk to her?"

"I did want to get a female's impression. When you've been married as long as I have, you come to appreciate the value of three different viewpoints."

"Ask your questions, and if I think it will help, I'll ping her."

"Very well," the Fillinduck ambassador said. "Would you accompany me back to the embassy? I understand that the security in this facility was recently compromised by an unidentified alien posing as an artificial person."

"Go ahead," Joe told them. "I can see how interested you are in the ship, John. I'll talk to Kevin for you, and I'll see how much Paul would be willing to credit you for trading in your old ship. Look for me when you get back."

Ptew made polite small talk about the failings of humanity during the walk and lift tube ride back to the EarthCent embassy where Donna was waiting for him to return.

"I've cleared all of your appointments for the afternoon, but Ambassador McAllister is going to be disappointed," she told the Fillinduck. "When you asked me to reschedule all of the cookbook business for Friday, I thought it was so you could get through it in one slog."

"My intention was always to roll over the meetings until Ambassador McAllister returned," the Fillinduck admitted. "Why she would think I'm interested in reviewing alien tribute recipes made from Earth ingredients is beyond me. Besides, I've been too busy working on high-level EarthCent diplomacy."

"Which you can't tell me about because it's secret."

"Exactly. Is the conference room available?"

"Daniel and the visiting ad hoc committee members just recessed to go out for lunch," Donna said. "They'll probably be a good two hours. And the station librarian pinged to say that Ellen is on her way."

"It wasn't me," Ptew said before John could open his mouth to complain. "Maybe EarthCent Intelligence has a bug on me and they intervened."

"You don't check yourself for surveillance technology?" John asked skeptically.

"Normally I would, and my amulet—" the Fillinduck fished out a dark orb on a necklace, "—would prevent most technological means of eavesdropping."

"It looks dead."

"I turn it off during my EarthCent work hours. It wouldn't be fair to the other species spying on you otherwise."

"Aabina is having her lunch in the conference room," Donna called after them. "She said you asked her to wait for you."

"If you ever have the chance to retain a Vergallian princess as a personal assistant, I highly recommend it," the Fillinduck ambassador told John. "If I was counting heads for a trio, I'd give her credit for two."

The conference room turned out to be empty, but then the door connecting to the new offices slid open, and Ptew jumped so high that he had to stick up his hands to avoid his head crashing into the ceiling.

"Was that because of me?" Ellen asked. "I stopped in to take a look at the new office the embassy is setting up for the Conference of Sovereign Communities, but it's as dead as a ghost in there."

"Please don't say 'dead' or 'ghost', at least not with that door open," the Fillinduck said. "There's something wrong with that room."

"You feel it too?" Aabina asked as she came out of the kitchenette with the salad she had brought for lunch. She set her food on the table and waved to close the door to the new office space. "You laughed when Daniel told you about the results from the probability dice."

"That's because the door was closed. Everybody knows that spirits can't enter a room unless you open the door and invite them in."

"Are you sure you aren't confusing spirits with vampires?" Ellen asked.

"What do fantasy creatures have to do with the spirit world?" Ptew asked. "Never mind. I find that when Humans attempt to explain metaphysics they invariably confuse themselves."

"Who pinged and told you to meet us?" John asked.

"Why do you think somebody pinged me?" Ellen asked in reply. "Semmi herded us all to the Physics Ride, and then she started flying circles around the kids just to show off. When somebody started shooting paintballs, I decided it was time for me to leave. I guess I'm too old for that kind of fun. The station librarian told me you'd be here."

"The ambassador wants to debrief us about our visit to Earth Two."

"Where is she?"

"I'm exchanging with Ambassador McAllister this week," the Fillinduck said smoothly. "If you check with your employer, they'll tell you it's all on the up-and-up."

Ellen didn't hesitate to take him up on the proposition. She pointed at her ear and began a subvoced conversation that ended with her saying out loud, "That's the dumbest thing I've ever heard, but if EarthCent says it's okay, who am I to disagree."

"Excellent," Ptew said, and settled into the chair at the head of the table. "Let me start by asking if you noticed anything on Earth Two that failed to match the Dollnick's description of the property."

"We didn't receive any details before Flower dropped us off," John said. "The first time I saw the official listing sheet was after we reported back to EarthCent."

"Of course," the Fillinduck muttered, obviously intending to be overheard. "Why would Humans proceed like normal planetary buyers and study the listing before-hand?"

"It all happened too fast," Ellen said defensively. "One minute we were with EarthCent's president watching the test of humanity's first interstellar jump drive, the next thing the Container Prince was inviting us to send a delegation to see Earth Two. Flower offered to drop us off, and we didn't even talk to the Dollnicks again until we arrived in-system."

"So they never gave you full disclosure?"

"The prince and his business agent came down to meet us not long after we landed. They gave us a pretty detailed rundown on things that had gone wrong when they started bringing in Earth fauna."

"Did you notice anything unsuitable about the planet between the time you landed and the time the Container Prince arrived?" Ptew asked.

"Well, now that you mention it, the Dollnick who told us where to land said that the gravity was nearly identical to Earth's, but I thought I felt a little heavy when we first put down."

"Do you have a recording of the Dollnick telling you about the gravity?"

Ellen shook her head. "I'm afraid not, though I wouldn't be surprised if Flower does. She's nosy."

The Fillinduck exchanged a glance with Aabina, who made a mental note to contact Flower and see if the recording existed. Then he asked, "How about abutters?"

Now it was the humans who exchanged a glance, and then John said, "I don't understand. Do you mean on Earth Two?"

"Abutters. Are there any other occupied planets in the system?"

162

"I don't—we didn't ask," John admitted sheepishly.

Ptew let out an explosive sigh. "My understanding is that the Alts will be seeking a variance from the terraforming planning board, which of course opens the door to input from abutting planets."

"How can planets be abutting?" Ellen demanded. "They're nowhere near each other and they're always moving."

"Near and moving are both relative terms. In the context of a star system, all planets, planetoids, and occupied moons in stable orbits are considered abutters."

"Flower will have imaged the entire system during her stop," Aabina put in. "I'll add it to the request."

"So you're saying that if another planet in the system is occupied, they can veto who can buy the world from the Dollnicks?" John asked.

"No, that would open the door to, say, discriminating against the Gem for being clones," the Fillinduck ambassador said. "The Container Prince is free to sell the world to anybody willing to pay as long as the buyer conforms to the existing uses. But if the new owner requests a variance, then it gets tricky."

"I get the gist of what you're saying, but I don't understand how it would apply on an interplanetary scale," Ellen said. "One of the reporters in the news syndicate I work with on Earth told me a long story about buying an old house in town that had been converted to office space a century ago. She wanted to create an apartment on the second floor and rent the first floor to other journalists to use as an office. It turned out that she could choose between all residential or all office by right of the zoning, but if she wanted to do mixed-use, she needed a variance."

"Was it granted?" Ptew asked.

"She had to bribe a few board members, but that's the way things are done on Earth. What I don't understand is why the hypothetical inhabitants of a planet that's light-minutes or light-hours away from Earth Two have a say over whether the surface is used for residential buildings or offices."

"Maybe it has to do with in-system traffic," John speculated.

The Fillinduck ambassador looked a bit startled and then gave the EarthCent Intelligence agent an approving nod. "Abutters have a say, but not an absolute veto, on issues that affect their own quality of life. For example, the Stryx will not establish a tunnel network connection in a system unless all of the occupied worlds agree."

"Who would be against getting connected?" Ellen asked. Then she recalled all of the species she was familiar with who hadn't joined the tunnel network. "Never mind."

"Generally it's the primitive species," Ptew replied as if she hadn't withdrawn the question. "The local advanced species who haven't joined the tunnel network, such as the Fleet Vergallians, Sharf, and Farlings, reject membership because they don't want to bind themselves to the treaty terms. But they're happy to gain access to the tunnel network, and I'm aware of a case where the Stryx provided one because the Human population on an open world was sufficient to merit connection. Primitive species are often xenophobic, and they have good reason to be, as exclusion zones are made to be broken."

"You mean that if a star system has a tunnel network connection, even if the Stryx prohibit contact with a world, eventually some unethical aliens will get through."

"Even if they have to jump into the system independently," the Fillinduck said. "Forbidden fruit is an added spice for cultural tourists, but out of sight is out of mind."

"Okay," Ellen said. "I can see where the neighbors should get to vote on tunnel network connections, but are there any otherwise conforming uses where they would have a say?"

"There was a case involving the Verlocks a few hundred thousand years ago where a Vergallian queen bought a terraformed planet from the Dollnicks to use as a tech-ban world," Aabina told her. "After a few millennia, one of her descendants decided to secede from the Empire of a Hundred Worlds, join Fleet, and drop the tech ban. The Verlocks have peculiar taste in planets and they prefer not to terraform, so they usually welcome other species to occupy the worlds they don't find suitable. But when the queen announced she was dropping the tech-ban, they objected, and it ended up in front of the terraforming subcommittee."

"But the Verlocks are probably the highest tech species on the tunnel network," John said. "Why did they object?"

"The academy on the Verlock world was given over almost entirely to astronomical observation," Aabina explained. "They were concerned about electromagnetic noise and light pollution. Some of their instruments are extraordinarily sensitive, and they had already gone to great expense to shield all of their own noise sources. During the public comment period after the initial hearing, one of the queen's sisters deposed her. The new queen reestablished the tech ban and rejoined the Empire of a Hundred Worlds, so the issue became moot."

"There's not much more I can suggest until we have all of the facts, at which point I'll no longer be your ambassador," the Fillinduck said. "But we could be onto something with possible abutters, so I'll leave instructions for the next exchange ambassador."

"Do you really think that zoning issues would affect whether or not the Alts will buy Earth Two?" Ellen asked.

"The threat of legal action is often more important than whether or not the grounds are legitimate," Ptew explained. "It's unfortunate that Humans have such shallow pockets. Money is the best advocate, and if it wasn't in short supply, you could just outbid the Alts and we wouldn't be having this discussion."

"It's a shame we can't just share the planet with them," John said. "There's more than enough room for both of our species. I doubt the Alts have the manpower to finish the terraforming work on the large continents in any reasonable amount of time without help."

"I did what I could, but a week on the Human calendar isn't enough time to heal tens of thousands of years of animosity," the Fillinduck said, and then glanced over his shoulder at the closed door leading to the new offices. "And you really should do something about that room."

Fourteen

"—and as a confidence-building measure to promote understanding between species, I can assure you from personal experience that there's nothing better than a cultural exchange," the ambassador concluded.

"I never thought I would hear such a compelling argument from a representative of EarthCent," Methan said. "You've laid out all of the facts in such a straightforward fashion that even if I wanted to refuse, I couldn't make a sound case for doing so."

"Then it's agreed," Affie said. She took the Alt's hand and placed it over the Drazen's hand in the fashion of Vergallian oath-taking. "I'll finalize the details with Aabina and the exchange will begin next Monday on the Human calendar."

"Sealed," Bork declared, and wriggled both of his thumbs. "Now that we have that out of the way, Methan, can I interest you in a visit to our embassy? We've just expanded to make space for visiting members of the Conference of Sovereign Human Communities, and there's quite an anomaly in the new office involving a failure of probability that may interest you as a scientist."

"As tempting as that sounds, my daughter is starting work today and I promised to be there to support her," the Alt said. "The whole concept of working for hourly pay at a business with millions of employees is very different from anything that we have back home, but she insists that it's practically a rite of passage for girls on Stryx stations."

"Let's see, your oldest is Meena if I recall," Bork said. "I remember seeing her on *Let's Make Friends* some years ago, so she must be in her early teens. It's the perfect age to start working for InstaSitter."

"How did you know I was talking about InstaSitter?"

Bork let out a hearty chuckle. "All of the teenage girls on Union Station work for them sooner or later, the business started here, you know. The founders are the daughters of our embassy manager, but the real tentacle pulling the strings these days is Tinka, a fine young Drazen who owns a minority share in the business."

"I had no idea that Humans could employ an individual from one of the advanced species in a business," Methan said. "My information is that most Humans who have left Earth are doing contract work for other tunnel network members."

"That's true, but only in the strict mathematical sense," Affie told him. "Increasing numbers of Humans are choosing to live and work on open worlds when they complete their contract employment. My own information suggests that within twenty years, the contract workers will be in the minority. This is exactly why I keep telling you that Alt needs an intelligence service."

"But spying just seems so dirty," Methan said.

"Have you considered subscribing to our intelligence database for businesses?" Bork asked. "You could choose the areas of information you're interested in and not get stuck wading through the sewer."

"The Drazens sell intelligence information to other species?"

"Under certain circumstances, but you've forgotten that I've exchanged with Ambassador McAllister this week. I'm talking about EarthCent Intelligence, which primarily funds its operations through selling information to businesses. I'd be happy to set up an appointment for you to talk with Clive Oxford, the director."

"It's a bit much for me to take in all at once, but I'll discuss it with Affie as soon as I return," Methan said. "I don't mean to rush off, but my daughter goes on the clock in ten minutes and I promised to accompany her."

"I'm heading back to the embassy myself, so let me come along with you as far as the lift tube," Bork said. "I'll show him out, Affie."

"You'll have to forgive me if I seem indecisive, but I'm a bit nervous about my daughter," Methan said as he followed the Drazen out of Affie's Vergallian embassy office. "Meena is a responsible girl and she's babysat innumerable times for her siblings and neighbors. I just don't understand how the station residents can trust their precious children to a complete stranger who shows up within minutes of the request."

"I think most parents leave extra time to interview the first few sitters the service sends out, and I understand that InstaSitter generally starts off new customers with a sitter from the same species. But it's also become quite common on Stryx stations for families to hire sitters just so their children spend time with an alien."

"You mean that somebody might request my Meena because they want to interact with an Alt?"

"For their children to interact with an Alt," Bork corrected him. "InstaSitter has strict rules about that. If an elderly person wants to hire help with cleaning or carrying groceries on a shopping trip, InstaSitter has a different

169

pool of employees who are interested in that work, most of them boys."

"I see there are many holes in my knowledge," Methan said. "Do you think there will be a problem with my escorting Meena?"

"Normally an adult would be an unwelcome addition, but I believe that as long as your daughter informed her manager beforehand, they'll match her with an appropriate assignment. Keep in mind that the local station librarians provide the back-office and monitoring for InstaSitter, which is why the business only operates on Stryx stations."

"I think I'll take you up on your offer of a meeting with EarthCent Intelligence after all," the Alt said as they reached the lift tube. "It's exactly these sorts of details that don't appear in the Galactic Free Press because it's assumed that everybody already knows how such ubiquitous services work."

"Excellent," Bork said. "You know where to find me the next three days." As the doors began to slide shut, the Alt heard the Drazen say, "Human deck. EarthCent embassy."

Methan hurried along the corridor to the Vergallian bed-and-breakfast where his family was staying and found Meena waiting in the small lobby as soon as he entered. She was wearing a special ear cuff translator supplied by InstaSitter, which immediately brought to her father's mind her recent request for an implant. He put aside his nervousness and gave her the traditional greeting hug.

"Did your mother already leave?" he asked.

"Yes. And she made Antha go with them even though he wanted to run around the station and explore on his own. Methanon is so lucky that he gets to be on *Let's Make*

Friends as long as we're here. Aisha is soooooo nice for a Human."

"As the hostess of the most popular children's show in the galaxy, I expect that Aisha is the exception that proves the rule," Methan said. "Are you on the clock yet?"

"One more Human minute," Meena said. "They told me not to be disappointed if I don't get a call because of my request to let you accompany me. I guess most families who hire an InstaSitter worry that if the sitter brings a friend they'll end up ignoring the children."

"I'm your father, not a friend," Methan protested. "Didn't you tell them?"

The Alt girl pointed at her ear cuff and tilted her head slightly to that side as she listened. Then she said, "Got it," and beamed at her father. "This must be my lucky day. A business just put in a call for a sitter to watch an infant and I earned the highest possible rating for holding babies when I took the InstaSitter test. They don't care if you come because the place is already full of grown-ups."

"What kind of business?"

"The dispatcher didn't say. The station librarian is going to supply directions over my ear cuff."

"Won't you need your external translation pendant?" her father asked as they headed out for the nearest lift tube. "I can run back in and get it for you."

"My client is a pre-verbal baby so I'll just make cooing sounds," Meena said.

"Aren't the parents the clients?"

"Not according to my InstaSitter training. We believe that the children are our clients."

"I thought that training for babysitters would be limited to safety considerations."

"Not babysitters, InstaSitters," his daughter corrected him as they entered the lift tube. "InstaSitter Meena. Please take me to work," she told the capsule, which set off as soon as the doors closed. "Of course we had safety training, but there was also a group discussion about the philosophy of the client-centric approach. Once I've completed ten assignments, I'll come off probation, and then I can start taking free courses and going along on InstaSitter outings."

"What kind of courses would you be interested in?" Methan asked.

The girl shrugged. "I don't know. I guess it will depend on how much longer we're going to stay on Union Station because I wouldn't want to start something and not finish."

"Don't you miss Alt and all of your friends at home?"

"Of course I do, but they'll still be there when I get back," Meena said. "While I'm here, I want to learn everything I can about the other species and make the best of the opportunities I've been given. The only thing that scares me is going home and having my friends ask why I never sang with a Drazen or meditated with a Verlock while I had the chance."

Methan looked wonderingly at his daughter as the capsule doors opened and she set off without the slightest hesitation. "Maybe your mother and I should start taking assertiveness training with Affie if she has the time. I can't get over how confident you've become."

"It's not just the training," Meena told him. "I am practically grown up now." She walked past a display panel on an easel in the corridor announcing training for franchisees in a half-dozen tunnel network languages and turned into the office.

"Are you the InstaSitter?" a young clone asked the Alt. "He woke up early from his nap and he won't go back to sleep, but I have a class in ten minutes."

"Is he yours?" the Alt asked, holding her arms out for the fidgeting baby, who seemed to be working himself up for a tantrum.

"Oh, no. I'm not even married yet," Myst said. "The baby's name is Richard, and he belongs to Dorothy, but she and the rest of our staff are helping with the training. Well, except for Baa and Jeeves, but they don't do babysitting. Will you be okay with him?"

"Of course," Meena said, settling the squirming baby in the crook of her arm. Richard immediately fell silent, stared up at the Alt with his blue eyes open wide, and smiled.

"I have to run," the Gem girl said. "We have a nursery back in our regular office but we rented this place for the day to do the training. If he's quiet, you can sit in the back and watch." With that, she hurried off for the lift tube.

"The baby isn't making you uncomfortable?" Methan asked his daughter. "You used to be very sensitive to Humans."

"Is he Human? I didn't even notice. Maybe he's too young to put out the scary vibes."

Methan held his hand out over the baby as if he was checking the temperature of a stove burner. "It's not strong, but I can sense it. You really don't feel it at all?"

Meena shook her head. "Nothing. Oh, look, he's fallen asleep. Shall we go in and find out what the training is all about?"

"The room may be full of adult Humans," he cautioned her.

"There can't be more than there are in the Grenouthian broadcast studio when I go to see Methanon on *Let's Make Friends*. Maybe I'm just getting used to Humans."

"I didn't think that was possible," her father muttered to himself. "Don't be surprised if you see Affie inside. When she's not working as a contract queen for us she's a designer for SBJ Fashions."

"You mean we're going to a fashion show?" Meena strode forward without any further hesitation, and the father and daughter took seats in the back of the hall so they could leave in a hurry if the baby woke up cranky.

"You've all seen what our nanofabric can do, so now we'll discuss the business model," Dorothy was saying. She looked up as the Alts came in and breathed a sigh of relief when she saw Richard sleeping in Meena's arms. "But first, are there any questions?"

A Horten in the audience stood up and said, "I have a question for your technical manager. Is it true that the nanofabric is locked?"

Lancelot moved up next to Dorothy to reply. "I haven't heard that term used in relation to nanotechnology, but I'll guess you're talking about access to the software. Our nanofabric is programmed so that it only forms dresses from the SBJ Fashions catalog."

"But that constitutes a restraint of trade!"

"We aren't selling the nanofabric outright, we're providing a catalog fitting kit under license," Dorothy explained. "I'm sure you all checked the tunnel network registry for available franchises before signing up for our seminar. SBJ's buy-in fee is lower than any other fashion franchise by an order of magnitude."

"Low pricing is usually a red flag," a Frunge spoke up.

"It's because we don't require you to purchase hundreds of outfits to stock a shop. There's also no forced ad buy to promote our brand because we believe in word-of-mouth. With our patented system for custom fitting any dress from our catalog, your customers aren't just seeing a hologram of themselves like in a Vergallian fitting room. They get to put on the nanofabric version of the real thing. The software created by our Gem expert ensures that the bespoke dress you receive within thirty days will fit perfectly."

"Thirty days!" the excitable Horten said in dismay. "Who would wait that long for a dress?"

"Thirty days is the outside figure we're using for shipping to the least trafficked worlds of the tunnel network," Dorothy explained. "In fact, one of you pointed out to me before we began that Vergallian law has a prohibition against franchises receiving exclusive territories, implying that our questionnaire could be construed as a violation. We only ask where you plan to operate to weed out locations where we can't keep our thirty-day promise."

"Who are you using for deliveries?" a woman asked.

Dorothy looked at Shaina, who rose from her front-row seat and turned to the audience. "SBJ Fashions is vendor-agnostic on deliveries, so in most cases, the fastest and least expensive option in your area will be a service you're already using. We are exploring relationships with direct connection courier services that can speed up deliveries by eliminating a tunnel network hub."

"But what if we want to open a walk-in boutique with inventory?" a successful-looking Vergallian asked. "I accept that your nanofabric is the most exciting technological innovation to hit this industry in my lifetime, and it's a perfect match for a door-to-door saleswoman or a pop-up mall kiosk offering a custom fit by mail order. But I have a few hundred years of experience in the boutique sector, and most customers like to look through the racks and hold dresses up next to each other. The whole shopping experience isn't the same without a store."

"Our primary distribution to this point has been through existing boutiques on tunnel network stations and we have legal agreements not to go into competition with them," Shaina said. "If you're interested in opening a shop on a planet or an orbital, that's another matter."

"I am, but as your designer pointed out just a few minutes ago, a franchise from one of the leading fashion houses costs as much as a small spaceship, and that's before you figure in the required ad spend. I wonder if you've looked at a hybrid model to support small boutiques with some ready-to-wear stock plus nanofabric fittings for the more particular customers."

"If you give me your information after the seminar, I'd like to invite you to our offices for a brainstorming session," Shaina said. "It sounds feasible, but we haven't explored the option."

"Any more questions before I continue?" Dorothy asked.

"How long will it take us to learn how to do the custom fittings?" a Frunge asked. "While I was watching the three of you do it, I couldn't help recalling the time I bought a very expensive knife after a demonstration by a chef, only to find out at home that my skills were lacking."

Most of the attendees tittered and nodded their heads at this admission, having had similar experiences themselves. Dorothy only hesitated a moment before saying, "Okay, let's do this. Come on up and you can do a fitting for one of us."

"Right now?" the Frunge asked in surprise, and her hair vines tightened around their low-rise trellis. "But what if I guess wrong and take a measurement in too far? Could I hurt you, or damage the nanofabric?"

"I'm glad you have your priorities straight," the EarthCent ambassador's daughter said with a laugh. "No, there are built-in safeties to prevent that, and Lance can explain them while I slip into something more comfortable."

The Frunge woman went up to the front of the room and accepted the hand-held controller from Lancelot while Dorothy retreated into the curtained-off changing booth. While the young Gem engineer began explaining the functionality of the controller, Dorothy swapped the dress she was wearing for nanofabric, giving thanks that the last volunteer model had been approximately her size.

"So we start with the standard sizes for our species, and then make the adjustments by changing the measurement numbers at the critical dimensions?" the Frunge asked Lancelot.

"That's correct," he said. "There's also the option to run a gradient between any two measurement points to distribute the alteration evenly, and I'm working on advanced algorithms for curve fitting on a species-specific basis. Here, let me switch it to Frunge."

"But it's all number-based. Wouldn't it be better to give us sliders, like on an audio mixing panel?"

"That would be easy," Lancelot said. "Nobody has asked before."

"That's because you're used to me or Flazint throwing numbers at you during the demonstrations," Dorothy said as she rejoined them. "Now that she's mentioned it, a slider would be a good idea."

"Why not a holo controller?" the Horten who had asked a question earlier called out. "Then we could operate the nanofabric with gesture controls."

"I suppose it's possible, but it would add to the cost," Lancelot said.

"Let's get through the rest of the presentation, and then we'd be happy to take all of your ideas for improvements, especially if you sign up as franchisees," Dorothy said. She glanced at the hand-printed nametag either she or one of the Hadad sisters had made for the Frunge during registration. "All right, Jazzet. Try to take my hips out a half size."

The Frunge woman concentrated on the controller with its lines of measurements, found the correct blank, and tapped in a number. The dress moved visibly as it hugged Dorothy's hips so tightly that she had difficulty moving.

"Oh, no," Jazzet said, looking from the dress to the controller. "I thought I was adding the increment but it took it as the whole value."

"I'm glad you did," Dorothy said. "If it wasn't for all of the safety features, I would have come squirting out of this dress like toothpaste from a tube. But you can see that it only shrank to a tight fit, no harm done."

The Frunge restored the original number, added a half, and then judging by eye, tweaked the critical measurements on each line. Dorothy did a twirl and an abortive ballet leap, which drew an appreciative laugh from the audience.

"That was easy, but sliders would still be better," Jazzet said, handing the controller back to Lancelot.

"I'll have them done by the next time you see it," the Gem promised. "There's actually a built-in graphical interface that I didn't enable because I didn't think any-body would use it."

As Dorothy launched into a detailed breakdown of the projected costs and profits involved in a franchise, Meena turned to her father and said, "I wish I could be that natural in front of an audience. Are all Human women so confident?"

"You can tell she's been doing presentations for years, and she's also the EarthCent ambassador's daughter, so I doubt she's typical," Methan replied.

"Isn't that sort of what you just said about Aisha?" Meena asked. "What if we've been judging Humans unfairly and they're all better than we expect them to be?"

The baby stirred in her arms, gave a happy peeping sound, and went back to sleep again.

Fifteen

Kelly escorted the disappointed Drazen woman to the door of Bork's office and told her, "The texture was really very nice, and you can't take my reaction as a proxy for all of humanity."

"Nobody has ever spit one of my creations out in a napkin before."

"It may have been prudent to test the flavors as you worked at developing the biscuit rather than going directly into production."

The Drazen shook her head. "Everybody told me that if I was going to market to Humans, the most important thing to get right was the packaging."

"The wrapper is a work of art," Kelly said and suppressed the urge to suggest that it probably would have tasted better than the biscuit. "I would encourage you to keep working at it, but bring in some tasters from the target species."

The Drazen woman turned around again in the doorway and asked, "Are you available?"

"Uh, I wish I could, but due to my involvement with the All Species Cookbook, it wouldn't be ethical."

The aspiring commercial baker moved slowly off through the embassy lobby, her body language obvious to all who saw her. A Drazen male carrying a large covered

180

tray in both hands approached Kelly before she could duck back into the office.

"Ambassador McAllister?"

"Yes, but you should think of me as Ambassador Bork because I'm here to do his job this week."

"Of course," the Drazen said, and employed his tentacle to hold up one side of the tray so he could offer Kelly a handshake. "Jilk. In that case, you and I go way back."

"We do? I mean, please come in," the EarthCent ambassador said, leading Jilk into the office.

The Drazen put the tray down on the desk and then did a quick circuit of the walls, examining all of the edged weapons Bork had on display. "Is this axe new?" he asked, taking down a massive double-headed weapon and giving it an experimental swing like a middle-aged man on Earth might do with a baseball bat. "Nice balance."

"I believe it's been on Bork's wall as long as I've known him, though I don't have a great eye for axes."

"All right, enough small talk," Jilk said. He replaced the axe and sat down across from Kelly. "I'm here about the Drazen edition of the All Species Cookbook."

Kelly kept a smile on her face, but inside she was screaming with frustration. "Why don't you come to the EarthCent embassy next week and we can discuss whatever it is? I don't want to be rude, but I'm here to do Drazen business."

"And why do you think I'm here? To do Horten business?" Jilk laughed at his own joke, and then he leaned forward in earnest. "I'm not a diplomat, and I can't claim to know how the other embassies do things, but assisting local businessmen with interspecies trade has always been one of Ambassador Bork's priorities. He helped get our friend set up on Earth with Drazen Foods, and these days

181

Glunk is one of the rising stars on the self-made entrepreneurs list. Have you met him?"

"Glunk? Yes, he's always been very supportive of EarthCent and our goals. You know him?"

"We're like this," the Drazen said, crossing both thumbs on the same hand to show how close they were. "I told him about this business idea the last time we met, and he suggested bringing an example to make it easier to explain."

"Oh, is that what you brought?" Kelly asked, looking at the tray. "I was afraid it was some new food product you wanted me to taste."

"Not my line of work." Jilk carefully removed the cover from the tray and set it aside, causing Kelly to gape at the three-dimensional paper pop-up of a robot performing some kind of prospecting operation on the surface of a rocky planet. "I'm a paper engineer and movable book designer. This is my sampler."

"It's unbelievable," Kelly said. "How can a pop-up book have movable elements? Is that a hand drill the robot is operating?"

"Bit of an inside trick there," the Drazen admitted. "Anything with a spiral like a drill bit gives the impression of more motion than is actually going on. Turn the page."

"There's no way this is going to fold down. I'm afraid I'll ruin it if I try."

"My books are guaranteed for ten thousand folding operations between failures. It's special paper."

Kelly felt for the edge of the page and was surprised to find that although rigid, it didn't feel any thicker than a normal book page. She slowly lifted, and the robot with his drill began to flatten as tabs slid through hidden slits she hadn't noticed. When the new page was perpendicular to the book, she finally pried her eyes off the collapsing scene to look at the unfolding vista coming up, and let out a little gasp of astonishment.

"They're harvesting grapes," she said, closing the page on the mining robot to fully expand the vineyard scene. "Oh, she's using her tentacle to reach for that high bunch. I've never seen anything like this."

"I know that EarthCent only took over the All Species Cookbook a couple of years ago, but even if you keep it for the next hundred millennia, the time to strike is while the axe is sharp," Jilk said. "Publishing is a funny game, and even for a long-lived product like a cookbook, it's important to keep the momentum going. If you'll allow me, I would suggest a two-pronged approach. For the high-end market and collectors, a movable version of the cookbook with hundreds of three-dimensional illustrations of cooking techniques and completed dishes. For the—"

"What would something like that cost?" Kelly interrupted.

"Do you mean the engineering, the printing cost, or the retail price?"

"I guess all three."

"My family has long since perfected the technique of creating movable art from two-dimensional illustrations," the Drazen said. "I took the liberty of working up an estimate for the design cost based on the current edition of the cookbook." He pulled a small tab off his belt, swiped it to life, tapped a few times, and then extended it to the EarthCent ambassador.

"How many zeros is that?" she asked after getting over her initial reaction.

"Seven," he told her. "But amortize that over a billion collector's edition cookbooks and it amounts to less than a cred per copy. Keep in mind that unlike text, the artwork is the same for all of the species."

"But that doesn't include the production cost!"

"No," he admitted, taking back the tab and tapping a few more times. "Here. I'll show it to you on a per-cookbook basis."

"Oh, that doesn't look so bad," Kelly said, though she couldn't help wondering how many buyers would be willing to pay over a hundred creds for a collector's edition of the cookbook. "What was the other prong you were going to tell me about?"

"Instead of engineering movable paper art from your existing illustrations, we can work with your marketing partners who will subsidize the inclusion of a few three-dimensional ads for the standard cookbook. As I mentioned earlier, I've talked with Glunk at Drazen Foods about this, and it would provide you with a whole new revenue stream."

"You're talking about pop-up ads?" Kelly grimaced. "They have a strong negative connotation on Earth."

"We're not on Earth, and readers can always skip a page if they don't want to see them," Jilk said, taking back his tab again. "I've worked up some numbers on the pop-up ads as well, and I'm so confident in the math that I can offer to finance the engineering for the collector's edition in return for a share of pop-up advertising space in future print runs of the standard cookbook."

"I don't know. It would be a big departure from our current business model, which is already going far better than I ever expected."

"So why don't we just twine tentacles on the collector's edition for now and you can think about the pop-up ads?"

"I can't make any decisions on behalf of EarthCent while I'm here representing Drazen interests," Kelly said decisively. "Thank you for coming, and I hope to see you at my own embassy next week, but I've already used too much of Bork's time on this."

Jilk was a good enough salesman to know when he had pushed as far as he could, so he replaced the cover on the tray and presented Kelly with a plastic chit. "That's got my direct ping address, and Ambassador Bork will always know where to get a hold of me." He rose and offered Kelly another handshake before picking up his tray. "Thank you for seeing me, Ambassador. I can show myself out."

Before the door had closed behind him, the hidden speaker on Bork's desk informed Kelly that her next appointment had arrived. She expected it to be another pitch for the All Species Cookbook and was pleasantly surprised when the head of Drazen Intelligence walked into the office.

"Herl," Kelly greeted him. "I haven't seen you in years. If you're on the station for a while I'll mention it to Joe and see if he can put together a poker game."

"I came specifically to deliver a briefing to the ambassador as per this embassy's request. You're exchanging with Bork?"

"Today is the last day," the EarthCent ambassador replied.

"Then I got here just in time," the spy chief said, and gave Kelly an exaggerated wink. "It will save some explaining if you tell me how much you know about the Alts."

"Do you mean their plans to purchase Earth Two? I understand that they have financing in place and they're

185

currently in negotiations with the Dollnicks, or rather, they've retained a Vergallian law firm to negotiate for them."

"But you know nothing about their long-term plans for populating the world?"

"No. I'm sure you're aware that EarthCent Intelligence made a strategic decision not to spy on the Alts for fear that it would deepen the paranoia they already feel towards humanity."

"A decision I didn't agree with," Herl told her. "Given that the Alts rarely leave their planet and they don't welcome Human guests, EarthCent has hardly expanded its knowledge of humanity's closest relatives since they first appeared on the galactic stage."

"That's true, but their children cry if we come too close, at least until they get used to us," Kelly said. "We don't even know if they grow more comfortable with time or if they just get better at hiding their visceral fear reaction."

"And the sad thing is that they aren't sure themselves because Humans and Alts have been doing such a good job avoiding each other. I understand that Methan is again serving as the chief representative of the Alts, though his people will no doubt hold the usual consultations once their legal team reaches a tentative agreement with the Container Prince."

"Yes, exactly. His family is living on the Vergallian deck, and Methan's youngest child has joined the cast of *Let's Make Friends*."

"And the older girl is working for InstaSitter," Herl informed her, chuckling at the ambassador's reaction. "No, we don't spy on InstaSitter, but I ran into Tinka and she mentioned it. Now let me fill you in on what our field agents have learned visiting Alt."

"You've sent undercover agents to their homeworld?" Kelly asked.

"Drazens couldn't pass as Alts without massive surgical modifications, which are hardly called for given that we've assigned the Alts the lowest threat assessment on our scale. In point of fact, we consider Humans more of a danger than Alts."

"But we're allies!"

"And they're congenitally nice. Our agents on the Alt homeworld gather information by identifying themselves and asking questions."

"You mean the Alts are willing to cooperate with alien spies?"

"They see it as a matter of being good hosts," Herl told her. "It turns out that they are comfortable talking about every subject under that yellow sun other than Humans, but with the right incentives, they'll even answer those questions."

"You tortured them for information?" Kelly asked in disbelief.

"Somebody has been watching too many dramas," the spy chief said. "I mean, somebody in addition to Bork."

"So you paid them."

"No. Their Vergallian contract queens use money for some of their business ventures, but the Alts still run the economy of their homeworld on the honor system."

"Honey traps?" Kelly guessed. "False flag operations?"

"The Alts respond to good manners, or perhaps I should say they incentivize our agents to behave well by repaying politeness with more detailed information," Herl explained. "We quickly learned that our agents could get whatever they wanted by being as nice as the Alts, but

187

unfortunately, that renders them useless for field work anywhere else in the galaxy."

"Can't you just give your agents a refresher course when they leave Alt?"

"It hasn't worked. For what it's worth, the other species with spies on Alt have run into the same problem, and there's some discussion of—I'm getting too far off-topic. The point is that the Alts left Earth with a rich oral history about the time they shared with Humans, and they developed a written language to preserve those stories soon after being transplanted to their new home. I'm afraid those histories paint a dark picture of your people."

"But that was tens of thousands of years ago," Kelly protested. "Surely they must understand that we've changed as much as they have."

"So that's the problem in a nutshell," Herl said. "The good manners, the community-based decision making, the respect for nature, the economic honor system? Apparently the Alts have been that way since before they left Earth. They haven't changed, they were always this nice."

"Oh." The EarthCent ambassador thought about that for a long moment, and then said, "We must have really taken advantage."

"I'm afraid so, and that's why when the Stryx rescued the Alts, their genome was already more Human than Neanderthal, not that there was ever a tremendous difference between the two from what M793qK tells me."

"You've been on Flower recently? Did you stop and see my son?"

"Yes," Herl replied. He rose and began casually inspecting Bork's weapons collection as he talked. "Samuel and Vivian were busy working with Flower and her team to put together a school for government associated with the

Open University. If it wasn't for the high percentage of Humans on board, I would have suggested that they try to bring in some Alt exchange students as a confidence-building measure."

"I agree to the principle, but—what kind of axe is that?" Kelly interrupted herself as the Drazen spy master took down a display and twirled it on the wrist strap.

"It's a broad-headed pickaxe. We use them for mining operations in soft stone. And that reminds me of why I'm here."

"You didn't arrange all this with Bork to fill me in about the Alts?"

"Such a calculated move would be an abuse of the exchange ambassador program," Herl said, returning the pickaxe to its place. "I came to discuss the economic possibilities of Earth Two in order to advance Drazen interests. As you happen to be exchanging with Bork, I thought it important to bring you up to speed. The real issue is that if the Alts take total possession of Earth Two, they will no doubt leave all of the business arrangements to whichever Vergallian princess they retain as a contract queen for the new colony."

Kelly took her notebook out of her purse and began to scribble frantically. "Just give me a minute, Herl," she said without looking up. "If I don't start writing this down it's all going to run together. The truth is I'm having trouble moving on from Jilk's presentation."

"Our impresario of moving books," the Drazen spymaster said sympathetically as he continued browsing Bork's collection. "His family's museum on our homeworld is one of the most popular destinations for school outings, but you better leave your programmable cred at home if you ever visit because the gift shop is murder."

"Alts themselves haven't studied their reactions to us because we systematically avoid each other," Kelly muttered as she completed her notes and underlined the last sentence. "So you're suggesting that Glunk would be interested in opening a new Drazen Foods business on Earth Two, and the other aliens with operations on Earth will be interested as well?"

"I can't speak for all of the other species, but if Earth Two falls entirely under the management of contract queens, there's a strong chance all of the new business opportunities will go to the Vergallians."

"But it's just one little planet among the thousands of occupied worlds on the tunnel network," the EarthCent ambassador pointed out. "Is getting your tentacle in the door really that important?"

"The business of the tunnel network is business," Herl reminded her, "In many ways, Earth Two has greater potential than Earth. Have you ever visited a strip-mining operation?"

"I think that's just the sort of thing humanity is hoping to avoid if we get a second chance."

"It's identical in many ways to a terraforming job. We Drazens have never made terraforming a major sector of our economy, but when we do take on a job, we pay close attention to sequencing. If you're going to scoop up billions of tons of iron ore, the time to do it is before you plant a forest or a prairie, not afterward. There are dozens of simple tricks like that which can help finance the ongoing activity needed to turn a barren planet into a home."

"But Earth Two isn't barren," Kelly pointed out. "The reports I've seen said it's an unspoiled paradise."

"That's just the one small continent, and I'm not sure unspoiled is the adjective I would use to describe an artificially created ecosystem that hasn't been in place long enough to find a balance," Herl said as he took down another bladed implement. "Besides, we aren't just about mining. He lowered the tool to the deck and worked the head as if he were loosening the dirt around plant stalks.

"It's a Drazen hoe?" Kelly guessed.

"A pole arm that's been converted for agricultural use," Herl told her. "You can see that the tip is a spear point that's been flattened. The axe blade was bent sideways to create a hoe."

"Oh. What's the hook for?"

"Pulling knights off their mounts, but I suspect it came in handy for shaking the branches of nut trees. I'd be willing to bet that Bork used this in one of those historical reenactments he participated in."

Kelly pursed her lips and thought while Herl continued to examine various other tools or weapons. "You're saying that it's in the interests of the Drazens and the other tunnel network species, with the exception of the Vergallians, that the Alts don't take sole possession of Earth Two."

"Given what I know about the internal politics of the Empire of a Hundred Worlds, I suspect that the Council of Queens isn't as crazy about the idea as their offer to finance the down-payment would suggest."

"Then why on earth would they put up so much money?"

"The Alts turning down full tunnel network membership in favor of management by contract queens was a huge political coup for the Vergallians, not to mention a boost for their egos," Herl said. "They're committed to making the relationship work, but as we discovered with

191

our field agents, too much contact with the Alts carries the risk of going native."

"Do you think Affie is in danger?" Kelly asked.

"The contract queens we've observed so far seem to be immune to spending so much time in close contact with the Alts, something we attribute to royal empathy training."

"How can being more empathetic protect you from people who are too nice?"

"Royal empathy training is about compartmentalization and always putting public policy before the individual," the Drazen spymaster told her. "Empathy is a natural talent among all of the tunnel network species—it's turning it off without becoming a sociopath that takes careful training."

Sixteen

"Good morning, Ambassador Czeros," Donna said to the back of the alien who was rummaging through the refrigerator in the EarthCent embassy's kitchen. "You're here bright and early."

"Bright and early in the late afternoon on my clock," the Frunge replied. "What kind of Humans don't have an open bottle of wine in the refrigerator? No, don't answer that," he continued, straightening up and turning around. "It was a rhetorical question."

"There's wine in the rack on the other side of the fridge."

"But I'm here as the EarthCent ambassador and Kelly would never open a bottle first thing in the morning." Czeros yawned and stretched, his limbs making creaking sounds a bit like a tree swaying in the winter wind. "So what am I going to do with myself all week while I'm waiting to be the special guest on your grandson's cooking show?"

"Kelly left a whole list of..." Donna trailed off when she saw the expression on the ambassador's face.

"You'll find that I'm fond of rhetorical questions," Czeros told her. "As it happens, I have a busy week planned. When will Daniel and Aabina be in?"

"I'm a little surprised that Aabina isn't here already, but Daniel usually stops out for coffee on Monday mornings because he needs that extra boost to start the week. I'm sure he'll be arriving any minute."

The Frunge ambassador took a moment to inspect the bottles in the wine rack before choosing one to pull all of the way out. "A fine lunch vintage. I'll just set this aside."

"Would you like me to make up a cheese platter?" Donna asked.

"That depends whether or not it falls within your normal scope of duties. I wouldn't want it to be said that I took advantage of the staff during my exchange."

"We aren't that formal here, Ambassador."

"Then I'll just have a seat in the conference room and prepare for the Monday morning meeting." Czeros hesitated in the doorway, and then turned back to ask, "When is lunch, anyway?"

Donna shooed him out of the kitchen just as Daniel arrived. The associate ambassador greeted the Frunge enthusiastically. "I've been waiting for your exchange week, Ambassador Czeros," Daniel said. "There are some issues related to mines on Kazard Five that I'm hoping to get straightened out. The Frunge owners are leasing them to a group of contract workers who want to start a sovereign human community there."

"If we have time," Czeros said noncommittally, and rather than taking a seat after shaking the associate ambassador's hand, he moved around to the other side of the table. "Is this the famous door into another reality?"

"It's not that big a deal," Daniel told him, leaving his take-out cup of coffee on the table and joining the ambassador. "Just a little problem with the probability." He waved open the door and entered the new office space, where he took the Thark ambassador's box of testing dice from his pocket. "I'll throw a few — Ambassador?"

"I can see just fine from out here," Czeros said from the conference room. "The furniture looks very comfortable."

"You're afraid to come in?"

"The better part of valor is discretion. Ambassador Bork told me he got that line from a Human play."

After six straight passes throwing the same outcome with both dice, Daniel gave up and returned to the conference room. "Still abnormal," he said. "On the one hand, I still can't help wondering if it's all an elaborate Thark prank. On the other hand, Aabina claims the new office has cold spots that can't be explained away. The other ambassadors who have exchanged with Kelly all thought there was something supernatural going on."

"I believe that the Verlock ambassador is next on the exchange schedule," the Frunge said, shooting Donna a look of gratitude as she placed a platter of cheese and the now-uncorked bottle of wine he had chosen on the table. "When I stuck my head through the door I felt something in the roots of my hair vines that I doubt can be explained by a technical glitch. Ask Srythlan to bring a Verlock mage with him. There aren't many of them so it pays to plan in advance."

"Don't tell me that you believe in that magic stuff too," Daniel said.

"If I have time while I'm here, I'll have to ask EarthCent Intelligence for a summary of humanity's experience with unexplained phenomena to find out why you're so—Good morning, Princess Affie. What are you doing here?"

"I'll be your special assistant for the week, Ambassador. Aabina and I originally intended to start the exchange next week, but Ambassador McAllister wanted to get it over with as soon as possible."

"But a contract queen for a special assistant is hardly an even exchange," Czeros pointed out. "Whose idea was it?"

"I believe Ambassador Aleeytis was the first to bring up the idea of a cultural exchange to help build confidence between the Alts and the Humans. The other ambassadors who have been here on exchange slowly pushed the idea forward. There was a lot of resistance from the Alt side, so Aabina and I thought we could serve as an ice breaker."

"So cultural exchange means that we send the Alts our Vergallian princess and they send us their Vergallian princess," Daniel said. "Why does that bring to mind an old joke about violinists?"

"I'm just surprised that Aabina didn't tell me you moved it up a week," Donna said, returning to the conference room carrying a tray with a wine goblet for Czeros and a tea service. "I made this mint tea for her without thinking," she continued. "Would you like something different, Affie?"

"Tea is fine, thank you," the Vergallian said. "Aabina told me about the problem you're having with the new offices for CoSHC. Any change?"

"I'm going to ask Ambassador Srythlan to bring a mage to check it out," Daniel told her. "He'll be here the week after next, but if that doesn't square things, I'm just going to move in. We've been paying rent the last two months and not getting any use out of the space."

"That's not exactly true," Donna said, returning from the kitchenette a third time with her own bit of Danish and a cup of fresh-brewed coffee. "If not for Crute, we'd still be renovating the space. It only seems like we're losing time because his contractor finished everything so quickly."

"I knew he must have had a good reason for going first," Czeros said. "Crute called in quite a few favors when we were setting the exchange order." The Frunge took a sip of the wine and pulled the cheese platter closer. Then he looked over at Daniel. "So where do we stand on Earth Two?"

"I'm holding weekly Stryxnet conference calls with the leaders of CoSHC, and I can report that the sovereign human communities are of two minds on the subject," Daniel said. "No, that oversimplifies the matter because they are really of half-dozen minds, if not more. But I'm loosely dividing them between those who are enthusiastic about the potential of having a new Earth to settle and those who see it as a distraction from making a home where they are."

Czeros swallowed, reached for another slice of cheese, and asked, "Any graphics?"

"Of course." Daniel stood up, took his tab from a Drazen-style belt pouch, and swept it to life. A moment later the conference room display synched up. "I like using Venn diagrams to identify what CoSHC members have in common since they're such diverse groups that it can be hard to keep track. The size of each circle indicates the population, and I used the colors to code which species are hosting each community."

"If I understand the labeling, the relative sizes of those circles indicate that less than two percent of expatriate Humans are living on Vergallian worlds," Affie said. "I would have guessed closer to thirty percent."

"The data is strictly for CoSHC members. You're correct that more Earth expatriates are living on Vergallian worlds than those of any other species, unless the Dollnicks have edged you out again, but those are all contract workers. The only sovereign human communities in Vergallian space are tech-ban colonies on three recently opened

197

worlds, and a large population on the Fleet world of Aarden that recently received a tunnel connection thanks to our presence."

"You should hire out," Czeros said.

"Excuse me?" Daniel turned away from his Venn diagram to look at the Frunge ambassador, who was refilling his wine goblet. "There are nearly five times as many humans employed as contract workers by other species as there are living in sovereign communities. We're hoping to move towards an equal balance in the coming decades."

"It's hiring out your CoSHC communities I'm talking about. Haven't you ever considered it as a business model?"

"Would the Stryx play along?" Affie asked. "I don't recall reading about anybody trying that before."

"I don't understand what you mean unless you're suggesting—" Daniel stopped mid-sentence, and a chill ran down his spine that felt not unlike the ones he'd been receiving in the new office space.

"Would somebody mind telling me what the three of you are on about?" Donna asked plaintively. "I know I'm getting old, but I'd like to think that my mind still functions."

"Czeros is suggesting that we could hire ourselves out to non-tunnel network species to get the Stryx to put in a tunnel connection," Daniel explained, wondering why none of them had ever thought of it before. "The Stryx treat our sovereign human communities on alien open worlds as if they were independent planets. Aarden is the Vergallian Fleet world where the Traders Guild held Rendezvous a couple of years ago, and it got a tunnel network connection thanks to the population and economic activity of its sovereign human community."

Donna's lips expanded in a perfect 'O' shape. "That could be incredibly lucrative if the Stryx went along. I'll have to ping Blythe as soon as the meeting is over."

"I try to come up with a good idea at least once per exchange," Czeros said modestly. "And speaking of your daughter, please ask for her to arrange an EarthCent Intelligence briefing for me while I'm here."

"Of course. All of the exchange ambassadors have requested one," Donna said.

"But the same logic would hold true for Earth Two," Affie said excitedly. "One of the major drawbacks for the Alts in purchasing a second world is that they aren't tunnel network members, so travel there would be limited to jump drives. While they did develop their own interstellar technology, it's barely a decade old. They would still have to get from Alt to the nearest tunnel network connection, but that would be far more efficient than hiring dedicated transport for end-to-end travel."

"So how were they planning on moving any of their population or their possessions to Earth Two if they close the deal?" Daniel asked.

"They were going to leave that up to the contract queens, which ultimately means they would have ended up renting cargo capacity from Vergallians. But it's not like Alt is overpopulated, and expanding to another world without a tunnel network connection just for the sake of —" Affie broke off suddenly.

"Sake of what?" Daniel prodded her.

"I couldn't say."

"Come on, you're here on a cultural exchange from the Alts. You're supposed to be open and honest so we can build confidence and trust in one another."

Affie looked down at her hands while weighing her options. "There's a distinct possibility that the primary reason the Alts are interested in buying Earth Two is to save it from Humans. I know that was the main value proposition in the Container Prince's sales pitch."

"That two-timing Dollnick," Daniel exploded. "All along we've been assuming that he tricked EarthCent's president into sending people to take a look because the Alts would see us as competition and raise their bid. Now it turns out he was using our people as a veiled threat to the environment."

"Buy this planet or we'll let your old persecutors trash it," Donna concurred. "I can see how that would be a highly effective strategy with the Alts."

"My mother was fond of saying that every problem presents an opportunity in disguise," the Frunge ambassador said. "If the Alts are primarily interested in Earth Two because of their fear that Humans will turn it into another Earth, I see an opportunity to lower the price for whoever takes the prize. You just have to convince the Alts that you've changed."

"Or that you're willing to accept civilized rules of conduct," Affie said. "The Alts must be the most law-abiding sentients in the galaxy, and because of that, they manage to get by with fewer laws than any other species I've heard of. I can't speak for them, of course, but I think if you were able to address their concerns by establishing a behavioral code and an enforcement mechanism, they would be open to negotiations."

"Why can't you speak for them?" Daniel asked. "I thought that's what they pay you for."

"This week they're employing Aabina and you're employing me," the Vergallian reminded him. "And I have to add that I'm shocked she's willing to work here for the money EarthCent pays."

"I imagine the educational experience is unmatched," Czeros said, pouring himself a third glass of wine. "Now that we have a plan, I'd like to see the rest of your Venn diagrams, Daniel. I'm curious whether the blue and yellow make green when they overlap."

"But you've just handed us the most exciting idea I've heard in twenty years," the associate ambassador protested. "Imagine what kind of concessions the Sharf would be willing to give a sovereign human community if it came with the promise of a tunnel connection. Or the Huktra. Or even the Farlings!"

"Or the Alts on Earth Two," Affie reminded him. "I understand your excitement, but I've visited Sharf, Huktra, and Farling worlds as part of my grandmother's retinue during her retirement tour. Humans would be able to breathe the air on most of them, but I'd be surprised if there was an available world better suited to your people in this galaxy than Earth Two."

"She's right, Daniel," Donna said. "Czeros has put a lot on our table, but we don't have to digest it all at once. I know that both of my daughters were excited about the possibility of humanity finding a second home of its own. I don't see a problem in sharing Earth Two with the Alts, even if we have to accept some rules for good behavior."

"I know they aren't enthusiastic about the idea of terraforming the unfinished continents," Affie said. "The Alts are happy to do manual labor, but there's a lot of heavy earthmoving and subterranean plumbing in store for whoever takes on the job."

"Our people love that kind of stuff," Daniel said. "Okay, where was I with the graphics?"

201

"The relative deficit of Vergallians," Affie reminded him.

"Right. This probably wasn't the best diagram to choose." Daniel swiped at his tab and a new Venn diagram appeared. "Most of our communities on open worlds are, to some extent, single purpose," he continued. He tapped different circles on the small screen, which caused them to zoom to the forefront of the conference room display. "The big five are agriculture, manufacturing, mining, academic, and theatrical."

"You've set up communities for theatre?" Czeros asked in amusement.

"The Grenouthians have allowed our people to establish sovereign communities on one of their production orbitals and on the worlds with the Human theme parks that tie in to their documentaries," Daniel explained. "It's hard to believe, but the theme parks on Earth don't have the capacity to handle all of the puerile interest the advanced species have in our history. As long as you brought it up, the theatrical communities showed no interest in Earth Two since there's no production industry there."

"Makes sense," the Frunge ambassador said. "Could you swap the colors you chose for the theatrical and mining communities?"

"Uh, all right," Daniel performed the task with a few swipes and taps. "Now, you won't be surprised to hear that the main interest in Earth Two comes from our mining and agricultural communities—that's why you wanted me to swap colors."

"The overlap does make a lovely green," Donna said.

"But our manufacturing communities are understandably put off by the notion of moving to a world with no modern infrastructure in place. Bob, who represents the floater factory city on a Dollnick open world, suggested that we ask them again in a couple of centuries after we've established a power grid and a supply chain."

Czeros nodded. "When colonizing worlds the old fashioned way, via colony ships, getting industry up and running takes second place only to agriculture. But if Humans gain access to Earth Two, your numbers will ramp up so rapidly that the Stryx will be connecting a tunnel almost immediately. As soon as that happens, importing manufactured goods will be more cost-efficient than making them locally for a long time to come."

"Maybe the Alts would be more comfortable with our being on Earth Two if we agreed for it to be a tech-ban world," Donna suggested. "I don't want to throw a wrench in the works for the Vergallian open worlds that recently started accepting us, especially since one of them belongs to Aabina's family, but she's mentioned that the emigration demand from Earth-based agricultural communities that have adopted a simpler way of life is quite high."

"I'm not familiar with the movement myself, other than a few things I've heard from the ambassador's family," Affie said. "Do any of these farming communities forswear cursing, violence, and intemperance?"

The Frunge ambassador, who had been about to pour himself a fourth glass of wine, instead pretended to be examining the label, and then set the bottle down again.

"I'm sure some of the religious communities would fit the bill, and probably followers of the Old Way as well," Daniel said. "I would suggest getting in touch with Lisbeth Townes, I'll give you her contact information. Her group hasn't left Earth yet, but for people who claim to avoid technology, they certainly send me a lot of questions over the Stryxnet."

Seventeen

"Today?" Kelly asked the embassy manager with a frown. "It seems unlike Czeros to schedule an event first thing in the morning on the Frunge clock, and my day will be up in less than an hour."

"I assure you that the station botany club is very near and dear to the ambassador's heart," the Frunge woman told her. "He almost swapped his exchange slot with the Verlock Ambassador when he realized he would miss the meeting, but Srythlan had another commitment this week."

"You're sure it had nothing to do with Czeros usurping my guest spot on Stone Soup this Friday when Jonah is devoting a show to wine?"

The embassy manager's hair vines stiffened. "If that's what you want to believe, there's nothing I can do to dissuade you."

"No, I was just joking," Kelly protested, but the Frunge woman was already on her way out the door. "I'll do the botany club thing. It will be an honor."

"Alright, then," the embassy manager said, all smiles as she reversed course. "Your next appointment is with the manager of an asteroid mining operation that's leasing their old habitat to Humans. He wants your opinion on the contract terms."

"I don't know anything about asteroid mining and I've never even visited a habitat," the EarthCent ambassador protested, but her words fell on deaf ears. She was once again struck by the similarities between the embassy manager and Beowulf. Both the Frunge woman and the Cayl hound had auditory organs far superior to Kelly's, yet they shared a gift for not hearing anything that wasn't convenient for them to hear. They were also experts at getting their own way in everything.

"Just wait in your office and I'll send him in as soon as he arrives," the embassy manager instructed her nominal boss. "And you may want to read up on Kazard Five. I've sent our intelligence file to your display desk."

Kelly waited until the embassy manager was gone before muttering to herself, "And I always thought Czeros drank because of his wife." Then she sat down at the display desk and swept her hand through the holographic control area. A representation of a planetary system sprang to life with incredibly dense text next to each planetary body or artificial structure. Kelly reached for the text associated with the nearer habitat, intending to spread her fingers in the standard expanding gesture. When she brought her thumb and forefinger together in preparation for the move, the Frunge controller misinterpreted the gesture and shrank the text out of existence.

"Libby?"

"Yes, Ambassador," the Stryx station librarian replied promptly.

"I was about to start reading a holographic Frunge intelligence report but I accidentally banished all of the text. Can you tell me how to reset it?"

"The embassy manager provided you with a one-time duplicate for security purposes. The only way for you to recover the text is to ask her to send it again."

"Maybe later," Kelly said. "Can you tell me anything about Kazard Five?"

"It's a mature mining world in the Kazard system belonging to the Frunge. Most of the planet's surface has been placed in the conservation category by its owners, but there's still a profitable gold mine operating, with much of the labor being supplied by a community of Humans. The ownership has been engaged in negotiating the operational turnover of the mine for some time, but it's hit a snag on security issues."

"Are you getting this information from Frunge Intelligence?"

"You know I can't supply you with species-confidential information," Libby said. "The situation on Kazard Five has been reported in the Galactic Free Press."

"But I'm officially the Frunge ambassador for the week. Why wouldn't you be able to give me their information?"

"For the same reason I haven't been alerting you to visitors at any of your exchange posts," Libby said. "The other species try to limit their reliance on my services, and I have to honor that intention while you're filling their shoes."

"I knew there was something off about all of these assignments but I just couldn't put my finger on it," Kelly said. She took out her notebook to add this latest information to the list of points she was making for any other EarthCent ambassadors who were offered an exchange in the future. She was just finishing when the office door opened and a sturdily built Frunge wearing an expensive business suit strode in.

"Executive Dzar to see you," the embassy manager announced via the hidden audio system about ten seconds too late for Kelly's taste.

Dzar did an exaggerated double-take when he saw the ambassador, a sure sign that the Frunge had been expecting her all along. "You've changed, my old friend," he said, motioning for Kelly to remain seated. "Please, give your weary knees a rest."

"I'm not *that* old," Kelly replied, though she didn't see the point in rising when the Frunge had already sat. "So you and Ambassador Czeros go back a ways?"

"We courted the same sapling, and fortunately for me, he won," Dzar said with a chuckle. "Our matchmakers and compatibility testing are supposed to save us from unhappy marriages, but when the system fails, it's usually in spectacular fashion."

"I met her a few times when I first came here and I gather she didn't care for aliens."

"Xenophobia isn't that uncommon among Frunge who never spend time around other species in their youth, but that's not what brought me to the embassy." Dzar leaned forward earnestly. "What do you know about Human mercenaries?"

"I'm married to one," Kelly told the executive. "He never talked about it much, but I gather that policing our workers on Frunge habitats and stations was one of his preferred assignments."

"And he was wealthy when you married? Maybe a stash of bullion that fell off a cargo ship?"

Kelly laughed. "He had more money than me, if that's what you mean. But I was in debt for my furniture, so it didn't take much."

"Have you ever met any of his former comrades in arms?"

"When Pyun Woojin, Joe's former commanding officer retired, we convinced him to work for EarthCent. He's currently the titular captain of the Dollnick colony ship we hired to visit sovereign human communities," Kelly said, knowing that the information was all in the public domain. "Mercenary companies were heavy recruiters on Earth in the decades after the Stryx opened the planet because there's always a demand for cannon fodder in the galaxy."

"I'll be blunt with you," Dzar said. "We're in negotiations to hand over a productive gold mine to the Human workers currently completing a twenty-year contract. They've proven themselves to be efficient and trustworthy, but our government won't pay to maintain a Frunge military garrison on the planet when our population falls below one hundred thousand individuals."

"Frunge individuals," Kelly surmised.

"Exactly. We've had a continuous presence on Kazard Five for almost half a million years, but ninety-five percent of the surface is now in a nature conservatorship. Taking any of the land back out for commercial purposes would require our equity partners to pay back taxes that would bankrupt a Dollnick prince."

"So you're worried about security for the gold mine when the Frunge military withdraws and you're thinking of hiring mercenaries."

"Not any mercenaries, Human mercenaries," Dzar said. "But I've been reading through an information dump about Humans provided by a friend," he paused to give Kelly a wink, "and I saw something about EarthCent working through a front business called Eccentric Enterprises to help establish police forces at Flower's stops."

"For several years now," Kelly confirmed. "But those were sovereign human communities on habitats leased from other species. I'm not aware of Eccentric Enterprises supplying retrained mercenaries as a police force to any communities on planets."

"Is there a reason for that?"

"Now that you ask, it's probably because all of the open worlds where we have sovereign human communities are majority populated by a host species which provides the policing."

"And how open do you think your Eccentric Enterprises would be to trying something new?" the Frunge asked.

The EarthCent ambassador thought for a moment. "I don't want to answer for them because I don't really know, and I am supposed to be here acting for Ambassador Czeros, after all. But I can suggest that you speak to Blythe Oxford, since Eccentric Enterprises is her business, at least on—" Kelly caught herself at the last second before saying 'paper' to the Frunge—"in the official documentation."

"Could I count on you for an introduction?"

"I'll talk to her this evening, and if she's willing, I'll invite her to meet with you in my office here tomorrow," Kelly offered. "Will that be satisfactory?"

"Splendid," Dzar said, rising to his feet. "I'm up for the next thirty hours so any time will be fine."

The EarthCent ambassador escorted the mining executive to the office door, and before she could go back in, the embassy manager intercepted her.

"That was the last appointment I could fit into your working hours so you can leave for the Botany Club meeting," the Frunge woman told her. "Early is on time."

"I suppose I may as well get it over with," Kelly agreed. She returned to the office to retrieve her purse and notebook. Then she remembered her promise to talk to Blythe and added a note to the daily to-do list she had trained herself to consult when she arrived home every night.

When Kelly reached the park deck, she navigated the woodsy path with step-by-step instructions from the station librarian. It quickly became apparent that leaving early had saved her from the indignity of showing up late. Approximately a quarter of the club members were Frunge, but there were also attendees from all of the other oxygen-breathing species on Union Station, including a sprinkling of humans, though none who Kelly recognized by name. She just had time to find herself an open spot to stand in the clearing when a Grenouthian wearing a brilliant green sash moved onto a small rise where he set down a large box and began talking.

"Fellow Botany Club members," the bunny boomed out in his native tongue without amplification. "It is my pleasure to introduce to you our guests of honor this evening, Ambassador Czeros, who you all know, and Rinla, representing an independent botany club on Alt. Would the two of you come up here?"

The club members offered polite applause in the style of their species as Rinla separated herself from her family and approached the natural stage. Kelly found herself joining in the applause until she remembered that she was attending in place of the Frunge ambassador. She hurried forward, being careful to keep the Grenouthian between herself and Rinla, and rapidly explained the situation to the large alien.

"He always finds a way to get out of survey days," the Grenouthian grumbled, and then relayed Kelly's news to the group. There was an audible groan, and Kelly thought she saw a few Frunge step back and blend into the greenery so they could sneak away. "As those of you who read the newsletter already know," the bunny continued, "instead of the usual lecture and workshop, today we'll be identifying plant species in the designated areas. The survey data will be used by the Open University botany department to determine if an intervention is required. Accuracy is more important than speed."

"Do we have to form teams?" a Drazen standing near the front asked the Grenouthian.

"We'll work in pairs, and this isn't a school recess, so I'll have none of the usual shilly-shallying about choosing sides," the club president replied. He pointed at a pair of clones standing at the edge of the group. "Starting with our new Gem members, each row counts off one-two, one-two, and those are the pairings. If you don't have a tab that will connect with the Open University input form, take a loaner from the box. We've cordoned off and numbered small sections of typical growth using red ribbon. Pick one section and the catering should be here by the time you input the first ten species you positively identify."

The club members had obviously been through the drill before because it only took them a minute to form all of the teams. Somehow, the club president ended up paired with a snow-white female Grenouthian with the silkiest fur Kelly had ever seen, and she couldn't help wondering how much botany they would get done.

"I guess we're the last two without partners," Kelly said to Rinla apologetically. "Do I make you feel uncomfortable?"

"I'll be fine, Ambassador," the Alt said. "I've been taking Methanon to Let's Make Friends every day so I suppose I'm getting used to Humans. Do you have a tab?"

"I have a paperback I take notes in, but I was never a big fan of devices with screens," Kelly said. "Do you?"

"Methan is the technology whiz in our family," Rinla said. "I prefer a wax tablet myself." She looked out at the dispersing crowd. "I see that my children are all paired with aliens who have tabs."

"They'll probably enjoy this more than a lecture. I know mine would have." Kelly retrieved a student tab from the box the Grenouthian had brought and swiped it to life. The screen opened on a form that was locked to the botany department, and a warning at the top stated that the tab couldn't be used for any other purpose. "I'm afraid I don't know too much about plants, much less all of the species from alien worlds on the ag decks."

"But this section is planted with Earth flora," Rinla said. "We have nearly the identical plants on Alt."

"Are you sure?"

"Our traditional education begins with six years of classes taught outdoors," the Alt explained as she led the way towards the nearest cordoned-off section that hadn't been claimed. "We start with plants and animals and move on to rocks and sky. When the time comes for the children to choose an area for deeper study, they're all well-grounded in the natural sciences."

"I believe some nations on Earth had a movement promoting that method of education a few centuries ago but it never gained wide traction," Kelly said. "Are you sure that's not an alien plant? I've never seen anything like it."

"It's from the yam family," Rinla said, crouching to look at the flowering plant. "Does *Tacca chantrieri* translate into anything for you?"

"A Latin classification," the EarthCent ambassador said, tapping it into the tab. The screen immediately changed into a viewfinder, so Kelly framed the plant and touched the shutter release icon, resulting in an image capture which she showed to her companion.

"A fine tool for cataloging. And this one is a *Musa acuminta*," Rinla said. "You can see a bunch of bananas beginning to form."

"So these are all tropical plants?"

"Yes, they appear to be, though I wouldn't necessarily expect to find them growing in such close proximity to each other in nature."

"That one has to be alien," Kelly asserted after inputting an image of the wild banana. "It reminds me of an open mouth."

The Alt laughed merrily. "*Anigozanthos rufus*, also known as red leaper paw. I have some in my own herb garden."

"I know it can't make up for my ancestors forcing the Stryx to rescue your ancestors, but it's a relief you were able to bring so much of home with you."

Rinla immediately stiffened, and then she made a visible effort to relax. She counted silently to ten before saying, "There's a debate about that very thing in philosophy clubs on Alt. Some of the younger members are putting forth a hypothesis that we couldn't have evolved into the species we are today without being forced to abandon our home."

"Do you think there's any merit to the idea?" Kelly asked.

The Alt forced herself to meet the EarthCent ambassador's eyes. "Of course. It's just difficult for us to accept the idea that our ancient persecutors may have been responsible for making us who we are."

"I can see where that would be painful. Until the Stryx opened Earth, I don't know if we ever went a generation without a major war. Much of our history was defined by groups forcing each other out of their lands in an endless chain of action and reaction."

"I don't see much evidence of it in the Galactic Free Press. Methan believes they suppress some of the most negative stories about Humans."

"I don't think that's the case, but I'd be happy to introduce you to the publisher if you'd like to meet her," Kelly said. "Besides, you can always watch the Grenouthian news if you want to make sure you aren't missing any wars."

Rinla shuddered. "No, the Grenouthian news is much too much for me. That one is *Colocasia esculenta*, which many people call wooly mammoth's ear. You can see the likeness."

"Alt still has wooly mammoths?"

"Doesn't Earth?" Rinla read Kelly's expression and said, "Oh, what a shame. Methan mentioned something about introducing them to Earth Two if they're amenable."

"You communicate with mammoths?"

"They're very intelligent," Rinla said. She bent an elbow to bring her forearm up in front of her chest with the wrist at her chin in an imitation of an elephant's trunk. "We share a sign language with over two thousand words."

Kelly captured an image of the wooly mammoth's ear and then spotted a plant she knew. "That's a fern, isn't it?"

"Very good, Ambassador. I'm not sure that we have an exact match on Alt, perhaps *Marattia cicutifolia*?" Rinla examined the fronds absent-mindedly and said, "Aabina is a jewel. I can imagine what a great help she must be to you."

"I've been relying on her more and more lately," Kelly said. "I suppose I should be embarrassed since I'm nearing the end of my career and she hasn't really started yet, but she's simply better informed than I am about most tunnel network issues."

"At first Methan was skeptical that exchanging our Vergallian princesses could improve our understanding of each other. Affie has always concentrated on business issues, but your Aabina is an active advocate for humanity. She presents a convincing case that joining the tunnel network had an outsized effect on your conduct."

"Keep in mind that the rest of the tunnel network species developed their own interstellar travel without help before being invited to join, and most of them contacted other species before accepting membership," Kelly said. "I wouldn't repeat this on the Grenouthian news, but I think that finding out that the galaxy was populated with other sentients who were more advanced than us in every way imaginable had a humbling effect that was long overdue. We always believed that we represented the ultimate triumph of evolution and then we found out that we were the laggards."

"And you accept that?" Rinla asked, fixing Kelly with an intense stare. "You aren't just saying what you think I want to hear?"

"It's self-evident, there's nothing to debate," the EarthCent ambassador said.

"Maybe Aabina is right and it would be possible for us to work together," Rinla said, half to herself.

Kelly was trying to decide whether it would be appropriate to respond when she spotted a few Gem guiding a floating catering cart into the clearing. Hunger focused her concentration, and she asked, "Isn't that one a hibiscus? Six down and four to go."

Eighteen

"Two-to-one she can't do it," the Thark ambassador offered the Grenouthian. "You'll never get better odds on an unknown proposition involving magic."

"Then why are you so confident?" the Grenouthian ambassador shot back. "If I'm going to take gold out of my pouch for such a random wager, I need at least five-to-one."

"I'll take a piece of that action at five-to-one," Bork said, and tapped the Frunge ambassador on the shoulder. "Czeros, the cheese platter can wait. We're betting on the exorcism."

"Not me," the Frunge ambassador said. "My father taught me never to gamble on anything supernatural. I don't have a clue what's going on in that office."

"Did anybody tell the Verlock mage that we're operating on the Human clock here?" Ambassador Aleeytis inquired. "We've been waiting almost five minutes."

"In all the time I've been on Union Station, I've never known Srythlan to be late to anything," the Grenouthian ambassador said. "Maybe—"

The corridor door to the conference room slid open, and the Verlock ambassador entered in the company of a strangely dressed female of his species. She was wearing a sort of costume with large silver buttons that looked like skulls and a necklace strung with what might have been finger bones. In one hand she carried a staff with a glowing gem at the top, and in the other, a large leather-bound book that could have been thousands of years old.

"My apologies," the Verlock ambassador addressed his colleagues. "Sylinda discovered that her malpractice insurance has a diplomatic exclusion, so she had to prepare a hold-harmless agreement."

"I usually avoid working magic outside the LARPing studios on Union Station," the mage added slowly. "Too much litigation exposure. Who leases the haunted office?"

"I guess that's me," Daniel said, breaking away from the Dollnick ambassador's latest attempt to earn a commission on some dubious service he was proposing for EarthCent. "Where do I sign?"

Sylinda placed the heavy book on the table, opened it to a bookmark, and drew a wicked-looking dagger from her bandolier. "Press a drop of blood on the bottom line," she told him, pointing to the appropriate spot.

Daniel grimaced, but the Verlock ambassador had made clear that mages worked according to their own terms or not at all, so he allowed her to prick the ball of his thumb and pressed it to the paper. The bloody fingerprint began to glow, and the associate ambassador heard himself recite out loud, "I, Daniel Cohan, EarthCent's Associate Ambassador on Union Station, do hereby indemnify and hold harmless Sylinda for any damage in the physical or spiritual realm resulting from her work in the new offices of the Conference of Sovereign Human Communities. I further agree to pay the sum of one thousand virtual gold pieces before the end of the current LARPing season if her exorcism is successful."

"A thousand?" the Grenouthian asked in astonishment. "That's rather generous."

"Hey, I didn't get to read the agreement first, it just came out like my mouth was running on automatic," Daniel complained. "Is the oath legally binding?"

"My old law firm could get you out of it, but it would cost a lot more than a thousand," Aleeytis informed him. "You can buy virtual gold at a discount from kids who pay for their LARPing studio time with what they earn on quests."

"Last chance to bet," the Thark ambassador proclaimed as Srythlan escorted the mage to the door that led into the new office space. "Three-to-one."

"No takers," the Grenouthian ambassador told him.

Sylinda muttered something untranslatable, and then employing both hands, began to spin her staff like a large baton. The glowing gem described a bright circular path that slowly solidified into a brilliant green disc of energy. Nodding in satisfaction with the results, the mage moved forward to trigger the door's proximity detector to open, and then she stepped into the room.

A bluish blur streaked towards the mage and bounced off the energy shield, which sputtered and dimmed. High-pitched sounds somewhere between hissing and yowling assaulted everyone's ears. The mage took a step back into the conference room and the door slid closed again.

"Is that it?" Daniel asked. "You're finished?"

"I'm done, if that's what you mean," Sylinda replied, looking more than a little shaken. "That thing knocked my staff down by ninety-six percent on the first hit."

"But what about our blood contract?"

"That was to protect me, not you," the mage told him, picking up her book. "My apologies, Ambassador," she said to Srythlan. "I expected a wandering spirit that

218

needed guidance to the other side. I don't even know what that was."

"Can you suggest somebody else?" Daniel called after her as she shuffled out the door. "How about two of you working together?"

"Forget it," Bork told him. "I checked with a friend who announces for the professional LARPing league and Sylinda's the only Verlock mage on the station."

"I knew she couldn't manage it," the Thark ambassador gloated. "You don't need more mages, you need a better mage."

"Is the office space leased directly from the Stryx?" the Vergallian ambassador asked Daniel. "If it's a sublet, I could probably break the lease for you, but those Stryx contracts are impregnable."

"I signed with—" Daniel broke off to answer a ping from his wife. He pointed at his ear and turned away for privacy, but being in the middle of a sentence, he forgot to start subvocalizing and continued speaking out loud. "Yes, Shaina. The mage was just here. No, it didn't work." He paused to listen for a long moment. "Baa's angry at me? What for?" Another pause and he paled. "She's on her way? I've got to go."

Daniel dropped his hand and turned back to the ambassadors just in time to see Crute crowding out the door behind the Fillinduck. With the exception of the Verlock ambassador, the conference room was empty of aliens.

"What happened?" he asked Srythlan.

"They didn't relish the idea of being here when an angry Terragram mage arrives," the Verlock said. "Some species are still traumatized by racial memories of visits from Baa's kind during their primitive periods."

219

"I wasn't going to mention anything to my wife about the exorcism until it was done, but the kids wanted to hear a scary story last night, so I made one up about the Ghost of Probability," Daniel explained. "After they went to sleep, Shaina insisted on hearing the details, and then she spilled the beans to Baa at work this morning."

"At least you'll get the problem fixed now."

"Are you sure? Then why didn't any of the exchange ambassadors suggest Baa in the first place?"

"Terragram mages do what they want, they don't come when you call them," Srythlan said. "I have no doubt Baa will be equal to whatever is living in your office, but I fear what it may cost us, whether in gold or in something entirely more precious."

"You don't need to be here, Ambassador," Daniel told the Verlock. "I'm the one on the lease, and Baa isn't going to do anything to me while she's in business with my wife and my sister-in-law."

"I'm here because Kelly would be here if she wasn't exchanging with me this week. We may as well prepare for the worst." Srythlan disappeared into the kitchenette and waddled out two minutes later with a small box of salt cod. "Last snack, just in case."

The doors between the embassy lobby and the conference room slid open, and Baa swept in with Affie at her heels, making an ineffectual protest at the intrusion.

"YOU!" the Terragram mage pronounced dramatically, pointing a finger at Daniel. "What were you thinking?"

"We have a problem that defies explanation and I thought that—"

"That you would turn to a hack Verlock mage who ekes out a living playing games?" Baa thundered. "I participated in a LARP with Sylinda just last month and watched her botch a spell to take control of a zombie army from a Master Lich. If I hadn't been there to pick up the pieces, the whole raiding party would have wiped."

"I don't really know what that means," Daniel admitted.

"The point is—just get out of my way," Baa cut herself off as she strode around the table.

"Don't you want to know what happened when Sylinda went in there?"

"She came, she saw, she fled. Typical LARPing mage."

Affie moved further into the conference room so the door to the embassy reception area would close, but Daniel noticed that she kept the bulky Verlock ambassador between herself and the new office. Baa twined her long fingers together and pushed out her palms to crack her knuckles.

"Could I get a cost estimate before you go in?" Daniel asked as the Terragram mage stepped forward.

"Time and materials, plus a performance bonus of my choosing," Baa replied over her shoulder. "Let the games begin."

As soon as she stepped through the door, a glowing ball of energy streaked towards Baa and attached itself to her shoulder. At first, the observers thought that the mage had been taken unawares and was feebly trying to remove her attacker, but soon it became clear that she was actually stroking the blob of blue energy, and even more shockingly, nuzzling it. Then she stepped back into the conference room and began to scold Daniel.

"You should have come to me months ago," the Terragram said. "This poor thing is practically starved for energy and affection."

"What is it?" Affie managed to ask.

"It's a Chatulbezeq. I don't suppose that translates into anything since they're unknown on the tunnel network, but you can think of him as a spectral cat."

"A cat?" Daniel asked. "As in, a meow-meow cat?"

"More like the god of cats, if you're going to push the comparison," Baa said. "Strangely enough, Geb spent the last few millennia on Earth helping a string of low-talent mediums access higher planes of existence. He could tell you tales about the ancient Egyptians that would make your hair stand on end."

"How did he come to be here?" Affie asked.

"Geb encouraged his last Human medium, Madame Zarathustra, to leave Earth and sublet that office space from the previous tenant. The psychic's readings became all too dramatic for Geb's taste and he stayed behind when she left. Then he found that your conference room and corridor reek of Cayl hounds so he was afraid to go out."

"It must be Queenie," Daniel said. "My kids often stop in to see me when they're taking her for a walk on the park deck. And I guess everything Kelly owns must smell like Beowulf."

A loud hissing came from the general area of Baa's shoulder. The mage stroked the blob of energy, saying, "There, there. Daniel is just a Human. He doesn't under-stand how you feel."

"Does your friend eat?" Srythlan asked. "While I'm ex-changing for Ambassador McAllister, I believe it falls to me to offer this new representative of an alien species the hospitality of our embassy."

"Maybe a dish of milk?" Affie ventured. "And I have salad in case he's vegan."

The sparkling mass of energy clinging to Baa's shoul-der seemed to be growing stronger with every stroke, and the mage nuzzled it again, making soft hissing sounds of her own. "Milk is fine," she said. "Geb developed a taste for it on Earth."

"Do you mind if I slip around the two of you and get in the office to try my dice?" Daniel asked.

Baa sighed and stepped to the side, allowing the associate ambassador to pass, and Srythlan moved over to the doorway to watch the results.

Daniel took out the Thark ambassador's special dice and threw them against the wall. "Light and dark," he reported the results as he scooped up the dice for another throw. "Dark and light," he groaned. "I've got a bad feeling about this."

"There's a fifty percent chance of rolling one light and one dark each time you throw," Srythlan reminded him. "Try again."

After the dice hit the wall, one of the cubes seemed to hesitate unnaturally on the rebound. It finally came up light, leading to one dark and one light again. "Stop that, Geb," Baa said, a tinkling laugh in her voice.

Daniel looked back at the mage to see that the energy was no longer clinging to her shoulder. Then he saw one of the dice moving out of the corner of his eye and turned back just in time to see it roll over to match its mate.

"So all this time the problem with probability was an invisible cat playing with the dice?" he demanded. "That means we could have moved into the office two months ago."

"Another reason you should have come to me first," Baa said, accepting the dish of milk from Affie and setting it on the conference table. Then she made a hissing sound, and added, "Maybe eating real food will allow him to manifest."

It wasn't clear that Geb had accepted the invitation until little ripples appeared on the surface of the milk where he was lapping it up. Then a sooty smudge seemed to form on the conference table. It grew in definition and bulk until a medium-sized cat with jet black fur had materialized, his paws on either side of the dish.

"Oh, he's beautiful," Affie said. "Can I touch him?"

"Not while he's eating," Baa warned her. "Now let's talk about my fee."

"Time and materials plus a bonus," Daniel repeated with a sigh. "Well, it didn't take you long, and we paid for the milk."

"Which leaves my bonus. But I have a soft spot for Flower, so I'll let you entertain her emissary and get back to you about the bonus later."

"What emissary?" Daniel asked as the doors to the embassy reception area slid open again.

"Emissary Dewey from Flower is here to see you," Donna announced. Then she saw the cat on the conference table and her eyes went wide.

Geb lapped up the last drop of milk on the plate and leapt onto Baa's shoulder. Then he blinked out of view as quickly as a Chert with an invisibility projector.

"We were just leaving," the Terragram mage told the startled embassy manager. Turning to Daniel, she added, "I've decided to take my bonus in canned tuna. Geb prefers the pull tabs so he can open them himself in a pinch."

As Baa exited into the corridor, Flower's emissary entered from the embassy's reception area. An artificial intelligence accidentally created by programmers on Bits, Dewey started life as a robot librarian but had since transferred into an alien-built android body with immersive star looks.

"You didn't tell me to wait so I followed you in," Dewey said, and then caught sight of the dice Daniel was carrying. "Are we shooting craps? I'm on an expense account and I could justify losing a neat sum in the theory that I'm buttering you up."

"Sounds like Flower has you bribing diplomats for her," Daniel said. He replaced the dice in the box and left them on the table so he'd remember to return them to the Thark ambassador at the end of the day.

"Greasing the skids of commerce, she calls it. The Dollnicks have turned diplomatic gift-giving into high art, though I've never had any luck getting Ambassador McAllister to take anything. Isn't she here?"

"I'm exchanging with the ambassador this week," Srythlan said. "Anything you'd say to her you can say to me."

"And Aabina?" Dewey asked.

"Same here," Affie said, half raising her hand. "Aabina and I are doing a cultural exchange for the month so she's with the Alts. We're trying to promote understanding between the two species."

"Please, sit," Daniel told the artificial person. "We've had a bit of excitement this morning, but it all seems to have resolved itself. Whatever Flower is proposing should be the perfect antidote to bring us back to reality."

Dewey helped himself to a chair and launched directly into his pitch. "It's simple. Flower is only approaching twenty percent of her passenger capacity which means she's running eighty percent empty. Ever since our brief visit to Earth Two, she's been working out schedules that would allow her to fulfill her current obligations while putting aside time to ferry the occasional group of settlers."

"Human settlers or Alt settlers?" the Verlock ambassador asked.

"Flower doesn't discriminate on account of species or origins, though in the case of Humans and the Alts, the former is barely differentiated and the latter is shared," Dewey said smoothly. "Whoever buys Earth Two, the Stryx are unlikely to give an advance on the tunnel connection, which requires at least twenty million settlers on the ground. Flower is in an excellent situation to drop them off."

"She'll be here in another week, right?" Daniel asked. "Why send you ahead when she's going to do what she wants anyway?"

"Before I can offer Flower's services to the Alts, I need to renegotiate our existing arrangement with Eccentric Enterprises. We found time in the schedule to make four jumps a year to Earth Two, perhaps even five if things go smoothly. But there's a problem with the logistics."

"Earth Two doesn't have an operational space elevator yet, and even large Dollnick shuttles only carry a thousand passengers at a time," Srythlan said slowly. "How many people a day does Flower estimate she can process?"

"Less than fifty thousand running her four shuttles around the clock," Dewey said. "You know how long boarding and disembarking takes. So if we filled every spare cabin with colonists, we'd be stuck in orbit at Earth Two for three months just to unload them, which obviously doesn't work."

"And another three months to pick them up, which means two trips a year would take every day of Flower's time, and she couldn't fulfill her commitments to visit the sovereign human communities," Affie said.

"Actually, it's the pick-ups I'm here to talk about. If groups of colonists are staged at each of the worlds which Flower is scheduled to visit, we could board them without any impact on our usual services, though it would be a bit busy."

"Hold on," Daniel said. "I think I see what's going on here. Flower doesn't care about whether or not Earth Two gets populated. She thinks that if she gets colonists on board and they're stuck waiting for months before they can disembark, some of them will decide to stay."

"It's win-win," Dewey said enthusiastically. "The more colonists stay on board, the less time she'll need to remain in orbit at Earth Two."

"How about a lighter?" Srythlan suggested.

"You want to smoke?" Daniel asked in surprise.

"A lighter," the Verlock repeated. "A ship for transferring passengers and goods from orbit to the surface. My people also use them for moving ore and other commodities off worlds without elevators. They tend to be ugly and have limited maneuverability, but reverse polarity gravity braking is one of the safest technologies for landing large masses."

"Are you saying you have spare capacity available for lease?" Dewey asked.

Srythlan shrugged. "I'm not in the business, but I know they exist. Don't be surprised if Flower isn't enthusiastic. The Dollnicks consider lighters to be an inelegant solution for any problem, but they've worked for us the last seven million years."

"What sort of capacity are we talking about?" Dewey asked.

"I seem to recall the standard passenger rating as twenty thousand, and given the mass difference between Verlocks and Humans, you could safely double that. If Flower ran a magnetic conveyer through an umbilical from her core, you could probably get the loading time under two hours and manage six drops a day."

"That's almost a million people transferred in a four-day stay, more if Flower used her shuttles as well," Daniel calculated. "What do you think, Dewey?"

"I think Flower will want to know how much it will cost to lease two lighters to double the throughput," the artificial person replied. "Now all we need is for somebody to convince the Alts to share Earth Two."

"We're trying," Affie said.

Nineteen

"Are you really going out like that?" Kevin asked Dorothy. "I'm not enthusiastic about the naked look."

"It's my cross-species version of a Grenouthian sash, and there's a separate top I'm not wearing because I was just nursing the baby."

"Aren't clothes supposed to cover both of your hips?"

"Men are such prudes," Dorothy retorted. She disappeared back into the bedroom and came out two minutes later wearing a flesh-colored spandex top under the sash to match the bottom. "Better?"

"I know that fashion is your thing, but I've noticed that the aliens aren't exactly exhibitionists. Even the Vergallians usually keep all the wobbly bits covered up."

"The bottom I'm wearing is much more conservative than a bikini, and I told Flazint and Marilla they could wear full-length bodystockings under the sash, though if you ask me, it spoils the effect."

"The Golden Ratio thing for cross-species branding?" Kevin asked.

"I mean the sash just isn't as sexy with the bodystocking," Dorothy said, slinging a large garment bag over her shoulder. "Richard will sleep for at least two hours, and Margie is at Aisha's playing with her cousins. We're going to be over at the training camp because I want to use their holo stage for backgrounds."

"You didn't eat much for dinner again. I could heat up some Zero-G rations in just a few seconds and—"

"Do you think I got back to my fighting weight six months after giving birth by cheating on my diet?" Dorothy threw her husband a withering look as she headed for the door.

"Good luck with the presentation," Kevin called after her.

In addition to Affie and Flazint, the Vergallian and Frunge designers who had been with SBJ Fashions since the start, Dorothy had drafted Marilla as the Horten model. Myst and her ever-present fiancé were already waiting on the holo stage when Dorothy arrived. The Gem girl eagerly took the prototype sash designed for her and disappeared into the changing room, which was really nothing more than an opaque hologram.

"We got here early so that Thomas could teach me how the holo stage works," Lancelot told Dorothy. "He had to go do some stuff that he couldn't tell me about because I'm an alien and all."

"You are? I mean, I'm surprised he cares. With Gwendolyn back as the Gem ambassador we're practically allies. Anyway, it's after hours, so he's probably just doing artificial person stuff."

"Thomas is artificial intelligence? But he has a Human girlfriend."

"Chance is an artificial person too," Dorothy explained. "You just haven't been around—what's wrong?" she asked, seeing the shocked expression on Lancelot's face as he stared over her shoulder.

"Like it?' Myst asked, doing a twirl.

"You're half-naked," Lancelot protested.

Dorothy let out a loud sigh. "Myst is neither half-naked nor half-dressed. She's fashionable. How can you have developed such puritanical notions when you're from the first generation of Gem males in thousands of years and you didn't have any sexist role models growing up? I always thought that males got this stuff from their fathers."

"I'll bet when I'm wearing the sash you'll finally be able to pick me out of a lineup of my sisters," Myst teased her fiancé.

"I could always recognize you anywhere," Lancelot protested. "It's just—never mind. You look great."

"I told you he's a fast learner," the Gem girl said to Dorothy in a stage whisper. Then she asked, "Did I put the sash on right? I wasn't sure which side was the front."

"Let me see." The EarthCent ambassador's daughter examined the sash more closely. "It's inside out and backward, but it hardly makes a difference since I used a Grenouthian joiner instead of stitching. Still, it would be better if you reversed it."

The young clone disappeared back into the holographic changing room just as Marilla arrived. The Horten girl's skin looked like a watercolor rainbow where the pigments had run together, a sign that she was embarrassed, excited, and nervous all at once.

"Easy, Marilla," Dorothy said. "You brought a bodystocking, didn't you?"

"I really tried," the Horten said. "I bought one, but my skin showed right through as soon as I changed color. Then my mother saw me and—"

"You still live at home?" Dorothy interrupted.

"Of course," Marilla said. "Where else would I live?"

"I just assumed that with your profit-sharing from Tunnel Trips you would have rented your own place by now. How about body paint?"

"For the rental ships?"

"For you," Dorothy said. "I have a couple of spray cans left from when we were doing fashion shows, but I don't know if it would have time to dry before you have to put the sash on."

"I am NOT letting you spray paint me," Marilla hissed. "Besides, my mother suggested a solution." She glanced self-consciously at Lancelot, who immediately got the message and set off for a stroll. The Horten girl took a white mass of fabric out of her shoulder bag and passed it to Dorothy.

"Is this a hazmat suit?" Dorothy guessed, puzzling over the white garment. "No, those are loose and this looks form-fitted. Pajamas?"

"It's a modesty suit," Marilla said. "You know, for visiting the doctor and such."

"You keep your clothes on when you visit the doctor?"

"Don't you? The different limbs and panels peel open for, uh, access," the Horten girl explained, and her mixed color changed to pure embarrassment.

"I can't even see the seams," Dorothy said. "What holds it together?"

"Molecular adhesion, but don't ask me to explain it because we're not allowed. Will it be all right?"

"I won't know for sure until you try it with the sash, but as long as it fits snugly it should be okay."

"Oh, it does," Marilla said with obvious relief. "They have to be very revealing since we wear them to medical appointments and school uniform fittings. I would never be seen in my modesty suit in public unless it was an emergency."

Dorothy handed over the sash she'd designed for the girl, who disappeared into the holographic dressing room that Myst had just emerged from.

"What do you think now?" the Gem girl asked, looking around for Lancelot.

"You know, it might have been right the first time," Dorothy admitted. "In any case, it's fine. Your better half went for a walk so that Marilla would stop changing colors. And here come Flazint and Tzachan."

"Let's get this over with," Flazint said, holding out her hand for a sash.

"There's the enthusiasm I like to see in my models," Dorothy said. "You may as well take the garment bag. Affie came by and picked up her sash earlier."

"What for?"

"She wanted to wear it out and see how people reacted."

"You mean she wanted to see how males reacted," Flazint said, accepting the garment bag. "She's such a Vergallian princess sometimes."

"Did you get my ping about the patents?" Tzachan asked Dorothy as his girlfriend headed for the changing room. "Even if you reduce it to practice, it's going to be tough putting in a claim for technology that we can't completely describe."

"Sorry, sorry," they heard Flazint apologizing to Marilla while backing out of the holographic changing room. "I didn't know anybody was in here."

"Just make another one," Dorothy told her. "They're holograms, after all."

"Do you know how?" the Frunge girl asked.

"Technically speaking, not really."

"I'll take a look at the control panel," Tzachan said, walking towards the instrument pit. "Read my ping, Dorothy."

The EarthCent ambassador's daughter sighed and invoked her heads-up display. She found it impossible to concentrate on the text while her surroundings were still visible in the background and quickly gave up, attributing her dislike of reading on heads-up displays to a genetic inheritance from her mother.

"Thank you," Flazint said to her boyfriend when a new changing room appeared.

A minute later Affie arrived, and even Dorothy had to admit that the Vergallian looked more than half-naked. Affie also appeared to be somewhat flustered, which was unusual for the royal-trained princess.

"What's wrong, Affie?" Dorothy asked in concern. "Did somebody make fun of the sash?"

"I went with Dietro to the bar that serves the fizzy blue drinks I like. There were a bunch of Humans from the professional LARPing league there celebrating a win and Dietro got into a fight with them."

"Why?"

Affie looked somewhat abashed and adjusted the sash. "I thought I'd try it without the top underneath just to see how it felt. They wouldn't stop staring."

"You went to a bar with one of your breasts exposed?" Myst asked. "Wow, you're my hero."

"Don't let Lance hear you say that," Dorothy told the young clone. "So what happened? Is he okay?"

"Dietro?" Affie snorted dismissively. "He had serious martial arts training when he was young. But they all got carried away and broke some furniture. The bar owner threatened to call the station management if they didn't pay for everything and clean up. I went home and got the top."

"You look really beautiful," Myst said. "Like you're gift wrapped."

"Thank you," the Vergallian replied, showing her dimples.

"All right, enough high-school drama," Dorothy said. "We only have ten minutes before the management gets here and I want to make sure we're all in sync. Are you ready yet, Flaz?" she hollered in the direction of the Frunge's changing room.

"Just a sec," Flazint called back, and when she emerged wearing the sash, her hair vines were suffused with chlorophyll. "Where's Marilla?"

"Here," the Horten girl said, stepping out of her own opaque hologram. "I was meditating to get control of my color."

"You look as white as a ghost," Dorothy said.

"Good. I was trying to match my modesty suit."

"Okay, line up on stage everybody. Not you, Tzachan."

"Aren't you going to join us?" Myst asked.

"Not until the four of you are synched up," Dorothy said. "Remember, no slouching, and keep your hands in front of your bodies until it's working. Lance," she called to the young clone who was still wandering about and trying to look anywhere other than the stage. "You have to get back here and run the holograms."

"I'm not seeing it," Tzachan said to Dorothy as the Gem, Horten, Vergallian, and Frunge formed a chorus line. "Are you sure about the proportions?"

"I got Dring to double-check my designs and he said they were within the necessary parameters." Dorothy turned sideways to the stage and twisted her head in the opposite direction, repeating the exercise in front of each of the models. "I can see the effect in my peripheral vision, it's just not strong enough against the metallic background. Could you bring up the savannah scene, Lance?"

The young Gem, slightly out of breath from sprinting back, enabled the gesture interface to the holographic controller and did something complicated with his hands.

"Better," Tzachan said after the hologram of lush grasslands replaced the changing rooms and hid the rest of the bulkhead. "Marilla and Flazint look matched, even though their sashes are different, but why are Affie and Myst wearing the same design?"

"They aren't," Dorothy said proudly. "Affie's sash is only half as wide as Myst's, and it fits much tighter over her hip. It would ride up on any of us if we tried to walk in it, but Affie's had royal training."

"In wearing revealing clothes?"

"It's a part of our diplomatic instruction," the Vergallian told him. "If you aren't prepared to use all of the means at your disposal to exert power you aren't fit to be a queen."

"Flazint, try bringing in your elbows," Dorothy called to the Frunge girl. "That's better. Marilla, stop trying to tuck your chin into your chest like a turtle. Just, uh, pretend we're all doctors."

"Strange," Tzachan said. "It's almost like looking through a telescope while changing the focus. If I hadn't been here from the start, I would have said the only difference between the sashes is the colors."

"Wait until after the show when we all take the sashes off and you can see them side by side on the stage."

"I am NOT taking the sash off in front of anybody," Flazint practically growled. "That would be lewd."

236

"Nobody is asking you to do a strip tease," Dorothy said. "We'll all change back to our regular clothes first. Now I'm going to join you, so, Tzachan—you and Lance will have to make sure I blend." She climbed up on the stage and went to stand next to Marilla.

"Something is off," the Frunge attorney reported. "Your sash looks like it's a hologram being disrupted by interference."

"Or illuminated by a strobe light, like at the disco Myst took me to," Lancelot contributed.

"There's something about the multi-species Golden Ratio that messes with our brains," Dorothy said, putting a crease in her sash at the shoulder, and then smoothing it across her chest in a widening taper. "Is that any better?"

"It's not blinking now, but I can't focus on it," Lancelot said.

The EarthCent ambassador's daughter looked down the line at the other models, turning her head to see them out of the corner of her eye. Then she pulled the sash a little higher on her hip and held it in place with a hand behind her back. "Is that better?"

"I think your shoulder position is ruining the drape," Tzachan reported.

"I've got some spare pins stuck in the back if somebody can fix it for me," Dorothy said.

The Horten girl carried out the operation, and after a few more back-and-forths, Tzachan and Lancelot both agreed that it looked like the models were all wearing essentially the same sash.

"Just in time," Flazint said. "Here comes the management."

Shaina, Brinda, and Baa approached slowly, stopping occasionally to point at the stage and exchange comments.

Then Jeeves caught up, and the four of them joined Tzachan. Lancelot returned to the equipment pit to run the holograms.

"Very impressive," Baa said. "I didn't think she could pull it off."

"Thank you," Dorothy said.

"I was talking about Marilla. I bet Jeeves she would be bright yellow by now."

"You've really nailed it, Dorothy," Shaina said. "It's almost as if instead of fitting the clothes to the species, you fit the species to the clothes. I would swear you're all wearing the exact same sash." Then she squinted and turned her head to the side. "Is the flicker supposed to be there?"

"Now that we're close, I'm getting a bit woozy," Brinda said. "I was about to say that the real test will be making it work with a Dollnick, a Verlock, a Fillinduck, and a Grenouthian, but you better check for health effects first."

"Maybe a different background will help," Dorothy said. "Lance?"

The young Gem began working through the program of holographic backgrounds Thomas had demonstrated, and while a solid black offered some relief, the waterfall made both Shaina and Brinda turn away.

"That's an interesting effect," Baa remarked. "You all look sort of runny, but being from older stock than the tunnel network members, I doubt I'm getting the full effect."

"You're melting," Shaina croaked, and then ran for the all-species bathroom.

"Shut it down, Lance," Dorothy instructed. "Sorry about that, guys. At least we know it doesn't affect the people wearing the sashes."

"That's because you didn't turn and look like I did," Affie choked out, and then visibly swallowed.

"But what would cause it? Did you see anything, Jeeves?"

"I'm able to synthesize the visual data I would receive if I relied on cone and rod cells for photoreception, but I can't say more than that," the young Stryx replied. "I think Brinda's point about testing for medical effects is the logical next step."

"It was like being motion sick while taking hallucinogenic drugs," Brinda said, still looking a bit green about the gills. "There's no need to rush the development, Dorothy. We have enough challenges gearing up to meet the demand from the new nanofabric franchises, and it's going to take me a while to get over seeing you all melt in front of my eyes."

"Did I miss something?" Thomas asked, joining the group. "I was watching the demonstration as I approached and I didn't see whatever effect you're talking about."

"You're lucky you're not a biological," Affie told him as Flazint and Marilla disappeared into the reestablished holographic changing rooms. "But now I have to wonder if the reason I almost caused a riot earlier wasn't that I looked so good but a side effect of the cross-species Golden Ratio."

"That's it," Dorothy said. "Thomas, you and Chance have to test-model the sashes for me. That way we'll find out if it's a mathematical error or if there's something about biologicals wearing the new Golden Ratio designs that's causing problems."

"But Thomas and Chance are indistinguishable from Humans, other than being a little too good looking," Affie said. "Why would the effect be any different?"

"I don't know, but I also don't know why it works in the first place. It's obvious that Jeeves isn't going to help, so the only thing I can do is start back at the beginning. We can use the process of elimination with boundary conditions to start narrowing in on a solution."

"You're suggesting that I'm a boundary condition?" Thomas asked, sounding quite amused. "I've never heard the term used that way before."

"Well, as an artificial person, you're right on the boundary between human and artificial intelligence," Dorothy reasoned. "If you and Chance can walk in front of the waterfall wearing the sashes and not make us all sick, at least I'll have a new starting point."

"That's very astute of you," Tzachan said. "I didn't realize you had such an analytical turn of mind."

"Paul suggested that I work my way into it step by step when I first asked him for help with the math, but I wanted to jump to the end and just try it already," Dorothy admitted. "Ever since I first noticed the effect in those old Gem pictures from Myst's history text, there's been this nagging question at the back of my mind that I haven't been able to answer."

"Which is?"

"How is it possible that with millions of years of fashion history the Vergallians never discovered the new Golden Ratio, not to mention the older species?"

"Next time you have a question nagging at the back of your mind, please let me know before the experiment," Shaina said as she rejoined the group.

Twenty

"Is there something wrong with the heat?" Kelly asked the embassy manager. "I feel like I'm freezing in my office."

"It's the same as always," Donna told her. "You're wearing a summer dress."

"Oh, you're right," the EarthCent ambassador said, looking down at the light material. "The Verlock embassy was so hot that I was tempted to strip down to my underwear."

"What was exchanging with Srythlan like? He was so deliberative while he was here that I imagine business in his embassy moves as slow as lava."

"Let me get a sweater from my office and then I'll tell you about my week. See you in the conference room."

By the time Kelly found where the Verlock ambassador had put away the sweater she'd left hanging on the back of her office chair, Donna had already preceded her into the conference room and was chatting with Aabina about the Alts. The doors to the new office space slid open and Daniel entered, looking extremely chipper for a Monday morning.

"Good news?" Kelly asked him.

"It's a long story. I got a ping last night informing me of an emergency terraforming planning board meeting so I was up hours ago."

"I'd forgotten that Ambassador Aleeytis stuck you with her seat. It worries you that much?"

"Huh?" Daniel lowered his take-out cup of coffee without drinking. "I already went to the meeting. It wrapped up twenty minutes ago at the Dollnick embassy."

"That means the planning board accepted Affie's request for an accelerated hearing schedule," Aabina said. "The lawyers put in for it while I was there, but they couldn't offer any guarantees."

"It seems that everybody is pushing for us to settle with the Alts and take Earth Two off the Container Prince's hands," Kelly said. "I spent the early part of last week doing an inspection tour of Verlock classrooms in Srythlan's place, and I have to admit their approach to education is fascinating. Then on Thursday afternoon, the heads of several academies came to the embassy and pitched me on the idea of setting up a model school system on the next planet we settle to give humanity a fresh start in learning."

"The Verlocks want to teach a generation of humans on Alt?" Donna asked.

"They have a plan to hire humans who have been living on their open academy worlds to do the teaching according to the Verlock system," Kelly said. "Of course, they presented the idea as if I were their ambassador, with the thin fiction that I would lobby EarthCent for them."

"Did you hear from any lighter salesmen?" Daniel asked.

"On Friday. It turns out that the Verlocks occupy some planets that are so active, geologically speaking, that maintaining space elevator stalks isn't worth the effort. So they have a surplus of these lighters, though I would have preferred to call them barges so I wouldn't keep getting confused."

"It's supposedly the best translation into English."

"They do have lighters available for rent," Kelly said. "Unfortunately, none of them are jump capable, so they have to be towed into orbit."

"Could the Verlocks tow them into position in time for Flower's visits to Earth Two and then pick them up after?" Aabina asked.

"Hold on a second," Kelly replied and pulled out her paperback with the alien romance cover to consult her notes. "Between the towing and the premium for short-term rentals, it's cheaper to lease a lighter for a year at a time and just leave it in orbit. The salesman knew more about the situation on Earth Two than I do, so either Verlock Intelligence is monitoring the situation or he's been in contact with Flower."

"I'd bet on both," Daniel said. "I'm not crazy about the way we're being led to the altar with the Alts, but I have to admit that access to Earth Two would be good for our sovereign communities, and even better for the Human Empire. Did you know that Dewey has been hanging around in the new office every day advocating for Flower with the CoSHC members who stop in to use the facilities? He keeps in daily contact with your son, and your daughter came in to give a little presentation."

"I can see Dewey and Samuel working together, but what does he want with Dorothy?" Kelly asked.

"Flower found out about the franchise network SBJ Fashions is launching with the Gem nanofabric and she wants in."

"Joe told me that they've approved Flower for a Tunnel Trips franchise and she'll be picking up her first allotment of rentals when she gets here, but why would a twenty-thousand-year-old Dollnick colony ship want to get involved in the retail fashion business? I don't think she'd have much success bullying women into buying dresses."

Daniel laughed. "She doesn't want an SBJ Fashions franchise, she wants to set up a sweat shop and manufacture dresses to the exact specifications as the orders come in. According to Dewey, Flower has been building out a courier network by paying independent traders to take deliveries, and she has a plan to take advantage of the Tunnel Trips rentals to reduce costs."

"Trying to keep up with Flower's schemes makes me dizzy," Kelly admitted. "Where's Dewey now?"

"Next door. If Dewey needed to sleep I guess he'd be sleeping there, but he said he considers it a waste of time."

"How does he get back in when you aren't at work?"

"Flower is a member of CoSHC, and Dewey is one of her official representatives, so the doors let him in and out anytime. Just into the new offices, though," Daniel added, "not into the conference room or the embassy. He's also been meeting with Methan there after hours when I'm not around."

"So the Alts have entered into direct negotiations with Flower?" Kelly frowned. "I'm not sure whether that's good news or bad news."

"Definitely good news," Aabina said. "Methan and Rinla both told me that being in close quarters with Humans is still slightly uncomfortable for them, but it seems that their children are almost completely over their fear of you, thanks to a few weeks of constant exposure."

"Dorothy mentioned that Methan came to an SBJ Fashions seminar for new franchisees with his daughter when InstaSitter sent her to take care of Richard. The girls hit it off, and now Methan and his wife will have to deal with being the parents of the first Alt fashionista in history."

"And their sons, Antha and Methanon, have started attending Libby's experimental school, so they'll be with Humans for hours every day," Aabina said. "Methan has been careful not to commit himself, but he agreed to meet directly with Flower and Samuel when they get here next week. If the Alts do make a deal, they'll want to work with the Human Empire rather than EarthCent."

"That makes sense," Daniel said. "EarthCent will be gone in another century or so. For an agreement involving a planet, the Alts will want to sign with a counterparty that plans to be around for the long term."

"So what happened at the terraforming meeting?" Kelly asked. "Did they grant the variance?"

"Like I said, it's a long story." Daniel took another sip from his coffee and looked to be composing his thoughts. "Maybe we should invite Dewey in. He was there presenting an amicus brief for Flower and she figures heavily into the ruling."

Kelly nodded, and Aabina jumped up and waved open the door to the new office and summoned Dewey. The artificial person was apparently expecting the invitation because he joined them in the conference room before the Vergallian girl returned to her chair.

"Have you told them about the meeting?" Dewey asked Daniel.

"Just about to start," the associate ambassador replied. "Have you been in contact with Flower since we returned?"

"She approved everything and authorized me to sign for her, though I don't think those Vergallian lawyers will have the agreement ready before she arrives. They're very thorough."

"They also get paid by the hour," Kelly pointed out. She found a blank page in her notebook, wrote 'Daniel's terraforming board,' at the top, and said, "Ready."

"I may as well start at the beginning," Daniel said. "Crute was the chairman, of course, and he started with a roll call for a quorum, without which they can't do much of anything. Bork, Czeros, Ptew, and Ortha were all there, and I could tell by the way they stopped talking all of a sudden when I showed up that they had something planned."

"How many ambassadors are required for a quorum?"

"Six, so counting the Dollnick ambassador and myself, we had enough. And even though I was early, Crute started reading the minutes from the last meeting as soon as I sat down. Those were short and sweet since they had recessed without a quorum."

"But I thought those were public hearings," Aabina said. "Shouldn't they have waited for the official starting time?"

"I asked Bork since he was sitting next to me, and he said that the rule doesn't apply for emergency hearings convened on short notice," Daniel explained. "Then Crute asked me to introduce myself and provide a brief biography for the record. I hadn't prepared anything, but it turned out that all he needed was the names of my parents and grandparents."

"Was Methan there?"

"Waiting in an acoustic isolation booth off to the side with his wife Rinla and their Vergallian attorney. Then Crute read out a summary of the variance the Alts were requesting and asked if any board members had a conflict of interest. I started to raise my hand to ask a question but Bork pulled it down with his tentacle."

"You thought you had a conflict?" Kelly asked.

"The way the variance request was worded, it was pretty clear that the 'second species' the Alts were referring to was humanity," Daniel explained. "Crute noticed, of course, and he asked me directly if EarthCent had any prearrangements with the Alts in the matter of the purchase of Earth Two. After I said we didn't, he told me to sit on my hands until he finished with the formalities."

"That's not very polite."

"It's just a legal expression from the Princely Rules of Order," Aabina told them.

"After that, Crute invited the attorney to present, and while she was getting ready, Czeros explained to me that if I had asked to recuse myself for a conflict of interest, the board would have to recess because there wouldn't be a quorum," Daniel said. "Then the lawyer read out some long statement, half of which was references to precedents and ordinances I had never heard of, but all of the ambassadors nodded along like she was making perfect sense. Then Crute asked if there were any questions, and they took turns asking about this or that subparagraph. The Vergallian lawyer had all of the right answers."

"That's the problem I had back when I sat in on a terraforming planning board meeting," Kelly put in. "I didn't have a clue what anybody was talking about, and I didn't see a way to get up to speed without neglecting all of my other duties."

Daniel took another sip of his coffee before continuing. "I was getting pretty antsy about the idea of being asked to vote on something I didn't understand, but after the questions period, it turned out that the lawyer was just reviewing the relevant case law and hadn't even gotten to the specific issue yet. Then Crute invited Methan and Rinla to join us, and after reading them into the record, he asked if they fully understood the request their representation was making on their behalf."

"He was being extra careful," Aabina said approvingly. "I've heard of rulings being tossed for buyer's remorse when the lawyers hadn't fully explained to their clients what they were getting into."

Daniel tilted his cup above the horizontal to get out the last drop of coffee. "Then Crute summarized the issue, which revolves around the fact that Earth Two is officially listed as terraforming-in-progress. That puts it into a risk class that requires any buyer to be a sophisticated investor by tunnel network standards."

"But why is that the responsibility of the terraforming planning board?" Kelly asked.

"After the meeting I asked Czeros, and he explained that it evolved from the goal of limiting planetary wastage. The idea is to use what amount to zoning regulations to prevent an unsophisticated buyer from purchasing a partially terraformed world that they wouldn't be able to complete."

"I thought that the watch phrase of tunnel network business is *caveat emptor*."

"Yes, buyer beware," Daniel said. "But terraforming is a special case because the laws also involve the neighbors, and the consequences of decisions can be permanent, in the sense of galactic time. I went into the meeting thinking we were going to be dealing with planetary engineering issues. Instead it was a hearing on whether or not the Alts had the financial resources and terraforming know-how in place to take on an unfinished project."

"I'd assume that the backing of the Empire of a Hundred Worlds would check all of the boxes," Kelly said.

"Crute himself brought up the fact that the Alts don't even use money on their homeworld. He even looked my way and took the time to explain the meaning of sophisticated investors in the context of terraforming as defined by tunnel network regulations. I'm sure in retrospect he was being explicit to head off any future objections."

"Is the definition related to what the Thark ambassador taught me about the difference between investing and gambling?"

"No, it was more specific," Daniel said. "Sophisticated investors must have a history of financial transactions on the scale of planetary acquisitions, plus at least one terraforming ship, either through direct ownership or contract. That left me wondering what we were all doing there since the Alts don't meet those requirements. Do you want to tell them what happened next, Dewey?"

"It would be my pleasure," the artificial person said. "I requested that the chair recognize me as the official representative of Flower. Then I gave a brief history of her eighteen thousand year career as a Dollnick colony ship before an unfortunate misunderstanding led her to pursue a more independent course."

"That's a nice way of putting it," Kelly commented.

"Then I ran through the terraforming jobs Flower had completed while she was working with the Dollnicks, including two that were essentially identical to Earth Two, if you ignore the details."

"What does that even mean?" Donna asked. "Identical if you ignore the details?"

"The basic work on the landmasses and oceans was complete, and one of the continents was almost finished,"

249

the artificial person explained. "Most of the oxygen in the atmosphere being produced by ocean algae, floating plants, and bacteria, qualifies that type of planet for the final stage of terraforming. Then the Dollnick ambassador asked how this was relevant to the proceedings, and I said that Flower was willing to contract with the Alts to provide terraforming support services."

"And then the lawyer produced the temporary suzerainty agreement the Alts made with the Vergallians," Daniel picked up the thread again. "She asked Crute to read it into the record as evidence that the Empire of a Hundred Worlds had a legitimate reason to extend the umbrella of their financial sophistication to cover the Alts."

"Both of which offers Crute accepted," Kelly said, nodding her head in understanding. "And then you voted?"

"Unanimously."

"Then the whole thing couldn't have taken more than fifteen minutes," Kelly said. "Why did you only get back a half-hour ago."

"I'd been wondering what the other species got out of showing up for an emergency planning board meeting on such short notice, and then Crute mentioned that as long as they had a quorum, there were a few other pending variance requests in the backlog they should clean up," Daniel said with a wry smile. "Purely technicalities, he called them. Over the course of the next two hours, I'll bet I voted in favor of more variances than the board has passed in the last decade, if not longer. All of the ambassadors must have had a couple of pet projects saved up that they were waiting to cram through at an unscheduled meeting without an audience."

"So you were their rubber stamp," Donna surmised.

"They were very nice about it," Daniel said. "Crute insisted on reading out a summary of each variance and the relevant precedents, not that I understood what ten percent of it was all about. But I figured if five tunnel network ambassadors were willing to sign off, who am I to object, even if they're all trading favors."

"They set you up, just like they set me up," Kelly said. "I wonder if the real reason Aleeytis stuck you with her seat was that she wasn't willing to go along with it."

"Vergallian attorneys have to take an oath about trading in quid pro quos," Aabina informed them. "It's a terrible nuisance for her as a diplomat, and I'm sure she can't wait for the cool-down period to expire."

"The oath has an expiration date?" Daniel asked.

"Of course. She's not working as a lawyer anymore. Aleeytis could have disavowed it when she became the ambassador, but then she would have had to requalify to practice if she ever returns to the law. Nobody wants to do all of that memorization twice in one lifetime."

Twenty One

Samuel noticed the Human Empire's Cayl mentor lowering her knitting needles, the signal that Krey had something to say. When Methan finished explaining that the Alts didn't have any experience with law enforcement agencies since they weren't needed, rather than responding, Samuel turned to the corner of his office where the Cayl emperor's granddaughter was sitting.

"You've made excellent progress for one day, but Flower is hosting another official dinner, so let's start wrapping things up," Krey said. "And I need you to stand, Methan, so I can check the sleeve length."

Methan rose from his seat across from Samuel's desk and obligingly approached the Cayl, who bore a frightening resemblance to a svelte polar bear. "I wish my daughter would take up knitting," he said to Krey. "Instead she wants to open the first SBJ franchise on Alt."

Samuel looked back down at his notes and continued. "We've agreed in principle to negotiate a set of planetwide laws with EarthCent Intelligence to provide a police force to ensure the compliance of non-Alts. Did you want to include a timeline for completion?"

Methan shook his head. "The important thing is to get the laws right, not to get them quickly. And whatever we come up with still has to be approved by the population of Alt."

"Of course," Samuel said. "Have you made up your mind about which financing option to choose?"

"Your mother's special assistant correctly predicted that the Container Prince would come down on the price after it became clear that we would be cooperating with you rather than purchasing Earth Two to prevent it from falling into Human hands," Methan said, holding his arms out at Krey's prompting. "If you can arrange for experienced terraforming workers who have completed Dollnick contracts to provide the labor for the unfinished work, the Container Prince is willing to credit back ten percent of the final purchase price."

"In addition to paying the workers?"

"Yes. It seems that Human labor is so much cheaper than any other biological option that the discount is justifiable."

"So we have that going for us." Samuel hesitated for a moment, and then asked, "Dewey told me that you had some specific worries about, uh, migration?"

Now it was the Alt's turn to look embarrassed. "It's just that back in the day, our ancestors tried to share Earth with your ancestors, but those agreements never lasted."

"Because our ancestors cheated."

"Well, yes. These weren't sophisticated agreements, mind you. More like, 'You stay on this side of big water, we go to that side.' Lashing a few logs together for a raft was the height of technology."

"So how did our ancestors even follow you?" Samuel asked.

"A volcano somewhere would blow up and bring a cold winter. The next thing you know, here come the Humans crossing the sea ice," Methan said. "Or there would be some geological activity and a temporary land bridge would rise out of the waves. I know that neither of our peoples had written languages at the time, but how hard could it be to remember one simple agreement?"

"No crossing sea ice or land bridges," the EarthCent ambassador's son tapped out on his tab.

"And of course, no crossing the center line on the shared continent without an invitation." The Cayl nodded that she was finished, and Methan returned to his chair across from Samuel.

"Do you want us to build a wall or a fence?"

Methan shook his head. "No, that wouldn't be fair to the buffalo or the other wildlife. A line of boundary markers through the grasslands would be best."

"Like poles with lights that can be seen in the dark?"

"I was thinking more along the lines of piled stones. We've found on Alt that using natural materials is the best way to ensure that migratory animals don't become confused. And artificial lights at night wreak havoc on the ability of some insects to navigate."

"But what about people traveling at night?" Samuel asked.

Methan laughed out loud for the first time in the meeting. "I see you've never lived on a planet with technology restrictions," he said. "Traveling any distance in the dark without paved roads or advanced vehicles is limited to emergencies. I don't believe those little moons in Earth Two's orbit will provide much by way of night light, though the lack of pollution means that as long as the weather is good, the starlight will be excellent."

"I hadn't thought of that."

"Neither of us will think of everything, First Administrator of the Human Empire," Methan said, employing Samuel's official title. "I'm grateful for the understanding you've shown for the little foibles of my people and am confident that we'll be able to bring these negotiations to a successful conclusion. I also appreciate Flower's willingness to prepare an Alt-exclusive deck for when she is carrying our colonists to Earth Two, and I hope that we can use the travel time to let our peoples meet under controlled circumstances."

"I understand," Samuel said. "And we'll start reaching out to some of the agricultural communities on Earth and in CoSHC that have expressed an interest in moving."

"This is your reminder not to be late to a dinner in your honor, Methan," Flower's synthesized voice came from the overhead speaker grille. "And your wife asked me to let you know that your daughter won't be joining us for the meal because she has an InstaSitter assignment on Union Station."

"I can't believe you were available on such short notice," Dorothy told the Alt girl. "I really never use InstaSitter at home, but I completely forgot we have to chaperone a date. Aisha and Paul are taking their children out to eat, and my parents are going to some diplomatic thing."

"You saved me from another one of Flower's boring banquets where everybody tries to cut business deals," Meena said. "I'm never going into diplomacy when I grow up." Then her eyes went wide and she asked, "Is that your dog?"

"Alexander, he's a Cayl hound. You don't have to worry if Margie wants to go out and play because he'll keep an eye on her." Dorothy threw her purse over her shoulder and then stooped to plant a kiss on Richard's forehead. "Put him in the cradle when he falls asleep. If you carry him around all night he'll get spoiled. And if you need anything, anything at all, just ask Libby to ping me and she'll hear you."

"Don't worry, I've been babysitting since I was six or seven," the Alt girl said. "Are you sure it's okay to play with your nanofabric after I put Richard to bed?"

"Absolutely. It's indestructible, and I'd appreciate hearing your thoughts on our catalog. Everything I know about Alt fashions is from Affie's travel pictures."

Kevin was just closing up at the chandlery when Dorothy got there, and together they hastened to the lift tubes and took a capsule to the Frunge deck. Five minutes later, they were seated with Flazint, Tzachan, Affie, and Dietro in an upscale garden café. Two bottles of red wine were already on the table, though Flazint and Tzachan each had a glass of juice in front of them.

"It's about time," Affie said. "I was beginning to think we'd have to uncork the second bottle of wine without you."

"She's having one of *those* nights," Flazint told Dorothy.

"I'm just decompressing," the Vergallian said. "If you think that contract queening for the nicest species in the galaxy is an easy gig, you're welcome to replace me."

"Why do you look so beat, Stick?" Kevin asked Dietro.

The head of outside sales for SBJ Fashions groaned. "Imagine being locked in a room for three hours negotiating with a twenty-thousand-year-old Dollnick AI over just-in-time manufacturing. I thought I was tough, but Flower is a maniac."

"Don't Shaina and Brinda usually handle those things?"

"They told me it would be a learning experience, and it was. I've learned to leave management to the owners and stick with sales," Dietro said.

"Three hours?" Affie asked. "But you've been gone since before I got up."

"After I caved in on everything she wanted, Flower hooked me up with a raiding party in her LARPing studio. It's not as good as on Union Station, but it was cool."

"I can't believe that Jeeves agreed to allow Flower to start handling some of our manufacturing," Flazint said. "I thought he loved working with Chintoo because everybody there is artificial intelligence."

"It will just be for the hand-sewn dresses that we've been contracting out on Union Station, not the hats and shoes," Dietro explained, and then he laughed. "Flower thought she could fool me with a factory floor she set up with Dollnick sewing machines, but even I could tell you needed at least three arms to operate one. Then one of her Humans, this girl, Julie, explained that they have a thousand sewing machines on order from a Frunge manufacturing world, but they won't be picking them up for another two months."

"Where is Flower going to get a thousand trained seamstresses?" Kevin asked.

"She bought a six-month contract for a dozen factory-certified trainers along with the machines, and knowing Flower, she'll probably try to keep them when their time is up," Dietro said. "Anyway, we're now officially in business with Flower Fashions, and I did get a legally binding promise that she wouldn't produce any knock-offs from SBJ's catalog."

"The exact agreement I wrote out for you?" Tzachan asked.

Dietro hesitated for a moment before replying. "Flower insisted on changing the sunset clause, but I figured with

Human lifespans, a whole century was kind of overkill in any case."

"How many years did you settle for?" the Frunge attorney demanded.

"Forty," the Vergallian admitted, and then drained his wine. "She kept on arguing and arguing, and the clock was running out on joining the raiding party to clear the dungeon. Besides, Dorothy always says that there are no secrets as fleeting as fashion secrets. It's not like a million other dressmakers won't be ripping us off within a year."

"Or before that," Kevin said. "Didn't anybody else see the story on the Grenouthian news about the Free Republic fashion show?"

"The pirates have fashion shows?" Dorothy asked.

"They used to, but this may be the last one for a while," her husband said. "I had the news on at the chandlery while you were showing the InstaSitter around and then I forgot to tell you. According to the Grenouthian announcer, it's the biggest event of the season for fashion knockoffs, but they tried including a new product line from a local designer and the whole audience got sick. The models looked like they were melting on the catwalk."

"My tab!" Dorothy exclaimed. "So my designs were pirated by real pirates."

"The fashion industry is a battlefield," Dietro commented, and refilled everybody's glasses.

Affie kicked the EarthCent ambassador's daughter under the table and gave her a slight nod. Dorothy blanked for a moment, and then she blurted out, "Speaking of battlefields, I hear you were some kind of fighting monk?"

Dietro froze in mid-motion as he was pouring a glass of wine, and Affie cried, "I knew it!"

Three decks away in the event room of an expensive vegan restaurant, a younger Vergallian princess began tapping on her water glass with her spoon. Several ambassadors joined in, forcing their neighbors to put conversation on hold, and then Aabina stood to speak.

"Before we move on to the official presentation, I have a short note from EarthCent's president to read." Even though she had the text memorized, Aabina looked down at her tab to reinforce the impression that she was merely delivering a message. "I want to express my thanks to the tunnel network ambassadors on Union Station for hosting exchanges with Ambassador McAllister, and for the quality diplomatic work you did while filling her large shoes. EarthCent welcomes all such opportunities to broaden our knowledge of galactic diplomacy, and we would welcome exchanges with our ambassadors on the other Stryx stations. If any of you find the occasion to visit Earth, you have an open invitation to stay with me in my home."

Aabina lowered the tab to indicate that the president's message was complete, and added, "I also want to thank the Stryx for updating the tunnel network treaty to allow a probationary member to take part in the traditional exchange. Jeeves is here representing his elders tonight, and I believe he wants to say a few words."

Jeeves floated up to the front of the room carrying a package wrapped with a ribbon. "Thank you, Aabina," he said. "Speaking for the record, the exchange program I've witnessed over the last few months was the most successful I've ever seen, in addition to being the first. I'm also honored that you have invited me to present the commemorative gift to Ambassador McAllister, even if that's only because you couldn't come to an agreement choosing amongst yourselves. So without further ado," Jeeves drifted to where Kelly and Joe sat at the head of the table and extended his pincer with the package, "from all of us to you."

"Thank you, everybody," Kelly managed to say, despite the emotion tightening her throat. "You undo the ribbon, Joe. I'm too nervous."

Joe deftly untied the bow and unfolded the silk fabric wrapping to expose a leather-bound book with a gold embossed title. "In Commemoration of EarthCent's First Ambassadorial Exchange."

"We all signed it," Czeros told Kelly. "It's not often I put pen to paper, as you can imagine."

"I wanted to give you a holographic scroll but I was outvoted," the Horten ambassador added.

"It's lovely," Kelly said and opened the cover. A three-dimensional scene unfolded of Ambassador Crute marking the opening for a door into the embassy conference room. "Oh, it's with pop-ups!"

"Look at the chalk line," Joe marveled. "It's pulled out taut." All of the ambassadors rose from their chairs and crowded around, the tallest in the back or looking on from the other side of the table. "Turn the page," Joe urged.

Kelly slowly lifted the next page, watching in amazement as the first pop-up fluidly collapsed in on itself. A new scene unfolded showing the EarthCent ambassador in the conference room of the Verlock embassy giving a presentation in place of Crute.

"We all contributed security system images to the book designer," Srythlan interjected.

The next page showed the Thark ambassador in the act of throwing his probability dice against the wall of the new office space, with a cat constructed from translucent paper reaching a paw towards one die. After that came a pop-up of the off-world-betting parlor, with Kelly triumphantly waving a betting slip in the air, her arm moving back and forth.

"Hey, that never happened," she objected.

"Artistic license," the Thark ambassador told her. "You did win, after all."

"This book must have cost more to engineer than my tug," Joe said, unable to get over the complex paper folds.

"Just the first copy," Bork told him. "We licensed Jilk to produce a run for the retail market in return for doing the engineering for free."

"You mean my commemorative book will be for sale to anybody?" Kelly asked.

"Yes, but the signatures in the retail books are just facsimiles," the Drazen ambassador told her. "It makes the original that much more valuable."

The next pop-up showed Aleeytis at her desk in the Vergallian embassy talking with an anorexic young woman. "Push down the lever on the side of her desk," Bork urged. Joe carefully depressed the paper lever and the Vergallian ambassador folded down to reveal Kelly.

"The stand-in technology was just like that," Kelly said. "I couldn't even tell it was me looking in a mirror."

Joe turned the page onto a new scene showing Aleeytis talking with Daniel in the EarthCent Embassy's conference room. The Vergallian ambassador's fingers kept crossing and uncrossing behind her back.

"I like to think that everybody benefitted when I replaced myself on the planning board with Daniel," Aleeytis said. "How would Flower put it?"

"Win-win-win," Aabina said.

Everybody applauded the next pop-up, which showed Fenna with a hand on the Van de Graaff generator at the Fillinduck science fair, her head surrounded by a halo of hair.

"Jilk used real hair for this one," Bork told her. "Press the dimple in the corner of the page to turn off the battery."

The EarthCent ambassador pressed the switch and Fenna's hair fell back around her shoulders. Then the paper-cutout version of Kelly raised her hands to pat the stray hairs back down on the girl's head.

"I hope the designer wins some kind of prize for this," Joe said.

"He'll enter it in the major book contests, but it's more about who you know than what you know," Bork said.

Kelly turned the page again, expecting to see the Fillinduck ambassador in her embassy, but instead it showed Ptew standing with Joe in front of the four-deck Grenouthian ship in Mac's Bones. After that came Bork with Methan and Affie in the Vergallian embassy, and the Thark ambassador said, "One will get you two that the next one is Ambassador McAllister in the Drazen embassy."

"You're on," Jeeves said. "I'll take all the action you'll give."

"Don't," Bork warned the Thark. "He probably X-rayed the book while he was carrying it."

The Thark gave the young Stryx a hard look, and then spread his empty hands, indicating he was declining the bet.

Kelly turned the page and a picture-perfect paper construction of Jilk rose, holding a document with 'Contract' printed on the top.

"It's a pop-up ad for Jilk's paper engineering services," Kelly said. "We've been negotiating for a collector's version of the cookbook, but with all of the exchanges going on, I haven't had time to finish my review."

"There's no time like the present," Jilk's voice declared, and Kelly turned to see the Drazen paper engineer holding a life-sized contract with the identical font as the one in the pop-up.

Kelly hesitated for a moment, and all of the ambassadors began chanting, "Sign, sign, sign." After glancing at Aabina, who nodded almost imperceptibly, Kelly gave in, accepted a pen from the Drazen, and scrawled her name on the signature line.

"I hope I'm doing the right thing," she said. "I prefer reading through every contract with Libby, but that would have taken hours."

"The business of the tunnel network is business," Bork repeated the slogan Kelly had heard from Herl just a few weeks earlier. "Sometimes you have to go with your guts, and this was clearly one of those times. Besides, after all the work the powers-that-be went to arranging for you to get the cookbook, do you really think they'd let a vendor pull a fast one on you?"

Kelly turned to Jeeves and asked, "Would you?"

"No comment," the young Stryx replied.

From the Author

The next book will be my first prequel, set two years before the first Union Station book. For notifications of new releases, sign up for the mailing list at www.ifitbreaks.com. You can find me on Facebook at facebook.com/E.M.Foner, and my e-mail is e_foner@yahoo.com.

The first sixteen EarthCent books, also known as the Union Station series, are numbered in order. Following the sixteenth book, **Last Night on Union Station**, the timeline order is the same as the publication date order:

- Independent Living (EarthCent Universe 1)
- Soup Night on Union Station (Union Station 17)
- Assisted Living (EarthCent Universe 2)
- Freelance on the Galactic Tunnel Network (EarthCent Auxiliaries 1)
- Con Living (EarthCent Universe 3)
- Empire Night on Union Station (Union Station 18)
- Space Living (EarthCent Universe 4)
- Traders on the Galactic Tunnel Network (EarthCent Auxiliaries 2)
- Orphans on the Galactic Tunnel Network (EarthCent Auxiliaries 3)
- Swap Night on Union Station

Made in the USA
Middletown, DE
23 July 2021